P▪O▪D

ALSO BY F. E. MAZUR

He's a Husband…Not a Friend

The Snoot

The Halftone Man

Unvisited Spaces and Twelve Other Stories

Spine

The Buckseller

F. E. MAZUR

P ■ O ■ D

ROYALTY RIDGE BOOKS
Springfield, Kentucky

This is a work of fiction. All of the characters, events, websites and their messages in this novel are either the products of the author's imagination or are used fictitiously.

Royalty Ridge Books
1610 Royalty Ridge
Willisburg, KY 40078

ISBN-13: 978-0692615287
ISBN-10: 0692615288

Cover Photo/Design by the Author

First Print Edition: January 2016
Second Print Edition: Novemeber. 2023

In memory of my brother Fred

and

for my sister Patty
whose bedroom bookshelf
was an early attraction

"Here's the most valuable piece of advice anyone will ever give you on the matter of contracts that seem too complex to understand: don't try to figure them out all by yourself."
—Scott Meredith
Writing to Sell

Chapter 1

I first learned of the murders when Snollygoster ignored his own reproach on copyright infringement. Instead of providing us the link as often advised, he'd copied the *Inquirer* story, unabridged, onto the ugly green pages of the Pixel-to-Paper website. Dead were H. Garnet Underwood, Spectra Suter, and Wade "Double M" Smmith. Published novelists out of the Philadelphia region, this threesome wrote in lockstep on the message boards whenever an issue turned controversial.

Each of the men had been discovered by a neighbor inside the front door of his home in an Everyman's rorschach of puddled blood. The cops found Suter sprawled outside her Lexus in a crumbling below-grade parking lot. Follow-up stories reported that their killer had shot each man dead-center in his forehead from mere inches away. For the woman he'd showed his gentlemanly side. He'd placed a bullet in her back.

On that mild mid-April morning in my quiet hometown of Valley Camp—population 27,000, give-or-take a few hundred Mexican immigrants who were laying foundations or ripping off wind-damaged roofs—the white blossoms of the serviceberry were emerging in the woodlot out behind the house, and the disturbing news put a damper on my yearly appreciation of their preamble to warmer weather. The news had also ripped a peristaltic shivering up and down my youthful bones, and many of the dedicated posters throughout the realm, I was sure, were experiencing the same. This was because the verbal war on book publisher Quotidian Release, undiminished in its third year and more vitriolic than ever, might finally have spun out of control. And only persons who turned their heads away from the wind would have argued that the whole nasty business couldn't ever lead to murder.

Of the scores of attackers carving up the writer boards at the time, this trio of Underwood, Suter, and Smmith had ridden together as a literary Janjaweed in their ruthless condemnation of Quotidian, whose detractors were mocking as Daily Release (more on this risible nugget later). They'd rebranded the rapidly expanding P O D house a "vanity" press and "author mill," and shot holes in any uplifting view to the contrary, this despite the fact its authors were not charged a hefty fee—or any fee at all, for that matter—to have their books published, the most touted of the differences between it and familiar vanity houses such as Willamette Press. And repeatedly they'd pilloried Quotidian's owner and company president. They'd first dressed him out as primordial sleaze with whom you wouldn't share even China's dirty air, later as a con man who was destroying the dreams of thousands of authors by lying about what they could expect from his publishing house.

Of the three, it was Smmith who was the most clever and virulent with his remarks, yet in efficacy my Patsy ranked him last. This, she said, was because he seemed unable to scratch out a paragraph without calling attention to himself. Such was the case in his response to a post by an

Appalachian writer in which he criticized the man's efforts to bring an end to the reprehensible coal mining practice in Kentucky and West Virginia of mountaintop removal as "weak, shallow as a spoon, and uninformed." Midway through the text (and for no particular reason I could make out) he informed his readers that he had added the second '*m*' to his last name because he was fond of the saucer-like candies that melts in one's mouth and he hoped his written words would achieve a similar absorption.

Reading his posts throughout the many months, I'd formed the opinion that Double M lived in his heart as a social malcontent who yearned to be on the side of David, an endless crusader in search of a serious cause that would finally give him the white hat, perhaps even the approval of his mother, as there had been hints in his postings that he remained tied to those old apron strings. He'd written westerns and action adventure tales involving heavy-handed mercenaries who gave terrorists their due, and a small independent publisher in Connecticut took him on. He had come to the attack late, but was granted a spot of some prominence on another forum after coining the word *"DRavlovian"* from the initials of Daily Release to describe, as he put it, *"those dogs in the filthy kennel"* who were not dissatisfied and refused to cross to the other side on the matter to add their own scorching denunciations.

Spectra Suter occupied the middle position for effectiveness, and she had come off as the most sincere among the criticizing trio, the one truly concerned that authors were getting ripped off. Her stamp-size picture on one of the boards hinted she was in her mid-thirties and very beautiful at the time of her death. She crafted wild erotica tales, often involving a husband or a paramour who behaved half-baked, and her postings suggested that more than one deadbeat publisher had withheld royalties after profiting from her work. As some illustration of this, she had penned two other books offering advice to writers on how to get published and what to be on the lookout out for regarding agents and contracts. One of these volumes remains to this day a steady performer on Amazon.

It was H. Garnet Underwood, however, who steamrollered the movement once it had gotten substantially underway, Patsy and I both agreed on this. Of the thousands of writers and wannabe authors frequenting the various boards, he had come across as the most successful, even claiming he once contracted for a six-figure advance. But in my estimation that was because he was skillful at stretching his facts while avoiding the appearance. He'd written horror and some fantasy, the 70- 80- thousand word novels published in mass paperback, the smaller books one finds in the supermarkets and drugstores. Patsy once purchased me a title—to see if I should be impressed. I wasn't. However, this was not because the story bombed. It's just that I submit to the echoing advice from my old high school teacher, Mr. Hazely: "With so little time on the globe, Falkner, why would you choose to read anything but the best?" From where I stood, his work, entertaining though it was, failed to reach that rarefied level.

Underwood was the one sure to rake the skin, eager to trade his bile for blood, when the argument reignited after some newbie, who had recently signed with Quotidian, would arrive on his favorite board to argue a defense. And with little exception, it was certain to be a newbie because most previous defenders of the P O D house had been rapidly ground down as the attackers vigorously supported each other, and there were sizable numbers of them who stormed over the cyber wall with their keyboards a-blazin', calling any writer who signed with Quotidian "naïve, desperate, and stupid." And these were just for starters.

In his posts denouncing the publisher, Underwood repeatedly had used the words *"fraud"* and *"scam"* and with regard to its advertising, *"false and misleading."* When he countered the positive claims offered by a supporter, he first quoted the disputable passage. If the supporter misspelled or mistyped a word, Patsy noted he would unfailingly include a (sic). Ordinarily, when a writer does this, his intention is to give simple notice to the readers on the periphery of the argument that the slipshoddiness is not of his making. But because he both indented and italicized the other's remark—an action that during the early iterations of the message board demanded meticulous attention for inserting HTML code into the web document—what Underwood had really been saying with the extra parenthetical alert was that the other writer was of a quality inferior to his own.

Yet he may have been a small-time scammer himself, this Mr. H. Garnet. While paying a visit to a much less popular board for scribes in the months before his demise, I ran across a post that shoveled dirt on the man. The poster, hiding behind a pseudonym (which, admittedly, brought the claim into question), asserted that Underwood's earliest titles, which were authored in collaboration with his younger brother, an Ivy League stuffed shirt, were in actuality authored wholly by the sibling. Adding H. Garnet's name, this poster had alleged, was to mask him with "the credibility he would need to run the highly profitable writers school he runs today." Oddly, Underwood's signature to his numerous posts on the AuthorsRetreat board, home to himself as well as Smmith and Suter, had mentioned nothing of his books; rather, they advertised the writing school by way of a T-shirt and coffee mug, both purchasable online, and today showing up on e-Bay where they sell for a few cents more, now that the man is dead.

Snollygoster, a displaced American who once claimed he perused thirty news websites every day as though he were expecting to be summoned home to assume the mantle of Secretary of State, lived across the pond at the time of the murders and so his post on the morning of the gruesome crimes had been on the board a few hours before others and myself read it. Routinely, by 10 a.m. Eastern Time, the board was energized and that was about when the first reaction appeared, followed soon by others. Anyone unfamiliar with the board's roster of everyday contributors would have read the early comments and viewed them as typical, the sort of expressions that result from a horrific event.

"Shocking,"

"How terrible!"

"Killing writers! What's this world coming to?"

They would have missed the real story!

The Pixel-to-Paper discussion board, you see, arose out of a handful of authors who had signed with the new Quotidian, but who would later accuse the company of lying to them after each of their works failed to sell even a most meager number of copies. They had aired their initial complaints on the publisher's own discussion board until it became apparent that public venue existed for the promotion of the company entirely to other authors seeking publication. The complainers unexpectedly found themselves banned without explanation from making further appearances. That insult, whereby they themselves became the focus of a diatribe slicing each of them apart and to which they could not respond, prompted the establishment of their own board and server. Once online with a set of rules favorable to themselves, they did not hold back. Their language describing the publisher and its adoring authors included all the terms anyone might expect from angry men and women, plus a lexicon of others, including the highly popular *scumbag* and our forty-first president's favorite for the his family's enemies, *slimeball.*

Soon enough, "trolls" began paying visits to the new board. These were writers coming to defend the publisher, label the complainers as whiners, and do it under a moniker or false name. They tossed out their own insults, usually *idiot, imbecile,* and *moron,* but a few of the most vocal egomaniacs felt no compunction against calling the regular PtPers *assholes, shit stains,* and *dumb fucks.* Yet because the PtPers regarded themselves as victims of an unscrupulous publisher, they remained professional in the face of their attackers' vulgarity and held to the linguistically moral high ground. They reprimanded the defenders for their "immature" language and advised them to crawl back under their bridge or return to their hole in the earth. They would also offer advice to one another, stating that the most effective way to discourage all trolls is to ignore them. Only it never happened. Patsy's contention was that many of them pathologically craved the final word. A common affliction, she added, for much of humanity, not just writers.

One very peculiar thing that eventually would develop out of the visitations by these unwelcome posters was that the PtPers began to think that many of them were the same person, and this person they were dead-sure was the publisher himself, Tor Schacter. Thus, a PtPer often began his reply this way: "Well, Tor ... ahem, Richard." And a few would find a special satisfaction when they were accused of posting something libelous. They would write, "So sue me, Tor ... ahem, Graham." Or "ahem ... Roger," or whoever.

Which was why several postings following the shootings were of a somewhat humorous interest because of what they weren't saying. Everyone on the board was chewing on the same thing, I would have wagered what little reputation I had on that: if Tor Schacter himself hadn't released the lethal slugs into Underwood and the others, you could well bet your ass he had ordered the hits and bankrolled the killer who did. And I knew there were a few people from the board who wanted to declare this to the entire world, shout it out, except if they yielded to the temptation and were wrong, then they legitimately could be sued for libel and what's more, they would lose, which could put that same ass out on the street. Even so, board history had instilled faith. Someone was bound to do it.

Dalton Ellis Post # 2056	Why dance around this! Is there anyone here who doesn't know who's responsible for these horrendous crimes? We can be reasonably sure the man didn't execute the deed himself since he doesn't have the courage to post his real name when showing up at this board. Remember last year's party? That alone points the finger.

Just as Underwood had been a daddy-figure to the AuthorsRetreat board, Dalton Ellis was striking me as wanting the same position of authority on his, except he was absent the writing credits. His only published novel was a Quotidian product featuring a P.I. of Zulu ancestry named Johnny Masai. In place of any fame, he soon metamorphosed into a kind of literary groupie, attending multiple conferences and workshops, and he reported back to the faithful his discussions with editors and successful authors whose works were bringing home real money.

His message to the Pixel-to-Paper brethren was calculated to keep him out of the courtroom kettle. Without mentioning a name, Ellis could explain his post in a variety of ways if ever questioned by Schacter's legal counsel. But I knew the president of Quotidian was on his mind and so too did the others, as the thread grew and dripped like polymers in flame.

Ned Cottrel Post # 850	Right on, Dalton! I'm thinking the same thing.
Thalia Dunne Post # 1817	Every writer who's been ripped off by that dishonest prick will reach the same conclusion once they learn of the murders. I feel sorry for the victims' families, and when the authorities catch up with him, I hope he fries.
Gerald Button Moderator Post # 1539	Burn, baby, burn!

Al Bartholomew Post # 1012	Dalton, your "party" reference escaped me for a sec. You're right about that event pointing a finger. Do you remember one of those muscular mesomorphs packing heat never left his side that entire weekend, even when he trekked to the john? The dude reminded me of the *Fargo* sickos, and that means, if he was the triggerman, he's too stupid to get away with the crimes. It means also he'll implicate Schacter
Tom Carlotti Post # 640	We shouldn't be too sure about that implication thing. This is the same dude who's detonated all paperwork in the publishing world. Everything is done over the Internet. Correspondence, manuscript submission, artwork, galleys, you name it. Plus, we all know he doesn't answer his own letters, but passes them off to his office lackeys, ahem ... editors. There's not likely to be a paper trail. At least not much of one.

The next post below Carlotti's was from a chronic smartass who called himself Disheveled and whose picon on another board showed a bald cranium spiked with red, white, and blue electrodes, or maybe they were lollipops, I never could decide which. I expected what he had to say would differ from the others and, sure enough, it redirected the fingerpointing. Without absolving Schacter, Disheveled reminded everyone of several "unreasonably stubborn" defenders of Quotidian and implied in that defense, he said, was "a motive to kill, believe it or not." He mentioned no one's name, yet he said the "sockpuppets," as he labeled them, were well known. I was among this group, but only because they had tagged me as one months earlier after I'd offered a blunt statement on the board to some personal criticism. I'd posted that I wasn't about to defend anyone who had tons more money than myself, as was the case with Tor Schacter. But that wasn't good enough as the attackers wanted everyone to fall in line and be strongly affirmative. Yet from all that I'd read, not a man or a woman of them had ever claimed they had talked to Schacter either in person or by phone. Not a one of them had ever asked a single question of the company prez. In other words, I didn't think they knew a goddamn thing more than I did.

"Screw you," I muttered to the screen. I then vacated the site in favor of the online BBC to learn what updates there were to the mess in Afghanistan. Wondering, too, what kind of mind was it that links *"murderer"* to *"sockpuppet."* For sure any titles by Disheveled wouldn't be showing up on any bookshelf of mine.

Chapter 2

During the occasional mellow stretch on the message boards, posters sometimes brought up the boards' addictive nature. This was particularly true when a hot-button issue stirred the slumbering egos, and this matter with Quotidian had been accelerant-hot, so that I couldn't exclude myself, much as I wanted to, because I was one of its authors—the title of my novel, *As I Lay Dreaming*. However, in recent weeks before the murders I had been forcing myself off the boards and back to the keyboard for work on a second book and to various household chores in need of attention. Live alone and soon enough you face the question, Do you want to live as a slob? If my mother were alive, she'd be proud of her boy.

I shut down my browser to the BBC after only a minute, thankful in a peculiar way that I wasn't watching the News Hour. Each week and in silence appeared the names along with the photos of the U. S. military men and women who had died in recent fighting or had just been trundling along a road hidden with explosives when they were blown apart. No matter what I was engaged in—whether detailing a storyboard, cooking pasta, toweling off after stepping from the shower, gathering the trash from the wastebaskets into a green garbage bag for the morning's pick-up, reading the works of others—no matter what I was doing, once the silence started, I stopped, stood, and stared at the images while taking note of the many cities and towns from which these fallen soldiers had hailed. I did so to show my respect. Yet several months into this practice I began to wonder how long this segment of the program could endure. How many more segments before I no longer remained still and resorted to doing whatever it was that I had been doing. How long, in other words, before respect was pushed to the side. The question troubled me, and one day I shorthanded a message in my notebook that it would foster a good story.

At the time of the murders I already had a good story in progress and I wanted to get back to it. Even so, I gathered up my dirty laundry of two weeks from the bedroom closet and stuffed it in the Kenmore, then went to scouring the toilet and bathroom sink because both were looking pretty ratty after an intestinal bug had attacked me earlier in the week following a night of too many brews. Outside, the incessant squawking of numerous crows, which for the past fortnight had been favoring my slowly awakening lawn, abruptly ceased and, moments later, came the reason as the heavy knock of a man shook the front door. A tiny, one-bedroom, ranch-style house, which sits in the middle of a neighborhood of similar homes and which right after quitting college I bought for a song because the surface of the exterior walls looked more like a thousand posted-notes than they did white paint, it was absent of numerous common amenities, including an electric doorbell. I hadn't gotten around to making any improvements other than a new metal roof and that was only because the old one had been leaking in a half-dozen locations following a fifteen-minute assault of rip-roaring straight-line wind in our section of Valley Camp.

I set aside the cleaning items and moved to answer the knock, never expecting that this would be the start of Patsy's and my involvement with the murders. I glanced through the window before opening the door. The crows, now resting in the bare branches of my neighbor's huge white oak and looking like a strange committee waiting for the crack of the gavel so they might resume their political pundit-like palaver, were attentive to the persons out front.

The man, who was of above-average height, rose like a modern architectural structure. His posture lacked the faintest vertical or horizontal kink. He looked to be twice my age, although there was an outside chance, because of the sharply receding hairline and a small choker of wrinkles around the neck, that he was pushing sixty, perhaps a year or two more. He gave off the impression by the turreted carry of his head, which advertised a machined finish, of a person under control, no matter the surroundings or circumstances. Nothing about his threads was slapdash either. He was wearing a long blue overcoat, unbuttoned because of the introduction of spring, and it fit him so well that it had to be tailor-made.

Behind him a half step loomed the woman, forced to because of the narrow concrete stoop at the entrance to the house. Her tight expression showed it wasn't customary. She was the younger by a decade at least and she too displayed a controlling air about her person. Her coat remained buttoned, except at the collar where a scarf was loosely tucked. Its tawny color matched the shade of abundant hair that swept backward in waves on each side of her head like the starched Old Glory left planted up on Tranquility Base decades ago. Obviously, she wasn't feeling that the temperature equated with warmth. Both had badges clipped to a lapel.

I left my sleeves bunched up to the elbow so they would know that I was busy at something. They were almost there anyway after I'd shrunk the shirt and some other togs in a recent hot-water wash. As I opened the door, a few words slipped from the left side of the man's mouth. The snide accompanying grin confirmed my read of his lips. He was figuring me to be just another grown-up child who couldn't make it on his own and went back to sponging off his folks. In other words, he knew my age or thereabouts. But the assumption he was making about the house, on this he didn't know squat.

"My parents aren't here!" I snarled.

Overcoat glanced at his partner with the greasy mien of I told you so and one of the crows in the big oak just then let out a raucous note.

"It's not them we're looking for, Ace." He shot out a finger at me, tucking it to his sternum where it carried the added screw of gotcha. "We're looking for you, Wyatt Falkner."

"You want to know why they're not here?"

"Not especially, Ace."

"They're dead. What's more, they never did live behind these walls. And I pay a monthly mortgage on this one-story house with a balloon facing me in less than seven years. So you can knock off with the 'Ace' thing."

A simple "Sorry" would do I told myself, while at the same time I couldn't keep from remembering, with some long lingering anger, the procrastinating nature of both my parents who died within months of each other and had never drawn up a will. Their beautiful house had gone into probate and my only sister, fourteen years my senior and with whom I had a zero relationship, had claimed it with the help of a well-connected lawyer.

"I'm Detective Dempsey. This is Detective Maines. We're with the Philadelphia Police Department. We have some questions regarding the murders of H. Garnet Underwood, Wade Smmith, and Spectra Suter."

I stared and seconds passed.

"This isn't news to you," he said, the voice musically deep and mellow. When later I learned that his first name was Harley, I thought it justly appropriate and for a moment even imagined his long form straddling a hog, although without the beany and leather jacket.

I scrapped my expectation of an apology. I said, "Okay, so you've been to the online message boards."

"We've read several hundred entries," Maines remarked while eyeing up what she could of the room at my back.

To that I did not respond, and Dempsey's eyes then narrowed as he may have understood that I was suddenly regarding it as very strange that two people claiming to be cops had appeared at my door. Their badges were polished and bright, and I wondered if that was the case with all cops. Or were these badges that I was now staring at fresh out of some box from Fingerhut?

"You want to inspect our i.d.s?"

I removed my gaze from the lapel to his face. The detective's eyes weren't cold, but they certainly weren't giving anything away.

"Mr. Falkner?"

"Forget it. My paranoia insists on a workout every now and then."

"Understandable. It's a crazy board."

"With a cast of players," Maines added. She'd completed her initial surveillance of the house and her attention now landed on me.

"So what is it you want?" I asked. "I've some writing I want to get back to."

"First off," said Dempsey, "let me apologize for my approach of a few seconds ago. It's never a cakewalk getting out of Philly traffic and that has a tendency to bring out the worst in me, despite it being a beautiful day with the sun out and all. You'd think I would know better." He threw a hand up to the blue sky, in the event I hadn't noticed, and even glanced in its direction. "Second, let me relieve any anxiety you may be experiencing. Although we'll be talking to some of your fellow writers from the online Pixel-to-Paper message board, we haven't yet. You're numero uno."

"Lucky me. Why's that?"

Maines spoke up. "No one likes you much on that message board."

"You picked up on that up, did you?"

"It wasn't difficult, Mr. Falkner," Dempsey said. "Anyway, we figured you for a good start on getting hold of some background information to get this investigation underway. Okay if we step inside?"

I waved them to follow me and invited them to sit, but they chose to stand. I took a seat on one of my sofa's armrests and ran a hand through my hair to get it out of my eyes. Maines resumed her visual exploration of the house interior, causing me to wonder if she'd once been a realtor. In fact, I was waiting for her to ask how many rooms were in the house and whether I had central air.

"I've a question. How did you make the connection to the board so quickly?"

It was back to Maines. At the same time she took notice of my favorite close-up photo of Patsy displayed on a corner bookshelf, she said, "In their respective homes several e-mail printouts were discovered. They mentioned your message board along with some others." Next to Patsy's picture was another photo, unframed, of a mountain camp owned by a friend of hers. She'd showed the snapshot to me, but then forgot to take it back. I saw the detective stretch her vision to look at it more closely.

"So what is it you want from me, detectives?"

"As already said, we've pored over quite a few threads," answered Dempsey. "What can you tell us about this 'party' that was mentioned?"

"It wasn't a party. The person who described it as such was covering for himself."

"So what was it then?"

"It was a gathering in downtown Philadelphia that included several self-marketing presentations and a few writing workshops for Quotidian authors. The publisher hosted it."

"Now there's something you can clue me in on. Most everyone on the boards refers to Quotidian Release as Daily Release. Why is that?'"

I grinned and looked to Detective Maines, but she was every bit as curious as Dempsey.

"Several aspiring authors like to bring up Ernest Hemingway," I began to explain. "Their point is that a reader never has to consult a dictionary to learn the definition of the words he used in his novels and many short stories. That, they claim, is what they are striving for in their own writing. However, others on the board are of the mind it's those writers themselves who never look up a word. They regard them as just a bunch of lazy bastards and probably wish they'd stop contributing. Anyway, some of the more active posters decided to do it for them."

"Quotidian's a synonym for 'daily'? Is that what you're

telling me?"

"Give us this day our quotidian bread," I said, clasping my hands together while mocking a look skyward.

Maines cracked a smile.

"Okay, I learned a new word. Always a plus. So back to this gathering sponsored by your publisher. Were you on hand?"

"Couldn't make it. Plus, I didn't want to. Presentations and workshops, understand, were being handled by Quotidian authors."

"And that turned you off?"

"How much do you know about Quotidian, Detective?"

"It's the reason we're here. Give us what you got."

"Then you should know they've signed 10,000 authors in under four years and have published their books in that same amount of time. They have contracts with some authors who are very good—"

"—Like yourself."

"Hey, I don't mean to brag, but—"

He raised the familiar hand of stoppage. "That was meant straight up, Mr. Falkner. A fellow officer, when he learned Detective Maines and I were off to ask you a few questions, said he read your book As I Lay something. He said it was great. He said he loved the part about the kid straddling the coffin and drilling holes into the lid so the old lady could breathe. He said the description was really graphic."

Fact was, my book's release date remained in the future, despite my promotion of it at my website and on the boards. "Thank you," I said with hesitant approval, while inside my head I was throwing up my hands and saying "Why not! If the creator of Vardaman Bundren were alive, he likely would find it amusing too."

"So they've signed some good writers," Maines said to get the questioning back on track.

"Yes, along with many who are not so good," I said. "In other words, if I decide to attend a marketing seminar and a writers' workshop, I want to know beforehand that the person conducting either knows what he or she is talking about. You don't want to go backwards in this business, and the fact is, there are a lot of people who are absolutely certain they know what they are talking about, and yet the truth is, they don't. Or at least I don't think they do."

Dempsey said, "Several of the posters stated that your publisher had a freak show of a few gun-carrying goons tailing him about throughout the whole affair."

"That's true, and that's where my relationship with the people on the board took another dive toward the south. Some of the regulars from the message board were in attendance and they claimed there were four men at hand to maintain order, and these regulars swear those men were packing heat. One fellow who drove down from Dearborn and who refers to himself as a 'gun lover' and boasts he's a weapons expert, said he was even shown a semiautomatic, a 9 millimeter Kimber Ultra Carry. Who could forget a name like that! Now on the publisher's own message board, some of those who'd attended scoffed at the claim and said there were no armed guards whatsoever at the gathering. But the PtPers swore to it. They pressed the matter on their board and later on the AuthorsRetreat discussion forums."

"What did you mean when you said your relationship with the others took another dive? Did you have words with them?"

"Words? That's what these message boards are all about. They're all words. There's no body language, no facial threats, no throwing of the middle finger. It's rare that anyone on the boards meets another from the boards in person."

"I'm talking nouns and verbs with a little chaser on the side."

"I didn't kill those writers, Detective, if by some crazy chance that's what is turning over in your head. Look, the arguments, disputes, the fights on the board? They're no different from a fight on the street. There you measure your opponent and if he's too beefy, you walk away unless you're a goddamn fool and are looking to get your butt kicked."

"And on the boards?"

"On the boards it comes down to whether or not you can whip the other person with some cool thinking and witty verbiage. Of course, ego usually plays a bigger part on the boards than on the street. Quite a few voices would do better to keep their fingers the fuck off their keyboards." I glanced at Maines and because the f-word had slipped from my tongue, added, "Sorry."

The detective faintly nodded her acceptance of my apology.

"I merely offered an alternative reason for the bodyguards and the firearms," I went on, "and it didn't go over well. You see, they interpreted the presence of gun-toting men as an attempt to silence any author who was disgruntled and angry, and who might have showed up at the event to create an embarrassing disturbance for the publisher. They further pushed the idea that it was an effort to intimidate other authors present from ever becoming troublemakers themselves. But I suggested that, because a great number of threats had already been made online by several very pissed-off authors in the Quotidian house—and it was not unreasonable to think that a few anonymous threats had been sent directly to the publisher—Schacter was merely taking precautions in order to guarantee the safety of all those in attendance. Even writers have been known to commit a violent act is the place I was coming from. Remember Mailer? Hindsight says I should have kept my mouth shut."

"We've all been there," Dempsey muttered, and I couldn't help but notice that it was said with the unmistakable inflection of bona fide commiseration, which made me smile as he hadn't struck me as a man who would ever let slip a secret of himself. "What can you tell us about this dispute between the authors and the publisher? It seems to be a topic that attracts more attention than the business of writing itself."

"Yeah, well, inform me of when your vacation begins and I'll answer the question," I said out of a straight face.

My reply brought a friendly understanding to his own and he immediately began to search a pocket of his coat. He pulled out a card and reached it out to me. Printed on it was his e-mail address along with the police department's phone number and his desk extension.

"Come on, Verlaine," he said to his partner. "This young man's got some keyboard pecking to do." I saw Maines glance a second time at Patsy's picture. I glanced at it, too, wondering yet again how I had gotten so lucky.

"When you can," Dempsey said, directing a finger at the card in my hand. "But better sooner than later. And again, Mr. Falkner, I'm sorry how this started out."

I waved the card above my head just as the whistle at the roll mill, several blocks to the west, sounded. "I'll get right on it," I said.

"So you're not a last-minute guy with the taxes," he said, grinning.

Not this year, I thought, while silently grinning in

return as I showed them out.

All the crows but one had departed from the big oak next door. It must have drawn the short straw and was required to stick around so that it could inform its black brethren when the area was clear and they could again invade the Falkner lawn.

Chapter 3

Patsy Lukehart (or "Pats" if you run across her byline—she wants first-time readers of her material to make their own gender presumption) is as fine a writer as they come, and that's not my opinion alone, no sir. On the work desk in her across-town home is a small sheaf holding complimentary letters from the managing editors of at least a dozen magazines. And while she is an eclectic reader of fiction, she has no interest in writing a novel, or even a short story. *("I'll leave that to you, Wyatt.")* Instead, she pens in-depth magazine articles on a variety of issues that range from politics to sports to the environment, loving the personal interviewing and investigative research end of it as much as the crafting of a strong sentence and a clear paragraph. She takes herself seriously as would be expected of anyone who might leap into a social issue with opposing sides, and yet not ever so seriously that she will not laugh when I point out something in one of her early drafts that isn't making sense, which isn't often.

Patsy, wearing her favorite rose-colored shades and a matching henley, her favorite cut for blouse and sweater, dropped by earlier in the day than expected and just as I was typing out my email to Dempsey. She studied my bookshelf and moved about my office in silence until I finished.

From: WyattFalkner@rouster.net
To: HarleyDempsey@phila.gov
Sub: War with Publisher Quotidian Release

Some history, Detective Dempsey, as I'm assuming you're in
the dark about book publishing. Until recent years,
books were published by the offset method. This
required hours of typesetting, plus the shooting and
development of large negatives, and finally a big
printing press. The setup costs alone forced these
publishers to print hundreds, even thousands more than
a single book. It also dictated that they promote the title
in order to sell a few copies and recapture their
investment. But with digital technology, this changed.
Today it is possible to print one book at a time. What
this means for publishers who travel this route is
reduced inventory. The new technology is known as
POD, or "print-on-demand." However, some detractors,
including other authors, have chosen to define it as
"publish-on- demand," a less than flattering term, and
that's where the first half of the problem began with
Quotidian and some of its writers.

In a previous life under a different name, Quotidian was a
"vanity press," a publisher who charged the author for
the publication of his book. This ran into thousands of
dollars so that only wealthy people who desired their
name on the spine of a book could afford it. But with
POD and its digital connection, things changed. In the
case of Quotidian, Tor Schacter stopped altogether
charging authors to publish their books. This meant a

dude dressing 'burgers and salting fries at McDonald's could have his manuscript published, if selected by his editors, and as I mentioned to you at the house, Quotidian offers a list of 10,000 titles, and that's after only four years. Which should tell you something about their selection process. By doing away with the charge to publish, Schacter declared himself to be a "traditional" publisher. This is where the second half of the problem began.

Quotidian defines the term "traditional" narrowly, whereas some of its angry authors were expecting their publisher to produce a catalog of its offerings, employ a sales force that would get their books into the brick-and-mortar bookstores all across the nation, send out review copies to the media, and participate in the Library of Congress Cataloging-in-Publication program, which most libraries require if one's book is ever to grace their shelves. Quotidian doesn't perform a single one of these actions. Other charges made against it are that the books are overpriced, editing is mostly non-existent, the publisher asks for a list of the author's friends and family to which a marketing letter is forwarded, and Schacter is primarily interested in selling numerous copies of books to the writers who wrote them rather than to the reading public.

Underwood, Suter, and Smmith—none of them under contract with Schacter, it's worth noting—promoted themselves as strong and dedicated writer advocates and vigorously encouraged those unhappy in his house to make their complaints known, often and everywhere. They advised writing to the Federal Trade Commission, the State's Attorney General's office, the Better Business

Bureau, various others. The whole thing rapidly escalated.

I went on to explain a little more for the detective's enlightenment, how the trolls began to emerge and so on, but cautioned myself against sounding like Thalia, an embittered and lonely woman who posted long vapid tomes interspersed with obscenities on the most insignificant matters. I figured Dempsey would contact me again if he was hungry for more. Finished, I hit the 'Send' button and stood up. That signaled Patsy we could talk.

"You're writing a police detective into your new novel?" She had glanced over my shoulder while I was typing.

I informed her of the murders and the posts that had shown up on the PtP message board that morning—she hadn't heard. She'd spent the hours putting the finishing touches to a piece on the Headstart program that would appear in the Sunday inserts. After that, I told her of the visit by Dempsey and Maines and the questions they had asked, along with everything I said in response.

"So what made them travel out to Valley Camp and seek out my man Leon?" she asked while leaning in to scan the entries of my email inbox after first giving me a kiss. (Patsy, at the time, sometimes addressed me by the first or last name of other novelists—some dead, some living, but all successful.)

"I was about to ask you the same," I said without the faintest grin. "What made Wyatt Falkner so special in the eyes of two police investigators from the big city of Philadelphia? That's what I'd like to know."

"You're troubled by it."

"I'm curious, Babes."

Finding no humor in me, she took to pondering. Finally

she answered. "Since they'd already been to the board before their visit with you, that tells me they must have discovered the pack mentality regarding your publisher. They most likely called on you to learn if there are any perspectives outside the party line, which you and I both know is all over the board each and every day."

Patsy did not think ill of the contributors to the PtP and AuthorsRetreat message boards. She had honest respect for anyone who worked the language and kept at it, people who truly wanted to write, not just to have written. But it was her opinion that independent thinking among them wasn't a thing you would easily run across.

"Wyatt, do you earnestly think Tor Schacter could be responsible for these murders? That's difficult for me to imagine."

"The man and his financial investment are undergoing a pounding on the boards of cyberspace. There's no disputing that."

"Even so. We're talking books."

"The business of books," I corrected her, after which, I changed the subject. "You're early. What's up?" We'd agreed I would cook that day and eat at my house, but that remained a few hours into the future.

She dropped the sunglasses into her tote, a functional piece of dark Argentine leather sufficiently roomy for an unpretentious woman, and dug deeper. Today was the 15th, Federal Tax Day. Patsy and I both were of the mind that a tax code should not require an outside party for the preparation and so we each did our own. But this time around we'd uncharacteristically switched roles. I'd completed mine online and sent it off a few weeks earlier than the usual last minute. Patsy was sticking with the paper and I figured she wasn't there yet and probably had a question about a line on a form, or maybe she was looking to get an extension, about which I was an expert. Instead, she withdrew a large pamphlet folded in half.

"Finished at midnight," she said proudly to my look of surprise.

"No kidding. Anything coming back this time around?"

"Enough for a fill-up."

"That's it?"

"Depending on the price of gas for the day, maybe a Butterfinger."

I chuckled and told her I was glad she got her taxes off the plate, then pointed at her hand. "So whatcha holding there? Looks interesting."

She raised her arm and shook the pamphlet in the air as though it were our ticket to the top. "Writers conference."

"Oh yeah? Whereabouts?"

"In the Finger Lakes region of beautiful upstate New York. I signed us up, I didn't think you'd mind. You don't, do you?"

"Anything special about this conference?"

"One of the editors who will address the audience is at Marley House and I roomed with her at college my first year. Wyatt, this business isn't entirely removed from others. If you can't write, hobnobbing and rubbing elbows with all the editors in the world won't mean a thing. But if you can, then it could make the difference. And you, Mr. Kurt, know how to tell a helluva story."

I bowed deeply and thanked her for the confidence she had in me. When I came up, I added, "Let's just hope I don't become another Dalton Ellis."

Patsy, although she rarely posted, was nonetheless familiar with the players at Pixel-to-Paper and elsewhere. She understood my reference and dismissed the remark under a facial pshaw. Then she delved back into her tote and produced a bottle of beer.

Chapter 4

If there's anything quirky about Patsy, it's that she downs a beer most every day during the morning hours. Just one and usually none for the remainder of the day unless we step out to a bar. And in recent weeks she had taken to sampling the many craft beers that were making the scene in Valley Camp. When she found one she liked, she brought a bottle over for me to try. Except for drafts, she always drank without a glass and at only 5 foot 4 with the slightest of womanly frames, when the bottle was a long-neck and she held it out front, it seemed she was no bigger. In the months ahead I imagined she would put together a magazine article on these many small breweries and the products they produced.

My Patsy, in addition to her eccentric routine for an a.m. beer, I want to say, is a beauty. And she's told me she's okay with my small expression of claim, certain I am not regarding her as an item to possess, which, to be perfectly frank, she wouldn't let happen in any event. Her flesh, whatever the day, is no more blemished than silk—in other words, it is perfect. It is also perpetually warm to my touch, and when troubled or out of sorts, I find it a comfort like no other when I rest against it. Its olive tone remains healthy throughout the suffocating afternoons of summer and even through the thoroughly desiccating air of the colder months. Her hair, the color of caramel and just as smooth, surrounds the softness of her face and all its magnetic features, even when she wakes. Patsy, thankfully, has never capitulated to those questionable fancies of the male stylist who frenzy the strands and place each in a harlot's tousle with the others.

She is most tempting when I see her standing and facing me from about ten feet away. A faint and deliberate angle to her slender hips. Her perky breasts, small but defined, insinuating themselves into whatever fabric separates them from myself. Her big blues gazing straight at me and into my heart. It's her most vulnerable moment because I cease listening to whatever she is saying and want only to jump her lithesome bones. And that's the reason, when she is on a roll about something, she strategically will put the breakfast counter, or a chair, or the coffee table between us. But she can be as inattentive as anyone, which explains how she came to be looking over my shoulder the next morning as I sat before my computer reading the latest mail.

"Metheny?"

"Yep."

"Why's Oliver Metheny writing to you?"

"I've quarreled with him regarding several of his posts," I said. "He's aware I've a book coming out with Quotidian. But it's more likely that I'm just included on one of his listservs with hundreds of others. Otherwise, he would have inserted a personal insult."

"He's not a fan?"

"An understatement."

I got up to refill my coffee cup and she slid into the seat at the desk.

"What's your opinion of Mr. Metheny?" she asked.

"Well, if I can persuade myself to overlook the crayon-like appearance of his web page," I said with a grunt, "I'm forced to admit that he provides an important service with Rottwriter. Having an online clearinghouse for the grievances from authors about their publishers and agents, any writer would be a fool to argue that isn't a worthwhile resource. Except with Quotidian it's become a fixation. On his website what you'll find is this single admonition in all caps that he's distilled from numerous complaints: 'STAY ABSOLUTELY CLEAR OF THIS PUBLISHER!' Yet on the boards he sounds off like some literary Limbaugh who's unable to turn off the switch. I'm inclined to think he has a few issues from his childhood that have evolved into something more distinct now that he's a man."

"Like maybe OCD?"

"Wouldn't surprise me. Wouldn't surprise me in the least."

"Are there guidelines?"

"Such as?"

"If I were to request a copy of his guidelines that determine whether and how a complaint gets aired online and, more importantly, what the requirements are for having it removed, would he send me a document outlined as Paragraph 1, Paragraph 2, and so on?"

"Not likely. As I said, his posts on the boards are longer than is warranted, and I suspect that's because he wants to appear more than a mere rumormonger, which a few others accuse him of. You know, some motor-mouth just passing on literary gossip to whoever will listen? He wants the respect that's goes along with being a true, hard-nosed investigator. Yet if you look carefully at those posts, what you'll find are paragraphs rife with phrases such as *'perhaps it's because, my guess is, my hunch is, didn't they, it seems, I really believe, it probably, in fact there's little doubt, you can almost bet, I wouldn't be surprised,* and more of the same. I've never run across his use of the phrase, *'according to.'* I once recommended that he enroll in a journalism class."

"What did he say to that?"

"I received an invite to kiss his fat ass."

"Now didn't you once tell me that you've never seen a photo of him? That you don't even know how old he is?"

"Babes, he talks out of it like he does, that ass got to be fat."

Patsy grinned. Then, without the hint of a stumble, she read the Metheny e-mail aloud:

"'As you probably know, I was the first to expose the fraudulent practices of this publisher who has taken advantage of thousands of authors, pretending to be a traditional publisher when in fact it is a new form of vanity press scamming to get the writer's money, with no intention to market any of their books, except to the author himself, and I will not rest until it is taken down, or changes its ways, in order to protect other authors from the same embarrassing disappointment.

"'Most of you know that three professional writers were murdered two days ago, and I've been informed that others were contacted by police, who are now aware that H. Garnet Underwood, Wade Smmith, and Spectra Suter, all three friends to me and countless others, were nearly as vocal and persistent in their criticism of Daily Release as I myself. I suppose I should be afraid, and many of you have warned me to be on my guard, but I am not, and perhaps it's because I don't have enough sense to be scared. Yet I prefer to think it is because our cause is just and that it will prevail and sustain me.

"'I'm writing to all of you today because those writers the police have interviewed conveyed to me that many of the questions from the authorities concerned the workshop Daily Release held last year and the strange imposing men who were present and concealing weapons. It seems obvious that the police suspect the very thing we all suspect: Tor Schacter ordered the killings. Although I have no reservations about making this statement in a private e-mail message, for obvious legal reasons I will not repeat it on any of the public forums and caution all of you against doing so. What I am asking for here, is this: if you attended the event in Philadelphia and know anything about Schacter's enforcers, even if it's only a first name or some detail you overheard them utter, I would urge that you pass it on to me. If you snapped photos or shot video and any of the bodyguards are included in the frames, please send those files along. I am offering myself as a collection point and will pass all information on to the police. You must know that Schacter, once questioned, will deny that he had employed gunmen at the workshop and he'll attempt to characterize all of us as nothing but bitter and resentful. We cannot allow him to get away with this. Please help me to secure justice for Spectra, Wade, and H. Garnet. Remember, they were working on behalf of your best interests.'"

I watched Patsy's arresting eyes move back to certain sections of the message. This time she read the passages to herself.

Chapter 5

Patsy left my house for her own around the same hour that she had showed up the previous day. With her absence I ceased trolling for fun inside my head regarding Oliver Metheny. In spite of my less than even regard for his watchdogging reportage of disreputable publishers and overall discrediting of Quotidian authors, I reminded myself that the message/discussion boards are safe havens for individuals to unleash their egos. That the boards are seldom used for the leaving of the typical message, such as *"I'll be along to retrieve your sorry carcass at 5"* or *"Don't forget to stop at Sheetz and pick up something for the morning."* That in reality they are not discussion forums at all because it is impossible to interrupt anyone once that person is under power in order to ask a question, or to request immediate clarification or even an example. I thought if our three dimensions were ever to meet in a bar, Metheny and I could probably enjoy a beer together. Maybe that was a stretch, but I thought the same for several others who often pissed me off with their posts, including Dalton Ellis and Ned Cottrell from the Pixel-to-Paper board. I wondered, too, if they harbored similar thoughts when I was pissing them off.

However, it was not my sense of fairness and interpretation of the cyberworld on social interactions that suddenly caused me to worry for Oliver Metheny. There was a killer on the loose and whoever it was had murdered three authors and not at the same location. Whoever was responsible had hung around like a Morlock beneath the city streets to shoot down Suter first, traveled an hour through terribly foul weather to the front entrance of Smmith's house, then another hour and to where the elevation increased to the rural enclave and wealthy estate of H. Garnet Underwood. And if the murders were in fact connected to the Quotidian war, the webmaster of Rottwriter.net might damn well be next.

Of the publisher's many critics cruising the boards at this time, nine had surfaced above the rest. Five of them, Patsy had observed, began referring to themselves, unabashedly and rooster-like, as "pros," three others were disgruntled Quotidian authors wanting their contracts cancelled and a reversion of all rights, and the last was Oliver Metheny. Together, they called themselves the Nemesis Nine, and the implied jocular tone attached to the use of the softball phrase suggested they believed they now had the publisher on the run, on the big defensive, especially as they reported that a damning article was soon to come out in one of the country's most widely circulated newspapers. Yet the numbers failed to support that Quotidian was on a downhill skid. From what I'd counted, it was continuing to release an astounding 250 books each month, and the voices and faces appearing on its own discussion board continued to change as new authors were steadily added. It seemed the relentless criticism hadn't made a crack. And if that were the case and Schacter was behind the killings, then perhaps the crimes weren't revengeful; maybe they were pre-emptive.

I removed Patsy's newest beer from the refrigerator, unscrewed the cap, and went to the AuthorsRetreat site where I clicked on the most active thread. Numerous posts since the announcement of the murders inundated its pages. Although it is not possible to always judge the tone of the messages revealed in cyberspace, this was not how it was that day. Where one was filled with anger, another showed the writer's deep sadness. Where a poster expressed fear, another had written words of profound confusion. The other boards reflected the same, even my publisher's.

I searched my desk for the card Detective Dempsey had left behind and telephoned. The phone seemed to ring endlessly and I was about to conclude I'd punched in the number wrongly when he picked up.

"Dempsey here."

"Detective, this is Wyatt Falkner."

"Mr. Falkner. You're calling me, so you must have something?" The voice was direct and warned of a controlled impatience.

"Nemesis Nine.' Do those words mean anything to you?"

"Should they?"

"You probably wouldn't have run across them on the Pixel-to-Paper board. But if you spent time on the other one, AuthorsRetreat, you might have."

"You have something or not?"

"Those two words referred to the biggest thorns in my publisher's ass. They included Underwood, Suter, and Smmith."

"Purvis?"

"Yes, Lillian Purvis, too. She's another."

Dempsey went silent and for a moment I thought I had

a dropped call on my landline, which would have been a first. "Hello? Detective?" However, I heard a noise, like the tapping of a pencil or a fingernail, and realized nothing was wrong with the connection. My novelist's mind then fired, and I knew intuitively at that moment Lillian Purvis was dead. Murdered, like the others. What's more, Dempsey was sitting at his desk, suddenly wondering because of my call, if it was remotely possible that I was involved. Was I one of those serial killers who enjoyed sparring with law enforcement's collective intellect? Had he read me wrong?

I put the bottle to my lips and took a big swallow of the beer. "Detective," I said, forcing myself. "I haven't been out of the county for over a month. Not to mention, after I make my mortgage payment, I've barely enough money left to pay for a hit on a goddamn squirrel."

I could barely hear the sniffle of a laugh.

"Who are the remaining five?" he then asked.

"Oliver Metheny, John Warner, Ruth Montgomery, Elizabeth Cotton, and Grimalkin."

"Who's that last?"

"Grimalkin. It's a board handle. I don't know the real name. I don't even know if it's a man or a woman. I'm not sure anyone does. "

Chapter 6

It was a gray, completely sunless day that grabbed hold of time and after speaking with Detective Dempsey, I took up my second novel. Only my mind was powerless to shake Lillian Purvis. I eventually closed the work-in-progress file and went online to the website of her regional newspaper.

Lillian Purvis had been a thirty-six year-old single mother of two, both in their first year of college, as she'd boasted on the board. At some hour in the morning her doorbell rang. She got out of bed, went to investigate, probably presuming a neighbor had an emergency and was in need of her help. She opened the door, and in a final heartbeat the wonderful dream of watching her kids receive their higher-education degrees was gone.

I searched out a post of hers on one of the boards and stared at the small photo, emphatically stark in contrast so that her hair and lashes displayed blacker than black. It wasn't the first time I'd stared and wondered why she did to her image what she had. The small selenium-tinted picture, entirely of her face, revealed a woman of some confidence, except that she had ripped herself apart into ragged quarters, then reassembled the pieces, seemingly by cupping her hands around their outer edge and moving them toward each other to impossibly and imperfectly form the original.

She'd been one of the angriest authors, always in a rage, and she'd sworn to exhaust everything in her power to bring Quotidian to its knees because the publisher, she charged, had misled her into believing her book, a semi-autobiographical romance novel heavily touched with brutality, would be promoted like many of the books coming out of the major houses. Only it never was.

Across the next few days as a residual chill returned to the air of Valley Camp and smoke was again rising from a few chimneys in homes where there was a woodstove or a fireplace, the many writers' boards on the Web grew cautiously lethargic, and most of the remaining living figures of the Nemesis Nine were suddenly silent. Someone identifying himself as Alioto wrote that Montgomery and Cotton had gone into seclusion because they were afraid for their lives. I suspected John Warner would do the same, if he hadn't already. Oliver Metheny was staying visible (well, not exactly visible, as it was impossible to find a photo of him on the Web) most likely because he had delegated himself to be the point man for the collection of information that might help to solve the case and put Schacter, my publisher, in prison and maybe even under the needle.

It was only Grimalkin's tune that hadn't changed. But why would it, I asked myself. If you clicked on the underlined board i.d. of all the posters to the AuthorsRetreat forum, you linked to their personal page. For some you found their christened name and the titles of any published works. For others, there was an e-mail address where you could contact them one-on-one. The word repeated in every box in the page for Grimalkin was private. Yet I thought also that it was just the kind of discretion that might protect Grimalkin's life, whoever he or she was.

Chapter 7

The following morning, the last day of the work week, I got out of bed early, even though a warm front had slipped into the region overnight and brought along a relaxing patter of rain on my metal roof that would normally cause me to linger. My first activity with my coffee in hand was to transfer a few pictures from my inexpensive digital camera to the iPhoto software on the Mac. A while back I began to realize that many of the story ideas I had jotted down in my notebook months earlier weren't even ticklers months later, particularly when I'd been stingy with their summarizations. I too often ended up scratching my head and muttering, "What the hell were you trying to tell yourself, Wyatt?" The "great idea" I'd had was nebulous at best and often entirely removed from the universe. I began to think that if I photographed the original prompt, the picture might help to assure its recollection.

In some instances these photographs the camera captured were nothing more than a series of captivating words that had appeared in a sign inside a store or as the striking graffiti on the wall of a building or the condensed quip of a bumper sticker, like the one that urged us to be *inferactive*, a step above the more familiar term. More recently it was the unintended message in the lawn box of a

Baptist church at the north end of Patsy's street. An ill-chosen homophone loomed as an important part of its religious message and it had roused me to laughing right there on the heavily trampled sidewalk of Valley Camp's Grant Avenue.

I brought the frame up full-screen.

Just as I did, the UPS step van drew up at the front of the house. I left the small room I maintain as an office and hurried to the door. The driver informed me that I had the day's distinction of receiving his first delivery.

In accordance with my contract the package he handed me contained the complimentary copies of my novel. I thanked him and after shutting the door, eagerly opened the box and, seconds later, held *As I Lay Dreaming* in my hands, my first novel. I stared at its front cover: a smoky, top-to-bottom mahogany backdrop with the title and the author's name—my name—in a large, white Bodoni typeface. I turned to the back cover where along with the descriptive blurb was a photo of myself, a candid Patsy had captured in which I held a large notebook in one hand while the other petted a neighborhood Llewellin Setter emerging from the brush behind the house. I turned the book away and ran a slow finger along the cleanly legible spine. I brought it back to the front where I carefully opened the volume and admired the inside layout and the typography. There was a tremendously satisfying feeling welling up inside of me, to be sure, yet all the dirt that was collecting and sticking to Quotidian would temper it. I returned to my office minutes later, opened a second window on the Mac, and went onto the homepage of my publisher's website where I located the cover's thumbnail. It signified that my first novel was now available for purchase.

I closed the window and quickly telephoned Pats with the news. Come the middle of the afternoon, she was at the house.

"Despite it being late in the day, I can see you have yet to get yourself together," she said in the manner of a major pronouncement after taking a gander at my figure. She shook her head as if she regretted knowing such a hopeless fellow. "Get in the shower, Wyatt. And shave!"

"What's going on, Babes?"

She looked about the room, which had metamorphosed into untidy since I'd agreed to work extra hours at the supermarket for a co-worker who wanted to visit an ailing sibling out of state. "I'll clean up here. You get yourself cleaned up," she said.

I didn't stray from where I was standing beside the Samsung watching a political candidate say that he wasn't in charge of an investment company after a certain date. I was waiting to learn if the reporter would ask my question, which was, "So tell us who was in charge and we can clear this matter up and move on."

"Turn that TV off!" she said. "I'm hosting a party for you and your book."

"A party? Now?"

She pretended to frown. Patsy knew if she had waited a few days and hosted such an event at an outside venue or even at her own house, I might not have made an appearance. I wasn't a party guy. Especially when I was to be the center of attention.

"There's nothing much in the house to eat or drink," I pointed out.

"There never is," she said with a roll of her eyes.

"Now now," I feigned a scolding. "Haven't you always managed to find a morsel of nutrition on the rug after only the briefest search?"

She ignored my attempt at levity. "The caterer's to deliver a few things within the next hour," she said. "Everyone will be here after they get off work. and most said they'll leave early, seeing it's the end of the week."

"Hold on a minute! What are we talking here, Babes? How many people did you invite? And who the hell are they?"

"Twenty-five, more or less."

"Who are they?"

"Well, your friends, of course, and some of mine," she said while removing several cleaning agents from under the kitchen sink and scowling at them because I didn't use vinegar and water like she did.

My friends, I didn't mind. Patsy's were another matter. She's always managed to know all too well an obnoxious bonehead or two. When I once questioned her as to why she keeps these people inside her friendly circle, she replied that she likes people of all kinds and from all walks of life and believes a motley crew is great karma for one's soul. I understood the explanation as her way of staying grounded, a translation of keeping one's head mixing with the angels while one's footsies were stirring the muck below.

"Where are you hiding the book?" she asked, again looking about the room.

"I received but three complimentary copies," I said, "and they're not for sale."

She grimaced like she hadn't realized I was stupid.

"What?"

"Wyatt, by some chance were you once an Amway dealer before we met? Is there something about you I don't know? Something you haven't told me?"

I wasn't sure I understood the connection, but I wasn't about to ask for an explanation either.

"Hey, I don't want a bunch of oily fingerprints all over their covers, that's all," I protested.

"Go! Jump in the shower. Lather up. Get the crud off, Mr. Hughes."

"Whoa....Stick with the authors," I cautioned while feigning a low, ominous voice.

"Go!" She stretched out her arm and pointed to the bathroom.

"The books are in the other room next to the Mac," I informed her. "And when I come out of the shower with just a towel around me, if there's time—"

"—There won't be!" she declared, cutting me off. She'd found the Swiffer and waved it at my crotch as though that was all it took to dismiss my licentious thoughts.

I emerged from the shower and the bathroom a short while later and everything was already under control, which anyone who knows Patsy would have predicted. She'd even exhumed a forgotten, partially depleted case of Straub's American Amber from the coolness of the basement, and on a round table set near the middle of the house's main room, on a small easel made for positioning papers, she had placed a single copy of my novel beneath a focused desk lamp.

The caterer arrived with a stack of pizzas and several liters of cola, and Patsy's best friend followed with a few bags of snacks, plus a huge salad in an enormous stainless steel bowl containing just about every vegetable offered in the local markets. A case of wine also appeared from out of nowhere. The first guests arrived soon after, and minutes later the rest, including the boneheads.

Once everyone had a plate and either a beer or a glass of wine in their hands, Patsy sidled over to the displayed copy of my book. She cleared her throat, not because she had to but because that's what many speakers do to get the attention of others (although it did strike me as unusual coming from a woman), and said, "I want to propose a toast to Wyatt. This novel is his first and I expect there will be many more in the years to come, each as creative and better than the previous one, but all contributing something positive to the body of American letters."

"Amen," said a middle-aged woman, a professor friend of Patsy's from the local college.

A friend of mine added, "I'm sure they will. Wyatt is a thoughtful man."

"Hear, hear," said the others.

"Why, thank you all," I said, feeling somewhat embarrassed. "I'll do my best."

There followed questions on what the book was about, how long had it taken to write, where did I find my characters, what else was I working on, and more of the usual. Finally, someone asked if the bookstore in town carried it, and I had to say "Probably not." I didn't want to get into an explanation of P O D, but at the same time I did want to encourage online sales. So I told them the bookstore would order a copy for them, but they might get it quicker and even cheaper from an online store. Many of the guests later made their way to the displayed copy where they read the back cover blurb, commented on my photo, and then went to the beginning where I could see them reading. I overheard a couple of Patsy's friends say, "It sounds really compelling" and another say "I like the pace it starts out at." After a while, smaller groups formed, and while some discussions continued along the line of authoring and book publishing, others talked of wine, sports, and even local politics. I was expecting someone to pull out a bit of illegal junk and start snorting, but no one did. I imagined Patsy had issued the invitation with the directive they not show up if any were thinking otherwise. About midway through the affair I withdrew and disappeared inside my office. Both boneheads were there, each with a copy of my book in his hands, and the smaller of them, whose top knob was remindful of a shrunken head come alive, was thumbing a corner of the cover while staring at the Mac.

"Why don't you perform that exercise on your dummy?" I said to him.

The screen before him was blank and he touched a key to bring it back to life.

"Have you been screwing around with my computer? Get away from there!"

"Have you seen this?"

"Get away from there I said."

It was the comical church sign. It had been up ever since the UPS man's arrival.

"Have you seen it?"

"Of course I've seen it. What do you think? Some leprechaun put it there while I was asleep?"

He laughed. So did bonehead #2, a ladle of a slob with a big body and whose big laugh suggested that he might let fly a dollop of phlegm.

"You know, I'm surprised you get the humor," I said to #1.

"Do you know you're in it, in the picture?"

I stared at him then, as I realized that, in fact, he didn't see the unintended joke. That he didn't know there was a less common definition of *alter*, which involved the removal of one's testicles.

I glanced at the monitor and even looked harder than I probably should have in some foolish act of appeasement. "I'm the one who snapped the picture and I'm not in it. Do you see me in it?" Then I said, while throwing out a hand to encompass the room, "The door to this room was shut for a reason. This is my office. Where I work. Where I write. Neither of you should be in here."

"You're in it," he said. "You just don't know it."

He placed the cursor over the adjust icon, tapped, and up came a list of several sliders to manipulate the image. He moved the cursor to shadows and fading into the picture was my mirror image holding up the camera.

"See?"

I reached across his arm and closed the case on the computer. Then I took the copy of my novel from his hand. The big slob, standing beside the window, showed his disrespect and returned the copy he was holding to my desk by way of a short sail through the air.

"How much did you have to cough up to have that thing published?" he asked at the same time the book smacked onto the surface of my desk.

"I didn't cough up anything."

They both laughed, and the noise from the ladle of a slob sounded again as if he might still let fly that dollop of phlegm.

"Come on now," he said. "What did it cost you? That's a vanity press."

"Used to be, when it was under a different name. Not any longer."

"Hey man! I watch the news. You're only saying that because you don't want to take a bullet to the brain."

"There's the door."

"Al Bartholomew ring any bells with you?" he asked. "Do you go on any of the writer message boards?"

"I know Bartholomew by way of the boards. He published with Quotidian. What about him?"

"He's my goddamn cousin from Buffalo and he tried to pull this same crap, except he actually tried to sell me a book out of his own stash."

"Did you buy it?"

"Are you serious? That company will publish anybody, and my cousin is proof. He knows it himself now. He bought a hundred copies of his own book and three-quarters of them are piled up in his mildewed basement where the only living things crawling across his words are the spiders and the roaches. He was swindled and admits it."

"Hey Wyatt," whispered bonehead #1, and I couldn't help but imagine the tiny head hanging from a string in a curio shop. "Don't you worry none. We won't say a word about this to any of those in the other room."

"But he's getting his revenge," said #2, "and you might want to do the same, Wyatt."

"What are you talking about?"

"My cousin. Al Bartholomew. He sent them another story and they gave him a contract and their big two-dollar bill advance."

"How is that revenge?"

He looked suddenly puzzled, and said to his fellow bonehead, "That's right, he didn't cough up anything either. They paid him with that big fat two-dollar bill they pay everybody with." He laughed out loud to himself before getting back to me. "Anyway, it's a story he wrote when he was but thirteen years old."

"Yeah?"

"It stinks."

I didn't know what the fuck he was babbling about and said as much.

"You know, from how Patsy bragged on you, I never expected you to be so thick. My cousin, see, he's not going to buy any of his books. He won't be making any effort to sell them either. He's just wanting.... What's that guy's name...?"

"Are you talking about Schacter?"

"That's him. Thor Schacter."

"Tor."

"Al says he's got people who run the software to set the book up, software to find misspellings, plus there's clerical work and other shit like that. See, Al says this Thor Schacter will have to pay those people for doing all that, yet he won't see a dime from the sale of the book because Al isn't planning on buying any. You get it now, Wyatt? You get the picture?"

Yeah, I get it, I said to myself. I also got that Tor Schacter wasn't likely to lose any sleep over cousin Bartholomew's big revenge plan!

Chapter 8

Goddamn it.

I uttered it under breath.

And it wasn't that the misfortune was unexpected. It was because it came less than a day after my book went on sale. But there it was, screaming at me, and with all the sharp screws anyone could imagine—the article on Quotidian Release. It accused the company of being a major scam, raking in millions of dollars from naïve writers who were desperate to claim they were a published author. I wanted to make a joke of it. I wanted to find the humor. There had to be a chuckle somewhere. No dice.

On AuthorsRetreat combative DR author John Warner, a balding man with bloodshot eyes that looked as if they'd escaped from a Jell-o mold, had announced the newspaper that published it was the *Chicago Star-Gazette*, and so I had gone to the giant daily's website to read the destruction. The headline on the first page of its business section alone would have triggered a hemorrhage if I hadn't been so stunned by the piece's sudden appearance.

Self-publishing, that's the term the reporter had applied in the title of her exposé, no doubt figuring it would be understood by the general readership, whereas vanity house and subsidy press would need definition. That's only to say these other labels were reserved for the copy beneath the header. Each carries its own baggage. All three together, that signalled a hatchet job.

"Will publish any manuscript it receives." This was in no way meant to imply that Quotidian publishes first-rate material. Quotidian publishes crap, kindling for the fire, floor paper for the birdcage. That's the message the reader was to take away. If you're thinking of purchasing a Quotidian book, "Forget it" was the advice being offered. Stick with the tried and true publishers who've given you the bestsellers you've enjoyed in the past.

"A re-invention of a vanity press." Even the writer of the article was astute enough to understand that authors passed no checks to the publisher with either their manuscripts or contracts. Instead, she went along with the line of thinking promoted by the Nemesis Nine: Quotidian marketed each author's book back to the man or woman who wrote it, and the money for those purchases was regarded as the same as a payment upfront.

"Widely regarded as an author mill." This line had first appeared on the boards and one rational observer, who was taking neither side in the ever more vicious dispute, posted that if the publisher was the object of their attack, why not instead a "book mill." There was no apology by the first poster. Rather, the writer sought absolution by claiming the term was not intended to disparage authors. This struck me as intellectual dishonesty in its slickest form and informed me that writers were no better than anyone else when it came to pettiness and jealousy.

I tried to determine how much of an attempt was made to balance the report. There were, after all, scores of Quotidian authors who had no complaints and stated the same publicly on the boards. But although two satisfied authors had been contacted to counter the damning remarks of Warner and Ruth Montgomery, the selected quotes of their words only served to drive home the prevailing themes: You couldn't be much of a writer if you signed with Quotidian. And, *No reader should waste his time.*

Three photographs accompanied the copy. The first showed the streetside exterior of the building that housed the offices of Schacter and his staff. The red brick structure was from an earlier time but its clean appearance made a statement as to the care it had received throughout its history. Above the entrance was the Quotidian Release sign. Its dimensions were not so big as to look ostentatious, yet it remained easily legible.

The second photograph framed two of Quotidian's thousands of authors, Timmy Norp from Montclair, California, and MaryLee Hubbard from Roulette, Pennsylvania. Neither was much under forty, so that the overly happy, gullible grins on each of their faces made the reader think they got what they deserved. In other words, they should have known better, as they weren't born yesterday.

The third and final picture was the so-called *proof of the pudding, smoking gun*, maybe even a kind of *coup de grace*. It showed a page from a Quotidian published book titled *The Adventures of Missy Potamia*. If you were a person who, after reading the article, held that the authors' complaints about inadequate sales were more about sour grapes because they had written lousy books and less about the publisher's intention to deceive them, the article's creator put that to rest by annotating the page. She called the reader's attention to more than thirty egregious errors in grammar and spelling.

I printed out a copy for Patsy and, while doing so, saw something I'd overlooked. The article was the creation of a writer who worked for a wire service. Put another way, the piece was likely to appear in newspapers all across the country.

That evening I showered and slipped on a clean pair of jeans, then drove over to Patsy's house. We hadn't done a thing together for the mere fun of it in a long time, and so we agreed to see a movie. I handed Patsy a copy of the article on the way. Although I wasn't muttering under my breath any longer, quite the contrary, actually, I had yet to make myself laugh.

"Vanity press, my ass!" I barked. "I haven't bought a copy of my book from Schacter, and I don't intend to."

"Shhh. Let me read."

"And with more than 10,000 writers under contract, you can rest assured I'm not the only one who isn't buying."

"Hush, Elmore!"

"MONEY FLOWS TO THE WRITER!" I shouted from inside the car and up to a woman with a brush pile of prismatic hair sitting inside a church van. "MONEY FLOWS TO WYATT FALKNER, OR IT DOESN'T FLOW AT ALL!" The woman diverted her eyes.

"Pipe down, I'm trying to concentrate. And keep your eyes on the road, will you, before we run over a dog or wind up in a ditch."

"And wouldn't you think, Pats, wouldn't you think that a bunch of authors—some write science fiction, others write fantasy—wouldn't you think these creative people would come up with a new term for this kind of publisher? Hell, I'll grant Quotidian Release isn't a 'traditional' publishing house like Knopf or Putnam, but neither is it a vanity press. Hell, off the top of my head I can come up with something that's much closer to an accurate description. How about a 'co-op' house, huh? How about that? Or I'll go so far even to call it a 'cooperative subsidy' house. What's that, you ask. Well, that's where you have some authors who will buy their books back from the publisher, authors who will be quite content to sell them at their club socials and Rotary luncheons, and who crave only a bit of local fame. But you'll also have the Wyatt Falkners who seek a readership far beyond local borders, and they want their books purchased online and at bookstores. The sales of the first group supports the publication of the second. Call it 'Marxist' publishing, for all I care. From each according to his wants to each according to his needs. Or how about this labeling? How about we call it a 'non-validating' publishing house, since it's something the Nemesis Nine and others have harped on as a method of belittling its authors? But then if we do, let's no longer call all the others traditional, all right? Let's begin to call them 'validating' houses, and then we'll see what connotations attach. What do you think, Pats? Do you like any of those?"

"This is really damaging," she said.

The week before, Conquest Cinemas had begun assigning one of its matchbox theaters to show a popular movie from the past. The new releases of all special effects with little plot and forgettable characters were of no interest, so Patsy opted for the resurrected classic *Five Easy Pieces*. I was okay with her choice because I didn't care what was thrown up on the big screen. During the showing, Patsy kept trying to silence me, but I couldn't help myself. The article was too upsetting and all I could see was my novel going nowhere fast, regardless of how much I was promoting it. It was like *As I Lay Dreaming* was an incredibly gorgeous woman, except for a bulging eight-inch scar stretching wildly from the forehead to the chin. It might attract attention, but nothing serious would come of it.

I didn't let up either when we returned to Patsy's home set inside an early development on the more populated north side of town, a two-bedroom dwelling that she had inherited upon the passing of a maiden aunt. She handed me a local beer that I traded for two fingers of a cheap whiskey she kept on hand for no particular reason. She gave the drink to me while I stood staring out a window at the street out front. Across the way a woman was at her door and staring back. I didn't know if she could make out if my lips were moving, but if she could, she probably was speculating about what I was going on about. Patsy's neighborhood was another one of those countless watch zones with its signs nailed to the utility poles, except here the residents were actively on duty because blinds were never shut, drapes never drawn, and inevitably there was always a figure looking out a window in at least one of the houses. Plus even after the sun disappeared and darkness prevailed you could count on little Jake Kotecki in his Phillies ball cap doing any of a dozen things in his front yard, the rare breed of contemporary child who hated staying inside his house and playing video games. Even now, I watched him chase his poodle around a tree. Each move he made, the dog made the same on the tree's opposite side and the kid could never get behind the animal.

"Aren't Jake and his dog having fun! You know, you could take a lesson," said Patsy.

"Pick your tree," I said.

"Wyatt, you need to settle down. You're letting this bend you out of shape."

"I can't help it. How am I to set up a signing in our

bookstore right here in Valley Camp or anywhere else? If anyone is sure to know about the article and what it says about Quotidian Books and its authors, it's the bookstore owners and managers. They aren't going to want to touch *As I Lay Dreaming*. It's not a historical work about the region. It's a novel, and I didn't set it anywhere near these parts. Look, Pats, I hadn't fooled myself about getting rich on this book. But I was hoping to schedule quite a number of book signings to sell myself, along with *Dreaming*. Schedule them around the state. Make it a fun trip. See some of the sites I haven't seen, except in a magazine spread or on television. I was going to ask you to come along. I figured if I could sell a thousand copies and more in six months, then I might interest a bigger publisher for my next book. But now, because of the article that's out there being read by millions of people, it seems such a tour would be folly. I mean, even if a few bookstores did agree to my appearance and order the books, still there would be customers who would now keep their distance from my table like I'm some kind of killer virus. And this bad press will be spread all over the Internet, too."

Patsy didn't say anything for a while, but I was pretty certain of what she was thinking. She had not wanted me to sign with Quotidian, at least not at the moment I did. She'd not been critical of them, but rather she'd adopted a wait-and-see attitude and she'd wanted me to do the same....

"Switching from a house that requires an upfront payment from its authors to one that doesn't charge a fee, the company all the same will need to make a payroll. That means it will be forced to publish books that shouldn't be published," she had explained. "And I've been to a number of websites established by Quotidian authors. Several include a chapter from their book and I can tell you candidly, too many of those authors are lacking both in talent and skill."

Nor had she faulted Quotidian for not promoting its books....

"How would a publisher, formerly a well-known vanity house, know which books to put some money behind? Of course, they wouldn't know and no one should expect otherwise. However, at some point they need to plunge into promotion and marketing. As time passes, you want to see evidence its rejection of manuscripts is growing and that it's getting behind a book or two by way of an ad in various book review publications and a timely interview of an author on early morning television. But if those signs fail to materialize, rest assured your book is dead."

And although Patsy was not fundamentally critical of P O D, when I'd first mentioned signings, she nevertheless reminded me that P O D books are nonreturnable, meaning bookstores weren't about to order a batch of books by an unknown author like myself and which they might get stuck with. But I had that covered. I figured I would ask each store to order fifty books, with my agreement that I would buy whatever remained and take them with me. If, at the end of the bookstore signings, I had a small collection of my own novel, well, there were open-air events coming up every summer in Valley Camp and nearby communities extending into Maryland and New Jersey at which various craftsmen, including writers, hawked their wares.

What Patsy had wanted me to do, instead of signing with Quotidian, was to continue querying agents and those publishers who still acted as their own gatekeepers. But nothing had turned out more frustrating, and it wasn't because of rejection, which is the standard for just about every writer. The frustration arose from the feeling that I was wasting my time, that I was even being scammed. To a score of publishers I had sent off the first thirty pages, in accordance with their requirements. Several had returned them within six months with a note indicating they had switched their areas of commercial interest from mysteries and mainstream fiction to either fantasy or to gay and lesbian literature. Another three or four had held onto the opening pages for almost a year before returning them with a standard rejection slip. Then there were the agents. Sixteen, that's how many to whose offices I'd sent out queries at the very start, hoping to find a representative for *As I Lay Dreaming* and myself. Seven replied they weren't interested while three said they were not taking on any new clients, this despite the names of their agencies appearing in every relevant writer's resource book focusing on getting published. The remaining six, to this day, have never responded. I once told Patsy how we could set ourselves up for free postage for the remainder of our lives. "We'll become agents," I lectured her, "We'll accept snail-mail queries only accompanied by a self-addressed, stamped envelope. Or, because writers are always warned to follow instructions to the letter, we'll insist they not glue the postage to save us the trouble of steaming off the stamps. One thousand queries per year, that's almost five hundred dollars in postage stamps." I remember she had laughed and shook her head dizzily, both amazed and amused by how my own head sometimes crazily worked. Anyway, all this together, plus my interest in the Internet and online sales of all kinds of items, eased me into signing with Tor Schacter and his Quotidian Books.

The contract for my book guaranteed that it would be published and available for sale in nine months. During that time while I began work on my second novel, I heeded Patsy's words and watched my publisher's website, both its online sale page of each day's new offerings and its message board for its authors. The issuance of books steadily increased over that period, and new authors in the house introduced themselves. I read the posts of many of these writers, the words contained therein a small measure of what I would later find at their personal websites in their bios, short stories, first chapters, and even in their poems. Too few were deserving of applause as most wallowed in poor diction, horrendous grammar, countless adverbs, and mere rant that was served up as dialogue. There were stories whose authors seemed to think that the most important feature of a character should be a unique name. But the others, the too few, were very good. These were books that would take a back seat in sales to the volumes put out by the big publishing conglomerates, but they were in no way of lesser quality in the writing. What's more, they were proof that a publisher such as Quotidian could be a beneficial thing if it so chose, because I thought as interesting and developed as these works were, conventional publishers would decline to publish them simply because they would not have foreseen an adequate financial return. It was part of an argument I had made on the board with those authors who championed the standby publishers, an argument of which the fulcrum was the level of culture. What I asserted was hardly unreasonable: if the reading level of the nation were ever to drop to an elementary grade—and weren't there already signs this was in progress—then even the best writers in the world, if they wanted to sell, would be forced to write in accordance.

I doubt it was the alcohol. I had merely grown tired from talking and all the discouragement that had come with it. I collapsed onto Patsy's sofa and slept the night. Still without finding a thing at which to laugh.

Chapter 9

Over the next few days, the damaging article appeared in newspapers all across America and throughout Canada, too. And once again, the boards were giddy with elation.

On PtP:

Thalia Dunne Post # 1912	Omigod, who would believe it! My little daily right here in New Mexico, has published the article on Daily Release, disclosing to everyone how big a fraud it is to aspiring writers. I'm overjoyed.
Ex-DR Dude Guest	It appeared in this morning's *Enterprise-Gazette* and not a word was cut from the original down-and-dirty.
Oliver Metheny Guest	It's right here in my morning paper. Doggone that John Warner and Ruth Montgomery! I'm after the title of "Quotidian's Most Hated Writer Advocate," and they're putting up a fight.

H.R. Gordon Post # 200	All of Detroit has likewise been warned. Hey Oliver, good luck with your campaign, but John and Ruth are highly motivated people. You have your work cut out! BTW, congratulations on Rottwriter's new web design.

On WritersUp.net:

Will Tatum	Attention, fellow scribes: Today's *Cleveland Plain-Messenger* includes the article on Daily Release although they call it by its real name. It's shorter than what I read in the *Star-Gazette* online edition. When I compared the two to see what my paper had excised, I found it was the so-called "balancing view." LOL
Holly Gee	The *Denver Times* has picked up the article. Plus there's a sidebar about three of its authors who reside in the area, and they all say their publisher lied and misrepresented itself.

And from AuthorsRetreat.com, following a barrage of posts announcing publication of the article by still more newspapers, came these messages of congratulations:

Growler	Let's give a standing ovation and round of applause to John Warner and Ruth Montgomery for their tireless efforts in bringing media attention to this scam publisher and his deceitful practices. I stand and tip my hat. Great job!

Grimalkin	Indeed, John and Ruth deserve the kudos. But let's not forget Garnet, Spectra, and Wade. They contributed greatly to reaching this important point. Lillian Purvis, too. All of them, independently and together, kept up the pressure.
Kevin Carson	And let me say to all that Grimalkin likewise deserves a share of the credit and a respectful tip of the hat. Too professional and modest to sound the horn? Then I will do it. Time and again, Grimalkin has demonstrated a commitment to exposing Daily Release through clear, rational responses to those who arrive at this board with an agenda to portray their publisher as respectable. But when a Howitzer was required, Grimalkin stepped forward and did not flinch.

It was extremely depressing. Even Patsy, who had read the same posts, had nothing to say. She must have reckoned an Out-of-Print label would soon be in order for *As I Lay Dreaming*.

Chapter 10

Shake it off! That's what my father would have said. He'd said it as much to himself as he did to me. And he followed his own advice each and every time so that I could never call him on it. So Shake it off! is what I told myself because, plain and simple, it was nothing more than a funk. Coming to terms with it was something I had to do alone.

My muse must have thought the same because she reminded her charge, who knew as a teenager that he wanted to be a writer and especially a novelist, that Mr. Hazely had said that James Hilton wrote the classic *Goodbye, Mr. Chips* in less than a week. I kept this marvelous achievement at the front of my consciousness as I pressed hard to finish my second novel. There was nothing I could do to bring an end to the war between Quotidian and its detractors. Nothing to do about the exposé. So I controlled what was possible, and that was myself. My intention was to take along a few copies of a finished manuscript to the upcoming conference for which Patsy had registered us. Between presentations, and while the agents and editors were away from their tables where they'd fulfilled appointments with other writers made months in advance, I planned on schmoozing with as many of them as possible to try and sell my story. If any expressed an interest, I could present to that person a chapter or two, or the entire narrative if they so wished. And if this occurred early in the conference, it was possible the manuscript might enjoy a reading before our return home and I would have some early word on its chance for publication. This could only be an extraordinary occurrence because agents and editors are not so easily charmed (or so I'd heard) but objectively as possible did I view my new creation, and I was convinced it was both a page-turner and relevant to the times. I was especially anticipating meeting Patsy's college roommate, an editor at giant Marley House.

Once under full power, I was writing up to 7,000 words a day, and when the process slowed, I revised what was already down. I created in a flurry, even in a maniacal euphoria at times, and dozens of pages were fancy tripe and were trashed without a second thought. Patsy, aware of what I was about and glad to see me working myself out of the doldrums fostered by others, stayed out of the way. I wrote through the night too, while at work stacking soup and flour and all variety of products on the shelves for the next day's customers. I kept paper and pen in my pocket and withdrew it to scribble down a passage that my mind just then clarified. One day before the conference I polished the end of the story. I printed out a copy, then hurried down to Kinko's and added two more. I was all set. So was Patsy. The following morning, a brilliantly blue specimen marked by a single cloud but lined with the long-lasting, intersecting contrails of numerous jets destined for airports across the East and further, I removed a collection of debris from the cargo area of my Subaru, tossed in a couple of bags and a little later a couple of hers and off the happy couple went.

The conference was being held at the Statler Inn and

Conference Center on the campus of Cornell University in upstate New York. The trip would take us some three hundred miles from our homes, and Patsy had worked out the route. This would not be our first journey together. Two summers before we had traveled to the Jersey shore, and the following year we drove westward to Churchill Downs for the Kentucky Derby where we learned it was virtually impossible to see the horses from the infield if you weren't another Dikembe Mutumbo. We'd learned we traveled well as a couple, neither one of us in a hurry, neither after the quickest and most direct route, neither unwilling to stop because of even a whim. In fact, it didn't upset one if the other said to turn the car around and backtrack over five, even ten miles to look closely at something we'd whizzed past earlier. We stopped often, too, occasionally just to stretch and feel the sun upon our flesh, at other times to eat, and Patsy sometimes packed a cooler of sandwiches and one or two beers for each of us.

We made Ithaca, where Cornell is located, without incident or long delays due to highway construction, and the Ru climbed one of the many steep hills to the university. The main campus overlooks Cayuga Lake, a very deep, long and narrow body of fresh water fed by numerous tributaries including some beautiful gorges with tragic histories of student suicide. Wherever one looked, university workers had groomed the landscape with harlequin care. We checked in at the Statler as the sun was beginning its daily plunge beyond the lake's western shore spread apart with numerous wineries and countless homes and cottages. Afterwards, we picked up our conference folders and i.d. tags.

Once in our room we flattened ourselves on the bed like a couple of dead fish beneath a replicated Winslow Homer watercolor emphasizing sailboats. It was a relief to be out of the car. Patsy was asleep in seconds.

Some three hours later my own eyes opened.

I nudged her.

"Babes, want to head downstairs?"

She screwed herself around and glanced at the clock radio on the stand beside the bed. It was nearing 10. She inhaled a slow breath while glancing at Homer's sailboats. Then, like a spark from a wood fire, she rose up off the bed and leaped to the floor in nothing less than a Superman single bound.

Men and women writers of various ages had already filled the Statler's lounge before we arrived and we joined them. Like ourselves, they were leaving the adoption of their identification badges until the morning. I spotted a slit of an opening at the bar, then attempted to chisel out space for Patsy.

"Too many Hemingways," the man on my right immediately said. He was short, widely pockmarked, and featured a barrel-like figure that seemed to be out of order with his abundant black and wavy hair. He did his utmost to cram further to the right so that I wouldn't feel like a sardine.

"How's that?" I said, fluttering a hand in the air for the bartender's attention while at the same time wondering if this was yet another writer who had no use for the dictionary.

"Look around. Quite a few hardcore drinkers," he said. "Would this whole affair were being held in Cuba. Or Key West at least."

"No argument there," I said and ordered a seven-and-seven for myself and a gin-and-tonic for Pats, our drinks away from the hometown.

"J.W. Cooker," he said ebulliently, then offered his hand as best he could under the crowded conditions. It was a gnarled appendage and testified to an early involvement with some form of abusive labor.

"Wyatt Falkner. This is Patsy Lukehart."

"You're writers?"

"You think we don't look it?"

"Easy, young man. Don't get your back up now. I put it the way I did only because some infatuated minglers have apparently infiltrated our hive."

Patsy smiled at him and asked, "What is it you write, Mr. Cooker?"

"Me, I busy myself with a detective series, Miss. However, my books are more popular with European readers than with the people here at home. I'm looking to change that. What about the two of you?"

"I've a novel just come out," I said. The grin my words produced on Cooker was too broad and I knew at once it was a sign of his instant recognition. A twinge of shame, unexpected, blew through me.

"Don't look embarrassed," he said with a jolt at my shoulder from the side of his fist. "I know that look is all. I've already seen it on several other faces. I'm guessing you're book is published with Quotidian."

All of a sudden the thought raced through my mind this weekend could become one of the worst of my life.

I felt a hand on my shoulder. "Relax, Wyatt. You think I'm about to make a judgment on your writing without running these over extended orbs of mine across a paragraph or two? Maybe you know what you're doing and maybe you're out in left field. Maybe your work should be flung into the fire. How the devil would I know? But your publisher as a topic of conversation at this conference is receiving prime billing, I can assure you of that." He looked past me to Patsy. "What about you, Miss Lukehart? Do you have a book for sale with the same outfit?"

Patsy mushed her lips and shook her head. The bartender delivered our drinks. I quickly sipped at the seven-and-seven, then swung around to look at the many groups that had formed in the room. There was chatter at each of them.

"You know there were some last-minute changes made to this conference, don't you?" said Cooker after taking a hit off his whiskey. "There's now a heavier emphasis on self-publishing. One of the organizers realized the industry is all over the place and that writers might want to hear about it from those who actually know something about the real developments and not from just other wannabe writers."

I nodded an interest and another writer behind us, eavesdropping, did the same.

"You know, Wyatt, there's plenty on hand like yourself. Quotidian books, that is. Quite a few in attendance who've signed with them. And that causes me to wonder which of you will be the one to write today's unfolding story?"

"What story is that?" I asked, not sure what he was referring to.

"What story!" He looked over at Patsy who wore a blank expression of her own, then laughed to the ceiling. "The two of you undoubtedly have been traveling all day and that's the reason you don't know. The allegation showed up online around mid-morning. The four authors who were murdered were having sex with one another. When you're back in your room, have a look."

"Where should we look?" Patsy inquired.

"By now, anywhere. But it debuted at WritersUp."

"Sex?"

"Yes, young man. Sex. And as you would expect, the word that comes next to mind is jealousy. And where's there's jealousy, there's often murder, isn't there?"

"That's hard to believe," I said.

"Much of what we read on the Internet is hard to believe. But all the same it's there, and who knows? It could be true."

"J.W., you'll have to excuse me. I'm going to circulate."

"Meet some people. Start networking. I recommend it," he said, nodding.

I backed out of my slot at the bar and Patsy tagged along after flashing a smile of farewell at Cooker.

Barely a minute later she put a hand on my arm and said, "Wyatt, you stay. I'm going back to the room."

"But we just got here," I protested.

"Yes, I know. However, this sex allegation interests me. I want to pull it up online and see what it's about."

"Why? Are YOU intending to write the story?" I threw this out entirely in jest, not knowing that Patsy was already doing exactly that and was waiting for the right time to tell me, and it wasn't now. "You really think there might be something to what he said?"

"I don't know."

"So why do you care anyway?"

"Later, Wyatt." She planted a quick smooch of dismissal on my cheek and moved out.

I knew better than to persist that she stay, and so I stood in place and watched her exit the lounge, carrying her drink along. Once she was gone, I took another look around. Finally, I shouldered my way through the crowd to a cluster of writers who were sitting around a table on comfortable brown leather settees while others lingered at their backs, glasses in hand. Yet before I could attune myself to their topic of conversation, from a window that offered a darkened view of the lake far below I overheard a male voice utter this: "It's unfair to say they'll publish anything without stating that 'anything' includes some very good books by some very good writers."

Another man scoffed. "Like who, Fletcher? Have you read any that you believe are good? Or are you thinking that with thousands of poorly written books, chance alone dictates you'll find a prize."

"I've read several, Tom, that were deserving of a thumbs-up review," said this Fletcher, and a half-dozen titles rolled off his tongue. The last was *As I Lay Dreaming*.

If that wasn't surprise enough, a third man standing with his back to me said, "I've read that novel. I especially liked the scene where the kid straddles the coffin and bores holes into the lid."

"I don't recall anything like that in its pages," Fletcher replied beneath a dubious brow. "Are you certain we're speaking of the same book?"

And even today I wonder which surprised me more. That no author in the group of eight had read William Faulkner's *As I Lay Dying*, or that Detective Harley Dempsey had showed up at the conference masquerading as a writer.

The detective then swung around in my direction, almost as if he were surveying and recording faces, and I stared at him from some twenty feet away. A woman at his side tapped a finger on his forearm. Until then, I had failed to recognize his partner Verlaine Maines, and the reason was that she was dressed much like you would expect a successful female writer to dress, with plunging top, dangling earrings and a gold necklace, and not at all like a cop—she looked exceptionally attractive. Rather discreetly, she nodded in my direction. I ended the starefest with a crack of a smile and started to maneuver my way toward them to say hello and anything else that might cross my mind, but they abruptly turned away after my second step. If I were of a fragile nature and a person who considers himself to be of significance in the lives of his fellow men and women, I would have been offended. Yet their instant rebuff at my approach signaled to me that they were undercover and did not want to risk being addressed as "Detective."

This explanation sufficing, I glanced into my glass and saw that my drink was down to a withering ice cube. Returning to the bar to order another, I noticed that J.W. Cooker had migrated to the far end and was now in a vigorous conversation with a woman whose air-inflated hairdo suggested that she was a romance writer. Cooker's drink was again filled to the top with ice and whiskey.

When the bartender, this one a young woman too adorned with a confection of makeup, set the new drink before me, the volume of sound from the most recessed corner of the lounge exploded, and she and I both threw our attention in that direction. A second startling burst followed and this time she met the eyes of the first bartender whose expression signaled the human interactions underway at the deep end of the room required a watchful eye.

I gave it all of mine, and as I did a silence unforeseen overtook the lounge as an unshaven, bohemian style of a man in a brown field coat with frayed corduroy cuffs and collar pushed himself from the perimeter of a compact group into its center. There he confronted a second man of undersized yet thick dimensions, and this other man was enjoyably smirking.

"You!" the man in the field coat said, pointing

accusingly. "You're responsible." He turned to his right and dialed the stiffened arm with an equally stiffened finger at a third man, possibly the only writer in the lounge donning a tie. "And so is he. And maybe a few others in this room."

"Schacter is responsible," groaned the smirker—it was a tiresome enunciation. He glanced with confidence at the others, but I saw a small warning sign in his expression that said he'd had enough of listening to contrary opinion on the subject. "That's who you should be angry with, Mister. Tor Schacter. Not us."

The man in the field coat inhaled his oxygen audibly, reminding me of a friendly old boxer an uncle had when I was growing up and with which I would sometimes wrestle. I could hear the barely controlled effort from where I was standing at the bar. Others were hearing it, too, as they exchanged questioning looks with each other and with me.

The man in the field coat pursued his lecture and its tone grew deeper on every word. "Schacter's policy makes it impossible to sell one's book in the brick-and-mortars. Sure, I'll give you that. I'll give you all of that. But it's you!" —The finger was out again—"It's you and the others who are ruining my chance of selling the book at the online stores because of your unfair attacks and endless barrage of lies and dishonest criticism on every goddamn message board and social website." He punctuated these last words by raising the rigid finger and sticking it into the smirker's face.

"Move it," the smirker warned, neither blinking nor flinching. "Best get it out of my sight if you intend that snout of yours to ever have use of it again."

The finger remained where it was for several seconds and did not slip or even flutter as the two men stared into each other's eyes. But eventually the small appendage was curled and the arm lowered.

"Wise decision," muttered the smaller man who, instead of losing the smirk, widened it. He even flashed the belittling expression to the rest of us throughout the lounge as if we were in agreement.

It was a stupid move of self-indulgence because with the reckless speed of pent-up rage, the arm inside the field coat shot up again and it was the entire hand at its end this time, not merely a finger, that took hold of the smirker's throat as though it were no more precious than a sewage pipe, and the field coat drove his captive backwards. The smirker, utterly surprised, stumbled like a fat stuffed puppet and unable to get his feet properly aligned, soon found himself slammed into a wall.

Others in the group reacted with a chorus of worried, inert objections. It was only Dempsey and Maines who jumped in, separating the pair as mere strangers in a crowd who didn't want to see anyone get injured. Then, after a few seconds, when it seemed their move was successful, I watched Dempsey look from one participant to the other and, in his mellow voice, say, "You know, you two squirrels are going to give us writers a bad name."

Chapter 11

The many writer websites, then and now, vary widely in their content and the amount of traffic they attract. While some act as a metaphorical backyard fence for gossip and trivia, others provide precise answers to important questions. One of the best for the latter continues to be WritersUp.net, a no-nonsense website hosted by an author who raises thoroughbreds in the heart of Kentucky's Bluegrass Region. Emoticons are non-existent and the contributors to the board know better than to pass along some joke or silly tale they received in their private e-mails, and a claim is seldom made that the poster hasn't already checked with Snopes. Its forums are many and include one confined to technical writing and another to the execution of queries and still another to nonfiction book proposals. There is even one for those wishing to exercise their lexical muscles in E-prime. Yet on this site, as on every other, a thread introduced long ago devoted itself to Quotidian. This came about because of the efforts of the Nemesis Nine, who left their home boards momentarily to engage themselves in the propagation of their faith. Seeing what they'd done sufficed as proof they were after more than mere aspersions. What they wanted was to shut forever

Quotidian's doors. I remember thinking, too, if that was how I saw it—ordinary citizen and supermarket stockboy Wyatt Falkner, whose biggest concern was for his novel— then certainly Tor Schacter, who had big capital invested, would see it the same and he might start to retaliate with every weapon at his disposal.

At home WritersUp never garnered a great amount of my attention because it is excruciatingly slow in loading on dial-up. More often than not I bailed after a minute. At the Statler this was not a problem.

It was past midnight when I returned to the hotel room from the lounge, and the screensaver of Hubble images on Patsy's computer was cycling. Patsy was asleep—or so I thought—as her pretty face was buried between two pillows like a sweetie of a kitten on a cold night.

"Touch a key to see what J.W. Cooker was alluding to," I heard her murmur.

"You're awake."

"For about the last half-hour."

Someone signed in on WritersUp as "Truth Serum" reported that the Philadelphia police were investigating a sexual connection among the four victims. The poster stated there was evidence to suggest that the four murdered victims were experimenting with each other in order to advance their writing careers.

"That's all of it?"

"That's it," she said. "Of course, it's getting stretched on the other boards."

I read the brief post a second time. It sounded more than a little bizarre.

"A new chapter for Write What You Know," I said. "If you can get yourself to believe it, it means Spectra Suter intended to add a dash of horror to her erotic novels. It means she wanted to experience first hand what an orgasm might be like with a knife at her throat. Same for Purvis and her romance material, I suppose. Underwood, on the other hand, must have wanted to experience what it's like to get off while a wooden stake is pushed through the heart."

"And what about Wade Smmith? What was he doing? Running around buck naked with a ten-gallon hat on his head and spurs on his heels, screaming 'Ride those fillies, Garnet'?"

Patsy slipped out of the bed and padded over next to me.

"Do you think it's actually possible?" I said.

"I don't know what to think, Wyatt. It was news to me to learn these people lived within driving distance of each other."

There were about two-dozen follow-up replies to Truth Serum's initial post. Interestingly enough, three accused Schacter of inventing the disparaging claim. They accused him of salting the website in order to take the focus of the crimes off himself.

I searched another site and Pats asked what I was looking for. I located the thread I was after and pulled it up on screen for her to read. I paged down near its end.

"There," I said, pointing.

Lillian Purvis Post # 485	Today's readers are demanding and can be difficult to please. They want to know that their authors have experienced what they are writing. Good news, my followers. Lillian Purvis's readers will have the certainty of knowing that all is not invented when they read a scene that includes a *ménage à trois*.

"Hmmm," said Patsy with a ducky purse of her lips.

"Hold your thought." I said. "Sample the other posts."

She did. "Everyone else is busy wisecracking," she said when finished.

"And so it might have been with Lillian Purvis. What I'm saying is, everything that woman placed on the boards was intensely dramatic. She may not have known how to tell a simple knock-knock joke."

"She's a very attractive woman. So was Spectra Suter. Let's have a look at Underwood and Smmith."

We went to AuthorsRetreat and found one of the countless posts belonging to H. Garnet Underwood. A thumbnail of his face was next to it. We examined it more closely than we'd ever done.

"Late 40s, maybe early 50s," mused Patsy. "More distinguished than handsome. How about Smmith?"

"No photo here, but he has a website."

I typed Wade Smmith into the Google box and up came his website link. I went directly to the site.

"Oh my," said Patsy, stifling an all-out laugh, and I was about to do the same, as her earlier image of a naked Wade Smmith in boots and cowboy hat came instantly to our minds, only with a startling alteration: Smmith's selfie showed him as outrageously pink.

"That's enough," Patsy said. "Close the window, please, or that broiler image is going to follow me to the grave."

I did as asked, but wasn't too sure I agreed with her depiction that carried with it the unspoken implication that overly pink flesh would rule out sex. As I recalled, Wyatt Falkner was pretty red-faced the first night he and Pats had hooked up.

Chapter 12

I held off informing Patsy of the surprising events that had played out in the lounge after her departure until the following morning. She listened to it all without asking a question, although I was sure the most fascinating of the items contained in the story was the presence of the two Philadelphia detectives and their pretending to be writers. Afterwards, we rode the elevator down to the restaurant before the many other writers in attendance began to show up.

Near a window that overlooked a street with a campus bus shelter at its corner was a table. We claimed it after filling our plates from the buffet. Before I had the chance to swipe a dollop of jam across my toast, Dempsey and Maines appeared alongside.

"Mind if we join you, Mr. Falkner?"

"By all means," I said to the detective. I pointed to the vacant seats. He held four stories of griddle cakes and stood straight as a marble column.

"Harley Dempsey," he said matter-of-factly for Patsy's benefit. He nodded at Maines across from him and to my right, and introduced her in the same matter-of-fact voice.

I introduced Patsy, and the detectives took a seat.

"It's a pleasure to meet you," Patsy responded, her eyes acknowledging one, then the other. "Wyatt told me of your visit to Valley Camp. He also reported on your heroics of last evening."

"Hardly heroic," said Dempsey, still matter-of-factly. "One would think writers would know better than to behave as they did."

A waitress, a student at the university, came by. She flipped our cups from the saucers and poured coffee after everyone nodded.

Right afterwards, while everyone sipped at their brew, I threw my head back and laughed. It was out of place and since my intention wasn't to make the detective feel uncomfortable, I immediately revealed the thought behind the mirth.

"Go on!" he said without the faintest amusement surfacing in the eyes. "There's no coffin scene anywhere in your book? No crazy kid with a brace and bit, straddling a coffin and boring holes?"

I shook my head.

"That screwball Dixon. I should've known," he said to his partner.

"Sergeant Dixon is a well-read guy," she remarked to Patsy. "Trouble is, he never remembers when a book was published and often mistakes one author for another."

Like Patsy and myself, both detectives this morning were displaying a white nametag that had been provided with the conference materials. Dempsey wore his on the right side of his chest at pocket level while Maines had pinned hers on the slope of her left breast. No title or rank accompanied either of their names.

Which led me to bring up the "undercover" thing.

"Keep it to yourselves," Dempsey said and it wasn't a

request.

Although I welcomed his confirmation of my suspicion, its reason eluded me. The same seemed to be true with Patsy who was looking questioningly at Maines.

The detective opened up. "When we first spoke with Mr. Falkner at his home," she began, "Detective Dempsey and myself had already worked our way through more posts on the message boards than you might imagine. Since then, we've combed through still more on just about every website where comments were written about the murders and Quotidian Release. Finally, we made out a comprehensive list of the writers we wanted to question. As it turned out, a surprisingly large number of them had signed up for this conference."

Dempsey was lifting each of his griddle cakes with a fork and slipping a pat of butter in between. I wasn't sure he was approving of his partner spelling out their strategy to a civilian. Even so, Maines was about to continue, except there wasn't a need because Patsy had figured things out.

"So by coming here this weekend," she said behind a respectful eye that again acknowledged each of them, "you're saving yourselves great amounts of both time and effort. Not to mention that pretending to be writers allows you to ask your questions without the worry the responses you receive were previously massaged and even invented. Smart."

Several seconds before, four participants to the conference had entered the room and the man among them approached a table near us. He beckoned to the others to join him, causing Dempsey to pause with the pitcher of maple syrup in mid-air. The women participants at the opposite side shook their heads to the man and called him back to a table where they stood. As he stepped away,

Dempsey released his thought. "Have you ever considered becoming a cop, Ms. Lukehart?"

That was Patsy's strength, for sure: the ability to instantly analyze. Plus, she was usually correct.

I, on the other hand, was not—quick to analyze. Although once I did, I was frequently on the mark myself, borne out on occasion by the corroboration of others. But what I couldn't help wondering at this moment was why the police were so eager to talk with writers. Seemed to me the detectives' time would be much better spent interrogating Schacter and his goons. I said as much.

Again, Dempsey paused and he looked at me with a cat's curiosity. "Any chance you've checked your novel at the online bookstores?"

"My novel? No. Not since it went on sale. Why?"

"Kenny Kershaw. Does that name ring a bell?"

"Kenny Kershaw published with Quotidian. His book came out maybe two or three months ago. He's not on the boards each and every day, but he posts routinely enough that everyone knows who he is. Why?"

"Robert Santoro. What about him?"

"Sure, Santoro is on the boards as well. He's a loser with a big mouth. At least, that's my opinion of him. What's this about?"

"Three reviews showed up at the online bookstores for Kershaw's book. They all panned it."

"And scathingly," added Maines. "One star, every one of them."

"Kershaw concluded it was Santoro who had written all three reviews, then posted each from a different IP address. Care to hazard a guess what he did?"

"He contacted the webmaster for those online bookstores and demanded the reviews be removed."

The detective grunted. "He wasn't that smart. No, what's this crazy Kershaw do? He searches out where Santoro lives and then he drives out there, several hundred miles, mind you, and attempts to run him down with his Explorer."

"He tried to kill him?" exclaimed Patsy.

"He denies that. He claims he was just trying to scare Santoro, but the Colorado D.A. isn't buying it."

"Why would anyone want to murder someone over a bad review?" I protested. "That's ridiculous."

"You writers are a screwed-up bunch is why," said Dempsey accusingly. "Too many think you're destined to become the next King or the next Grisham."

"Maybe, but we don't all believe it," I said.

"Kershaw did."

I shook my head and returned to my plate.

"I'm not done with the story," Dempsey interrupted. "There's a plot twist to the matter that you'll appreciate. Santoro wasn't the critic."

"Who was?"

"That's up in the air. Furthermore, the people running the online bookstores couldn't care less."

Patsy then asked what I was thinking. "Were the reviews in any way legitimate, Detective?"

"No," Maines answered for him. "I was curious about that myself, and so I accessed each of them. Whoever posted those reviews, I'm quite sure, never read the story, let alone purchased the book. Yet several others who later read those same reviews indicated they were helpful, so I can understand why such dishonesty would anger an author. What I don't understand is why the readers themselves aren't more skeptical of such severe criticism. To trust without question that it's true and accurate ... they're being censored by a stranger and they're saying they're okay with that."

"So does that answer your question, Mr. Falkner?" said Dempsey. "Scores of writers on the boards who hate Schacter and Quotidian. But quite a few others who hate their fellow writers in equal measure. And you already know where you stand."

"All right," I conceded, "so the police have reason to proceed as they are. Now what about the recent story that says the four victims were having sexual relations with one another?"

"What about it?"

"Well, is there anything to it? Or is it all nonsense?"

"Too soon to know," he said, shrugging. And on that he bent to the pleasure of the food before him.

I was about to join him in the activity because it appeared any pointed discussion among us was at an end, except I noticed that Patsy was staring at Dempsey across the lip of her coffee cup. She waited until he had finished a forkful of griddle cake and washed it down, before speaking.

"Detective, have you forgotten why you asked to sit with us? I'm thinking that you had a question you wanted to ask of Wyatt."

Dempsey hesitated to return to his stack of griddle cakes and an expression of appreciation spread across his face. He regarded his partner and there was Detective Maines throwing her head back out of her own appreciation.

"Thank you for reminding me, Ms. Lukehart," he said, smiling. "Yes, there is something we hope Mr. Falkner can help us with."

"What's that?" I asked.

"We got caught up in other things and it totally slipped

our minds. Does the phrase 'riding shotgun' mean anything to you?"

"Unless you're talking about a stagecoach with a strongbox on top—"

"—I'm fairly confident Wells Fargo is not involved."

"Can you give me anything more?" I'd heard the phrase as it related to sitting in the passenger front seat of a car, but that didn't seem any better a connection than did the Wild West.

"It was a P.S. to a message left on Underwood's phone," Dempsey explained. "It was from the woman Suter, but it doesn't appear to have anything to do with the message itself. It's more like it was an afterthought to an earlier talk between them. The entire statement was, 'He'll flip out when he learns of riding shotgun' Did you ever run across that phrase on any of the boards?"

Nothing struck my mind and I said I didn't recall ever seeing the phrase in a post.

Dempsey turned his attention to Patsy. She likewise couldn't make anything out of the statement.

"It likely doesn't mean a thing," he said and went back to putting away his breakfast.

There wasn't much conversation among us after that and all four breakfasts soon vanished from our plates. Finally, Dempsey said to his partner, "Let's get started." He drained the last of his coffee and swiped his napkin across his mouth a couple of times, then got up from the table. Detective Maines finished the last of her coffee as well and did the same.

As they stepped away, Dempsey raised an abbreviated hand in goodbye while Maines said she would be ordering my book.

Left alone, there was nothing then for Patsy and me to

do but to get up from the table ourselves, exit the restaurant, and become involved in the opening presentation, after which, because of the numerous individualized workshops and seminars, we went our separate ways for the remainder of the day.

Chapter 13

The conference came to a close on Sunday morning and I reminded myself that Patsy had signed me up for it because she had said that I was good on my feet and believed engaging face-to-face with editors and agents would benefit my writing endeavors. But until we were in the car and on our way back to Valley Camp, it had not occurred to me that she'd had her own reason for attending.

"So, did you pitch your story?" she asked me from behind her rose-colored shades.

"It's horror that your old roomie handles," I informed her.

"Well, that's a new wrinkle," she said, surprised, as she lowered her window all the way. "She was handling your kind of material a few months ago. I'm sorry, Wyatt."

"No need for that. She was gracious enough to accept the manuscript. She said she would pass it on to a colleague who's an acquisition editor for mainstream and thriller fiction. Did you have a chance to reminisce with her? She seemed very nice."

"We talked briefly. Although we roomed together, you know we never really hanged together. She had her circle of freshmen that first year of college and I had mine. In the remaining semesters, I saw her on campus but rarely. I only learned about her position at Marley from an editor at one of the magazines."

It was a sunny a.m. and few cars were on the route. I was letting the Ru cruise at sixty-five. If I'd owned a convertible, the top would have been down—that's how perfect a spring day it was. Sun, mild breeze any time we stopped, pleasant temperature, plus a sweet scent to the air from whatever was in early bloom along the shoulders, birds in the sky, horses grazing, cattle already lolling in the fields. Patsy's hair was getting flicked every which way but it didn't seem to bother her. She looked beautiful as always.

"What happened to you these past couple of days?" I asked and reached out to rest a hand on the outside mirror. The air hitting it felt cool and healthy, and all of me was experiencing an upbeat feeling inside and out.

"I don't know if you're going to like this," she replied.

"Now, Babes, when has there ever been anything about you I didn't like?"

"This is different, Wyatt."

"I'm all set to listen," I said. I pulled my hand back inside, shifted my position a degree to the right and leaned on the door. "Not to mention, there's a boatload of understanding that comes with it," I added.

She smiled at my effort to charm, maybe even nodded but hardly vertically, before she removed her shades and said, "For some time now, Wyatt—perhaps you took notice, perhaps not (I hadn't)— I've been stacking screen shots of the never-ending posts penned by the indignant men and women from the many message boards for writers where the ever present storm is Quotidian. These are ordinary human beings who hurl abuse upon abuse at each other, and yet not so long ago they practiced a mutual respect.

Why is that, I began to ask. And then I realized there's a kind of control freak behind it all, and these scores of men and women are unaware of its influence on their behavior."

"You're referring to Schacter," I said.

In spite of her young age, Patsy is well read. Better than myself. And among the countless authors she'd consumed was Studs Terkel, and it was her intention, she told me as we rode along, to model a book after his most famous in which he had included the transcripts of his recorded conversations with everyday working men and women—waitresses, boilermakers, roofers, secretaries, truck drivers, electricians, and so on. Patsy's plan was to interview many of the same people who had posted—those writers who used their real names and didn't hide behind some anonymous handle—then introduce a transcript of that interview alongside the earlier post, and follow up with some words of her own. I understood her assumption without her stating it, and that's because I know that she believes people are good at heart. In other words, when facing these people across a table or a desk, she anticipated they would come off as polite and civilized instead of hateful and vindictive, as was often the case on the boards. Schacter might be the freak, but the message boards were the catalyst—that was part and parcel of what she would be attempting to get at with her book.

The trouble was, she hadn't convinced herself such a book would interest anyone, and I was having the identical thought while listening to her. The book would work, I believed, only if what she herself had to say was insightful. As for what the posters had to offer, I was skeptical. I felt too many would still come off as jerks even when sitting across a table from my lovely Patsy, and how many jerks are required before you tell yourself, "I don't want to read anything more about this kind of person." I must have sounded flip when I said as much to Pats, but she said she'd had similar thoughts and that was the reason she decided to get other opinions, which meant the conference and the editors who would be on hand.

"So what is it you think I won't like, Pats? It's not your own reservations. I'm in agreement with them."

"Wyatt, I was already reaching the conclusion that the book couldn't stand as I just described it. It needed something more, something—"

"—Like maybe a group of authors having sex with one another? C'mon. What's this all about."

I slowed the car so that I could give greater attention to and more frequent looks at my woman.

"Okay," she said. "I'll explain. At the conference I sat down with only one editor and within seconds I thought he wasn't listening to a word I was saying and was brushing me off. But on the contrary, he knew everything about me. At least when it came to what has my byline attached. He'd worked for Time-Warner and Conde Nast and he said he was a big fan of Pats Lukehart, not only of my writing, but also of how my head seemed to work. He thought the idea to deliver a Terkel-style book on the nasty interchanges prevailing throughout the numerous message boards for writers would be a winner. But he added something. He wants me to weight my questions to the persons I interview so that they underscore the murders."

"He what?"

She repeated herself.

"He's hoping you'll somehow solve the crimes is what he wants," I said with scantily clad astonishment. "You're not a cop! Don't make the mistake of taking Dempsey's compliment to heart."

"I don't believe he's hoping that," she objected.

"Okay, maybe I'm stretching. But he is looking to smear Schacter, don't say he isn't."

She began to explain, but I cut her off in mid-sentence.

I've stated that I am not a person who is quick with analysis, but that doesn't mean I am never quick, that the proverbial mental light bulb unfailingly relies on some slowly warming ballast to produce a sickly yellow globe at one end and I gotta smack the fixture at the other end to boost the yellow to the revealing white. I knew what her editor was thinking and when she said he liked her idea, he was hedging and probably was lukewarm about it, the same as I. Only he realized that a market for such a book did exist if the spotlight focused on Schacter who was hated by so many of the authors he had published. Eliciting hundreds of comments and suspicions about what was behind the murders and who they believed was responsible from Quotidian supporters and detractors alike had more than the promise of just selling thousands of books; it carried with it the possibility of putting Schacter and Quotidian out of business. And if Patsy and her editor were responsible for that ... well, the blessings from others, both publishers and professional authors, was out there. It would mean that the twenty dollars an individual was spending on a Quotidian book, which in too many instances wasn't worth the paper it was printed on, might be spent on books that actually reward a reader's investment in time and money.

Of course I understood that such a victory, if it happened, would mean the burial of my own book, and while this thought was naturally off-putting, more so was another that probably hadn't crossed her editor's mind— Schacter might not have had anything to do with the killings. And wasn't Dempsey's and Maine's questioning of so many writers at the conference even supporting this possibility? Furthermore, what if there were sexual escapades among the four as was alleged in the post on WritersUp? That would naturally invite the consideration of spouses and boyfriends as the murderer. And beyond all of that it was possible that the killings were done by a total stranger and for reasons which no one yet had a scope on. And if her editor wasn't thinking about any of this, then it wasn't going to cross his mind either what might happen if Patsy were to ask her questions to the wrong person.

But they were crossing mine. Because who could guarantee that an answer to one of those questions wouldn't place her life in danger?

I said nothing further because in my heart I already knew that she would do the book and that she would do it along the lines of her editor's recommendation. Nothing I had to say would change that. I already knew this.

I swung back to where I was fully facing the road out front. I touched the brake going into a sharp turn, then accelerated out of it.

"Wyatt?"

"Apart from the book, anything else?"

"Then you're okay with it?"

"Promise me you'll be careful, Pats. You might get to knocking around in something that neither one of us understands."

"You have my word."

I studied her face an extra second. "All right then. Anything else you'd like to tell me about this weekend?"

"Yes," she said without the least hesitation. "What do you know about Oliver Metheny?"

The question struck me as coming out of nowhere.

"What about Oliver Metheny?"

"He was a no-show with the editor I spoke with. At least there's the possibility it was him. On the pad it read 'O. Matheny.' No first name, just the initial. And the last name was spelled with an 'a' in place of the first 'e'. I asked the editor about it, but his secretary had made out the list."

"Even if it was Metheny, why the question?"

"Didn't you tell me he writes fiction?"

"I don't think he writes much of anything beyond what he scribbles out on the boards regarding Quotidian."

"You once connected him to Tarzan."

"He's supposedly a big Edgar Rice Burroughs fan, and he developed a similar character, except he had to put his creation on an alien planet in some far-out star cluster. It's a self-published e-book. I don't know if it's worth one's time or not. However, I once checked on Amazon and B&N just to see if was listed."

"Was it?"

"It was listed, all right, but there wasn't any sales ranking. And no customer had reviewed it."

Patsy nodded soberly at the information. "Okay, that's all of my stories for the weekend," she said. "Now let's have the rest of yours."

"I met Dalton Ellis," I said.

Chapter 14

The final workshop for which I'd signed up was hardly a workshop at all. It was more a question-and-answer session and it focused on book reviews. In light of the subject, I hadn't anticipated more than a handful of participants. To my surprise the room was packed and the sole unclaimed seat was next to my own. A latecomer occupied it and that was Dalton Ellis who was several inches taller than how I pictured him from his thumbnail and the thousands of words he had posted on Pixel-to-Paper.

He nodded at me as he took the seat. On the table in front he stacked the many materials he had collected at the conference. These included two detective tales by J. W. Cooker. He had also a copy of his own novel and this he placed at the top of the pile.

"What have I missed?" he whispered to me, except his voice maintained a throaty harshness that made whispering futile.

"They just started," I said in a muted tone. "You're Ellis from the Pixel-to-Paper board, aren't you?"

He stretched his head around to read my nametag and nodded again as his eyes, below which hung a puffy curtain, came up to meet my own. The talk at the front picked up and we both fell silent.

Conducting the session was an attractive blonde with large elegant curls dressing her ears and a fragile male sidekick sporting black suspenders and an unremarkable red goatee. They stood several feet apart at the front of the room with a portable whiteboard behind them, which they would never employ. The blonde, who edited a university-sponsored literary journal according to the conference's advance brochure, was speaking of book reviews before the birth of the Worldwide Web. She mentioned the numerous magazines and newspapers with a general readership that either once carried book reviews in their pages or continued to. She then went on to list off other publications that courted a specific audience: women, health and fitness enthusiasts, sports lovers, travelers, woodworkers and hobbyists, and so on.

"The problem surrounding the special reviews that appeared in the pages of these magazines is easily identified," she said. "To read them, you either subscribed, patronized your local library, or selected one from the table while waiting in a doctor's reception area. The Internet changed all that."

"But we can't fully address the subject of book reviews on the Internet," her partner intervened, "without bringing in P O D which has allowed for the publication of countless additional volumes, all of whose authors want their books to be reviewed."

"Many of you who came up to us before we convened"—it was back to the blonde—"indicated you were already operating a website devoted to the reviewing of books. Others stated your intention to start one of your own. Still others we spoke with are writing reviews. Let's have a show of hands for each to get a feel for what we have here today."

To my astonishment, a dozen of the participants had book review websites in operation, and almost that same number of hands went up from those who were planning to create one. Scattered throughout were those who were either writing reviews or wanted to. Plain old curiosity brought up the hands from the rest of us, like myself—you didn't see book review sessions listed in the promos for writers' conferences.

The exception to it all was Ellis. He'd kept his hands at rest around the perimeter of his novel.

Like co-anchors of a local news show, the blonde and the goatee alternated frequently with their presentation. They covered considerable territory too, including the advice that a reviewing website is enhanced when it offers related material such as news, advice, even commercial ads. In all instances, these extra items needed to relate to books and writing, they stressed, and their source had to be credible.

"Credibility is at the heart of the reviews as well," the blonde emphasized. "Readers want to feel confident that the reviews they are consulting are coming from the minds of people who are widely read not only in the genre they're reviewing, but also in other genres. Now that doesn't mean they have to be experts across the entire literary continuum. But if you make the mistake of permitting just anyone to review, you run the risk of having scorn heaped upon all your reviewers and soon your site will be a thing of the past because readers will no longer trust it. You should be careful also about recommending or not recommending a book. A review in its entirety should advance the reader that information. There isn't any reason to point out the direction of your thumb to the interested person as though he or she is incapable of making their own inference from your words."

From the back corner on the opposite side an aging woman's voice interjected, although once I looked at her I saw that it wasn't a match for her actual age, which was much younger. "But don't you think that great numbers of these books should not be reviewed in the first place? And those that are ... well, I think the reader should be warned not to waste their time or, worse, their money."

The goatee smiled and advanced a step as he stroked his facial decor. "You're referring to a lot of the P O D books that are either self-published or the new vanity offerings?"

"Yes," the woman said. "Those books are often poorly written to begin with, and the editing just as often is nonexistent. Yet they frequently get reviewed, if not by a website dedicated to the practice, then by way of customer reviews at the online bookstores. And the reviews are just rave. 'Don't miss this one.' 'We'll be hearing a lot from so and so author,' and on and on. Then you spend your hard earned dollars to order a copy and before you finish Chapter One, you realize you've been hoodwinked."

The goatee dared to ask the woman, "And what reason would you give for those rave reviews?"

"That's easy," chimed in a male voice from the center of the room. "They're being written by other authors who have their own vanity or self-published book they're trying to hawk. It's another example of 'You scratch my back, I'll scratch yours.' Except with this it's dishonest and takes advantage of the trust of strangers who are the readers."

Ellis jumped to his feet, surprising everyone who was seated. "It works the other way, too!" he shouted across the room. He was a middle-aged man still thicker in the chest than abdomen and with a face dry and grossly grooved, which complemented the rough resonance of his voice.

"What is it you're saying, sir?" the goatee asked.

"There are some great books out there," stressed Ellis, "and they're getting slammed. They're getting slammed intentionally with the goal in mind of sinking the book so that no one buys it. This isn't scratching the back. This is a knife in the back, and its other writers, jealous ones, who are responsible."

"Is that what happened to you?" inquired another woman. "Do you have a book that was panned?"

"You bet I do!" he shouted, and he raised his novel off the desk. He held it high. He swung it to his right, then back to his left. There was no rush to the movement. He held the book so that the title, his name, the silhouette of his Masai private eye holding a gun in the air and all of the bright yellow cover were visible. Before he returned it to rest, he angled it downward for my benefit.

The two presenters glanced at each other, and as they looked away, a most peculiar expression inhabited the goatee and he stared at Ellis an extra second before singling out a man with frameless glasses slid far down his nose.

The man addressed Ellis. "I don't know you and so have no reason to insult you, sir. But how do you know those terrible reviews of your book aren't for real?"

Several heads with the identical thought inside them nodded.

"Just read them," said Ellis. "It doesn't take a rocket scientist to conclude the reviewer never had the book in the first place. Besides"—he reached down for the novel to show the group a second time, except I had it open; I closed it clumsily and elevated it above my head like a priest with a chalice— "Besides, I've personally called dozens of books bestsellers before they were bestsellers, so I think I know what I'm talking about when I say my novel Darker than Pitch will sell a minimum of 50,000 copies if just given the chance."

Patsy couldn't hold back her laugh. "So he used fellow writer Wyatt Falkner in his marketing plan."

"He did indeed."

"You said you had the book open."

"You're wondering, was I reading? Chance of a lifetime."

"And what's the verdict? Is it worthy of the 50,000 copies like he said?"

"On page two his main character was already staring into the mirror and solemnly reflecting. Except it wasn't the closeness of his shave or the graying at his temples that he was having thoughts about. It was his life."

Patsy's head bowed, shook a little, and then she gazed out the open window, her head still shaking, the hair still flying, and there was even a low guffaw.

My woman may not have written fiction, but she recognized the handling of backstory by an amateur.

Chapter 15

Before the week was out Patsy had packed her bags and collected the materials and the equipment she would need to interview scores of people. She was eager to head out, even giddy, mostly because this was her first opportunity for a book. Of course I was happy for her in spite of remaining uneasy about the whole venture, but I was envious as well. With my novel Quotidian had offered a mere token advance, the same advance all its authors received and who some commemoratively framed under glass rather than spend as they believed it to be a sign they were on their way to the Pulitzer. Patsy for her first book, and without the plug of an agent, had contracted for a $5,000 advance. Seed money in the amount of two grand had arrived two days after the conference, just as her editor had promised. It was this money that was permitting her to travel and gather her material. It was this money, too, that allowed her to rent a car and not depend on her own, an early model that had upwards of a hundred thousand miles on its four cylinders and about which I was guilty of nagging her because I feared she would break down one day in the middle of nowhere.

I kissed and hugged her for the send-off outside her

house on Grant Avenue and told her to make sure she telephoned on her cell, and I again showed her mine as a reminder. Earlier in the week, I had terminated all service with my landline, signed up for cable for speedier Internet downloads, patched in a router for Wi-Fi, and bought a cell phone. I'd done so out of worry, although I wasn't admitting this to Pats. But if she was intending to pose questions to people regarding the murders—people who were strangers, not so in the strictest sense of the word, but strangers all the same—I wanted her to know that she could get a hold of me at anytime, including when I worked the overnight.

And then seconds later, cool and beautiful in her blue slacks and cream linen henley, she slipped behind the wheel of the car. She started the engine, shifted to drive, and gave a last little wave. I watched and listened until the car disappeared in the distance of the road that spearheaded east out of Valley Camp, loving her all the more because on the rear bumper of that rental she had attached this sticker she'd made as a surprise:

Wyatt Falkner's
AS I LAY DREAMING
"Dare to read it!"

Late that evening, while I crouched over my desk, scribbling out the monthly checks for the various utilities and a spring rain was hitting the windows, my cell sounded. It was Patsy calling to say that she had reached her destination without a hitch, but that the drive had been exhausting because of several road construction projects underway.

And then I wouldn't hear from her again until twenty-four hours later, and the exhaustion was a thing of the past.

"Wyatt, I've already interviewed so many people, and all but one had me in stitches. The funniest was someone you've met. Douglas Robinson."

"Sorry, Pats. You're mistaken. I don't know any Douglas Robinson."

"Sure you do. His pen name is Rex Atherton."

"You're kidding. And he was funny?"

I was skeptical as I recalled my interaction with the man several months prior. He had been the author for a seasonal book signing at Valley Camp's only bookstore and Patsy and I had gone to get his signature on his latest title. Then, to my astonishment, she suggested he join us for a drink afterwards at the Welcomian, a flat-roofed, T-iii-sided box of a building that was a popular hangout midway between our respective homes, famous for its cold draft beer, huge whitefish sandwich and a clientele of adversaries, such as management and labor. Patsy, I'd realized eventually, was doing this for my benefit. She'd figured a little hobnobbing and networking with a successful author couldn't be anything but beneficial to someone starting out, except that once Atherton learned I was to be published by Quotidian, he promptly dismissed me as a loser and endeavored to weaken me in front of Patsy, dreaming he might bed her.

I thought I would hold off on any agreement regarding him.

"Wyatt, you there? Listen, I have several additional interviews within driving range of where I presently am, which is two hours outside of Philly. After that I'm into the city for quite a few more."

The next morning I made a cup of decaf, then downloaded her e-mail before turning on the morning news. It included an attachment containing two of the interviews.

Before leaving Valley Camp she had invested in a handheld digital audio recorder, good for several hours, after which, using the accompanying software, she could transfer the recordings to her traveling laptop.

"Great entertainment here," her message read. "Be sure to listen."

One of the interviews was with Atherton, and when I searched several of the writer websites with message boards, I did indeed come across a D. Robinson and, while he didn't post except where there was controversy, he lacerated the opposition at will. That evening I tuned up my MacBook to listen to the recordings. I must admit Patsy seemed to be correct in her assessment of the mystery author. He sounded entirely different from how I remembered him the past winter's night, energized and convivial on the recording, telling a couple of really funny writer jokes, and he did in fact have Patsy laughing like I've seldom heard her laugh myself, which worried me that he was up to his old trick of trying to nail Pats. For all of that, though, I could concentrate on the interview for only so long, and when that moment came, I got up and went into the kitchen to make a snack for the night while leaving Patsy and Atherton still talking and yucking it up in the office area of his house. But while sprinkling the cinnamon sugar across my two slices of toasted wheat bread, I heard Atherton in the outer room utter the words "riding shotgun" and it caught me up short because these were the curious words Detective Dempsey had asked about at the Statler, words discovered among the phone messages of H. Garnet Underwood. And I'd have wagered the phrase would have caught Patsy up just as short, and that she would have pursued its use. In fact, I was already wondering why she hadn't mentioned it on the phone.

Taking my snack along, I returned to my desk and played back the recent bytes of the interview, during which I learned that Patsy had excused herself to visit Atherton's bathroom, which is the reason she had not mentioned his use of the phrase. The truth was, she hadn't heard it. When next we talked, I brought up the matter.

"He said he never was one who required an audience, and when I got up to go that he would just continue to ramble on. And you're saying that's what he did?"

"Apparently."

She laughed.

"Are you certain 'riding shotgun' is what he said?"

"It seems he was moving away from the recorder at the time, but yes, I think that is what I heard. Also, does he own a bird? Something like a bird sounded off when he spoke. I heard a squawk."

"Then it's nothing."

"How so?"

"You haven't listened to the entire interview?"

"No."

"When I returned from his bathroom, he began to brag about his parrot. Moses, that's the bird's name, accompanies him just about everywhere he goes, sometimes even to a signing, and it loves to ride in the car upfront. He said it stays planted there like a little Grenadier Guard until they get to his destination. That's what he must have been referring to. He must have been referring to Moses riding shotgun in the car."

"You're probably right."

"Although...."

It was a curious although. I'd heard it before. "Although what?" I asked.

"Wyatt, are you thinking this phrase 'riding shotgun' is

somehow connected to those murders?"

"I don't know, Pats. But if you recall, Detective Dempsey said it was a postscript to a message left on Underwood's phone by Suter, and it referred to a third party, a man, who Suter said would 'flip out.' Why do you ask?"

"The last thing Atherton and I talked about was the murders." I could hear her deliberately and slowly inhale. "Wyatt, I hadn't yet got around to asking my questions."

And with that I smiled to myself. Because, just like her editor, I knew how Patsy's head worked. I knew what she was thinking. Atherton's use of the curious phrase might have greased the skid for their final discussion. In other words, it was quite possible 'riding shotgun' was connected to the killings.

Chapter 16

My grandfather on my mother's side worked as a public schoolteacher. He taught social studies, Problems of Democracy—or, coincidentally enough, POD as we the students called it—in a community much smaller than Valley Camp. While in his twenties, a local bartender well tutored in the martial arts persuaded his instructor, a Grandmaster and Chinese-Dutch man by the name of Willem Reeders, to visit the town and offer lessons. Those who signed up were mostly young male teachers like my grandfather who found little other than drink to entertain them across nine months of the year. Unfortunately, instruction began late in the second semester and when the summer break arrived, too many had to leave for college classes in order to extend their professional certification so they could continue to teach in the fall. The lessons came to an abrupt end and were never restarted. Even so, my grandfather was proud of a singular move that Reeders had complimented him on, not once, but twice. The move was such that an attacker wielding a knife or a gun would soon be free of it by a lightning-quick, downward plunge of my grandfather's left hand while his right swung immediately up behind it, bare hard knuckles to the front, and pulverized the attacker's face.

"Fast *riken*! Fast *riken*!" my grandfather would quote Reeders when he was telling the story and include all the excitement of the Grandmaster's approval.

Although this same move was often out in the wind, just as often he enjoyed perpetrating it on his grandson, those bony knuckles surprising me each time and stopping just a microchip away from my nose, certainly close enough that his daughter, my mother, was continually asking, at times begging, him to cease and desist. And eventually he did. But not before he taught the move to me and assured me that I, too, had a fast *riken*.

I had never employed the defensive move at any time in my life and it had only come to mind because Rex Atherton was in my head now and wouldn't quit. At the Welcomian he had demonstrated a most annoying habit of pointing his right index finger with a raised thumb at you when he was attempting to preach or make clear his position on a matter. The move would start at belt level as if he were a gunslinger holding you at bay, but would soon elevate to the level of the chest, and finally the finger was in your face just as he was reaching what he thought was an inarguable conclusion. If he had extended it another inch the night he had joined Patsy and me for a drink and conversation, he would have touched my nose, and I can't say incontrovertibly that he wouldn't have triggered the *riken*.

Patsy's next call came after making the City of Brotherly Love.

"Guess what," she said. "Tomorrow I'm meeting with Tor Schacter."

"You're not! How did you arrange that?" I asked with great amazement.

"Well, it's not actually arranged," she confessed.

For some reason I couldn't help but laugh, and Patsy explained that earlier in the day she had interviewed Jan Sherman, a name that meant nothing until she mentioned the woman's board handle. Sherman, a.k.a. Nine Lives, had been an employee at Quotidian Release until her pregnancy. Because she did some writing of her own, she found the message board at AuthorsRetreat around the same time the attacks on her employer took a leap to include everyday employees like herself. No longer was it to be Schacter alone subjected to blanket incriminations; now anyone working at the publishing house would endure the same and find their character under attack. Sherman, as anyone without an axe to grind would expect, attempted to defend her former co-workers, and she was both reasoned and measured in what she posted. In no manner did she attempt to explain the business model of Quotidian, stressing it was a new twist on book publishing, but never stating that its policies were beyond question. When another poster asked why she had quit, she answered truthfully, but it was pounced upon as a lie and another bellicose voice then wrote he wouldn't be surprised if Schacter was the father of her child. This post was removed from the board, although not before an entire day had passed and hundreds of others had read it and lengthened the thread with dozens of additional comments, many with a vilifying thrust. Moreover, the anonymous assassin was permitted to continue to post on the board without offering an apology.

Nine Lives had told Patsy that to meet Schacter she need only show herself at his place of business. His office was at the rear of the building and made entirely of glass, so that he would have no trouble noticing her entrance. And once he did, Nine Lives assured Patsy she would be waved to the rear. In other words, Schacter liked his women.

"Okay," I said. "Only Pats? Remember a lot of people are convinced this guy orchestrated the murders. So be careful what you ask him."

When we finished talking this time and I shut off my phone, a weird feeling out of nowhere came over me.

Right along, the remarks coming off the message boards were that Quotidian Release was operating as a business and while it might not be breaking any law, it was a fraudulent moneymaking racket all the same, and its list of suckers was made up of wannabe authors. And I was beginning to hold with the view myself as it was getting punched at me enough. Yet there continued to remain some restraint to my perspective because of the nature of the boards themselves, particularly AuthorsRetreat. Unlike the Pixel-to-Paper board where there was never a single advertisement, the pages of AuthorsRetreat had more than its share. These ads appeared on every one of its web pages and they were offers by other P O D publishers to publish one's book, by agents who weren't flooded with clients, by people sitting at home wanting to "professionally" edit your manuscript for a hefty fee before you sent it off. There were enticements in the form of commercial endorsements inviting writers to conferences all around the country, urging them to attend a workshop and maybe even enroll in a university program that would bestow on them an MFA. There were pop-up ads for writing-related software, some promising a plot if you lacked the imagination to come up with one on your own. These ads made for a business, a web business in the form of a message board, and a business intends to make a profit. Someone was making a buck by running these ads, and I was sure whoever it was wanted to keep on making it, along with many more. So wasn't it in that person's interest to keep the board attractive and exciting, even angry and provocative, perhaps taking a page out of Limbaugh and Hannity and similar others who perpetually stirred the political pot and emotions of distinct groups of people in order to keep their paychecks coming around? Perhaps Suter, Smith, and Underwood—throw in Lillian Purvis as well—had been altruistic defenders of the writer—I wanted to think that! Yet it was somewhat bothersome that, except for Purvis, none of the others had a contractual relationship with Quotidian, so that the question arose, had they one with the owner of AuthorsRetreat? Was it possible they had been some kind of web shill? And even if they hadn't been, were there others who were?

This feeling wasn't altogether distressing to myself; it was Patsy for whom I worried. I feared that she was involving herself in a matter that might easily fool her, a situation where there was clarity at the surface, but a short immersion below would reveal a world treacherous and steaming with danger.

Because I harbored these troublesome thoughts, I kept the cell phone on my person throughout the day, and soon after her visit to the Quotidian Release offices, she called. And she was again excited. Only she begged off on her report to me because her morning interview in New York was forced to reschedule for that evening.

"I'm sorry, Wyatt, but I just have to get my tush in gear."

"Wish I were there to see it," I said.

"I'll call you first thing tomorrow morning. Then I'll unload everything Schacter said."

"I'll be waiting."

Except the next morning dawned and she did not call. Nor the next afternoon and evening. Neither did she return my calls. And there was nothing from her in my email inbox.

And then it was that the nightmare began.

Patsy was # 1 on my cell phone's speed dial and I kept punching it in throughout the second day and leaving messages, but nothing was coming back. To be honest I was willing to allow my fears the benefit of the doubt. Good things might have exploded for my Pats and I knew from experience she would surf whatever wave was rushing in her favor until it flattened out; that she would let nothing and nobody get in her way, including me. I was first in her life, as she was first in mine, but we both understood first did not mean always first. We weren't husband and wife. We weren't even formally engaged. First could, on occasion, ride second. The city was New York, too, and her publisher had offices in Manhattan, I reminded myself. It was not difficult to imagine her stopping by to see her editor, which might have led to an unexpected opportunity to attend a real party celebration of a new book about to be released by a well-known author, an event offering a great deal more than pizza, mediocre wine, and boneheads.

Yet at the same time I was restraining my fears, the voice inside me was saying her phone was a cell and that she could ring me up from just about anywhere. So why hadn't she?

And then to worsen the feeling, the downside of the big city came crashing to mind. Could something terrible and unthinkable have happened to Pats?

I had to get control of my head. Letting it drift in every direction wasn't helping, and thus I began to think like the novelist on which I prided myself to be. The first thing I realized is that I couldn't be at all certain she had left Philadelphia. Raking through the memory of our last conversation, I was unable to recall the name of the hotel where she had stayed until I ran the alphabet across the brain. Then I found the number online and called at once. I learned Patsy had checked out just forty-five minutes after her call to me. But that didn't provide any relief, although it pretty much ruled out Philadelphia. Still, I couldn't categorically put a line through this because something could have happened as she went from the hotel to her rental. Even so, this possible exception was set aside. What I figured could be ruled out was a car accident. Because if she had been in a serious wreck between Philadelphia and New York, news of it would have reached Valley Camp.

All right, she's in New York, I told myself. I would go with that. But where? Just as Patsy and I knew we would not, out of habit, call the other every day and night, we also did not insist that I become aware of her itinerary, where she would be staying and with whom she would be meeting. Moreover, while Patsy had scheduled many interviews before she'd left Valley Camp, she also had a list of others from the boards and if there was time, it was a foregone conclusion that she would contact them for some additional question and answer.

I glanced at the mirror above the dresser, if only to consult another human form. All my reflection signaled was that I had been running my hand through my hair so many times that I was starting to resemble a devil of a character.

"What are you going to do, Wyatt?"

And as a freakishly impulsive answer to my question, I remembered that Patsy had some relatives living in other parts of the country and I considered contacting them to determine if they might know anything. But I just as quickly dismissed the idea. She was on good terms, what little they were, with all of them; however, she had said that they were an uninterested group of people who read their local newspaper and not much else, and she wouldn't think of discussing her work with any of them.

That left Dr. Stoddard down at the community college, with whom Patsy often conferred after gathering her preliminary information on an assigned, upcoming magazine article.

"I'm sorry, Wyatt," she said when I phoned. "She mentioned Philly and some neighboring towns and suburbs she was intending to visit, but not the interviewees. I know she had scheduled many a meeting before she left, but she was hoping also to schedule others once there. You know Patsy. She wanted to make full use of her time on the project. Are you worried about her?"

"It's unlike her not to call or send an email," I said.

I still had nothing. And it was becoming impossible not to think that something terrible had befallen the woman I loved.

Ah, Babes. Where are ya?

Chapter 17

Much of another empty day slid by after talking with Dr. Stoddard. You have to act, I scolded myself. Do something!

One thing only came to mind.

"Good afternoon. Quotidian Release. This is Kristen speaking. How may I help you?"

"This is Wyatt Falkner. I need to speak with Tor Schacter. It's extremely important."

"I'm sorry, Mr. Schacter doesn't take calls from just anyone," the female voice said.

"I'm one of his authors. Listen, my girlfriend interviewed Mr. Schacter a few days ago and I haven't heard from her since. I'm worried that something's happened."

"If you'll put your concerns in an email, Mr. Falkner, I'll make sure Mr. Schacter gets it."

"Didn't you hear what I said? She might be missing. I'm worried sick. Mr. Schacter might be able to help."

"Control yourself, Mr. Falkner. Are you certain this woman is your girlfriend?"

"What?"

"Please state your concerns in an email. I'll see that it gets to Mr. Schacter's desk."

The woman hung up on me. This treatment strongly suggested that Quotidian's critics weren't over-the-top with what they were writing on the websites about my publisher. I waited most of a minute for my anger to subside and rang up the number again.

"Good afternoon, this is Amy. How may I help you?"

I hesitated a moment. Amy sounded a lot like Kristen. This was yet another charge against Quotidian I'd read about on the boards: a caller couldn't be sure that the person on the other end was who they said they were.

"Tor Schacter, please."

"Mr. Falkner, I believe Kristen already informed you to put your concerns in an email."

"Forget that," I said firmly. "This involves my book. You tell Mr. Schacter my plans are to order 250 copies for sale at four open-air events at which I've arranged to participate. That number alone should cover his investment and make him a nice profit from *As I Lay Dreaming*."

"That's terrific, Mr. Falkner. I'll let him know."

"Fine. But you can tell him also that I won't be ordering squat if he doesn't call me back in ten minutes."

It was a lie as I wasn't intending to order any of my books, but they didn't know that. Yet in that fraction of a second before I flipped the cover on the phone, I heard a titter.

I waited the ten minutes and quite a few more with the cell in hand in case Schacter was of the type who refuses to have others ever set his timetable.

He never called.

Which is when I began to consider that the Nemesis Nine, those dead and those still living, weren't even close to understanding the heart and head of Tor Schacter. What kind of a man wouldn't return a phone call after learning the caller was deeply upset and concerned about the welfare of someone close?

I knew then what I had to do, and so I called my boss at the supermarket. I told him I was taking time off to do something that couldn't wait and that I hoped my job would still be there for me upon my return. After that, I phoned the only people who could possibly help. Dempsey was away.

"Is there an extension for Detective Maines?" I asked.

I first reminded the detective that she had met Patsy at the Cornell Statler and informed her that she was doing interviews for a book and that she hadn't been in contact.

"She was driving up to New York from Philadelphia," I informed her. "She'd interviewed Tor Schacter. It wasn't one of her scheduled interviews, yet when the opportunity presented itself, she couldn't pass it up in light of the murders and all that's swirling around his possible involvement. But she checked out of the hotel in Philadelphia, and that's the last I heard from her."

"Who's her publisher?" Maines asked businesslike.

I gave her the name and she said she would call in case Patsy had made contact with them. I told her too about the rental car. After that, she rattled off a physical description of Patsy to see if it agreed with my own and inquired of what she was wearing the last time we'd been together. I knew what was behind this and didn't like it, but that was only because it could make one start to think on the dark side too prematurely. Patsy was alive and until there was evidence to the contrary, I would avoid thinking the worst.

Late that evening I loaded the car, locked the house, and sped off into the spreading darkness. There was nothing to go on as to where I might locate Patsy, but I thought Schacter might have the answer. And so I headed for Philadelphia and the offices of Quotidian Release Book Publishing where I planned to confront him in person.

I drove throughout the night, windows down as the outside temperature was pleasantly warm, stopping for a coffee-to-go now and then, once breaking the run to drop back the seats on the Subaru and sleep for an hour at a roadside rest. When I awoke, I got out and shuffled inside the octagonal outpost to the restrooms, plus I wanted something from the vending machines. On the wall next to them was a bulletin board and tacked to it was a flyer for a book, one whose title I recognized. Incredulous, I stared at the flyer. Was this what one of Schacter's authors must do to promote his or her work? Why not take it a step further, I thought with growing disgust, and tape additional flyers to the inside of the toilet stalls? If anxiety over Patsy hadn't been occupying my mind, I would have become thoroughly depressed about my future.

I arrived in the vicinity of the building that housed Quotidian around seven the next morning and found a parking spot that permitted an unobstructed view of the front entrance. It was a three-story red brick building that had been on the street for a long time, but it obviously had been cared for with great solicitude over the years as there was no patina of industrial smoke and crud, and any old graffiti had been sandblasted away. It looked as it had in the photo for the exposé, except some sections near the top stood out as their mortar had been recently repointed to insure public safety on the sidewalk below. Similar structures were to its left and right, except they housed families instead of a business. Something suggested it was a quiet neighborhood, perhaps inspired by the presence of books close by.

At a quarter to 8 a woman strode up to the entrance.

She was in her early to mid-forties with dark hair cropped too close to her skull and she wore a plain green shift that hadn't been allotted much attention beyond its length. She walked like a well-tuned wrestler emerging out of the tunnel. She produced a key from a pocket on the loose garment and unlocked the doors. Minutes later, others followed, men and women who couldn't have been much over twenty-one, if they were that. Kids was my first thought. I'd expected their number to be greater, although I don't know why, because with all the changes Schacter had employed to streamline communications and manuscript submissions, it made sense that those who were editing, illustrating, and otherwise designing the book could easily do it on their computers at home and at a reduced cost to Quotidian Release.

I stayed seated in the car, and then on the half-hour Schacter himself showed. Rare photos of him had displayed on the boards, and these had been searched for arduously by those who had posted. The pix, as I recalled, didn't reveal much below the shoulders, so that in person he appeared considerably smaller in all dimensions, though far from being the runt of the litter. His hair, I could clearly see, was thinning and his skin sallow, sending the message that he'd passed too much time indoors with most of the locations poorly lit. The jaw was round like a big cherry and even heading toward the assigned color, light or no light. The eyes were quintessentially remote. With a strong handle like Tor Schacter, I'd been expecting more, although at the same time an air was coming off him, like a laughable fart from a steadfast growling dog, that said only a fool would dismiss the company president so readily.

With him was a man who was obviously a weightlifter, except the somewhat loose and cavalier fit of his shirt about the waist suggested that he might not be in quite the great shape he was intending to project. He qualified as Muscle and I was betting with myself that he was one of those goons at the so-called party who was said to have been packing heat. I scrutinized his person as carefully as was possible from the distance I was at to see if there was any hint of a gun. I was pretty sure there wasn't, but that didn't mean one wouldn't be close at hand inside the offices, and after what had occurred with the phone and Kristen the day before, the feeling was developing that I might have to go through this guy to get to Schacter. I might have become immediately apprehensive about this but for the paltry advance of the Jefferson bill he'd sent to me and each of his authors. It was telling me through simple extrapolation that Schacter probably hadn't rolled out the big bills either for a top-of-the-line bodyguard.

At the entrance, Schacter paused. He swung around and looked down the street in my direction. I didn't know if he was searching for something or if the move was just a whim and something done every morning before entering the place, like maybe he'd sniffed the odor of something he wanted to identify. In any case, I doubted he could see inside my car. On the dash above the speedometer I had set an empty coffee cup and the wrinkled wrapper from a Sausage McMuffin.

He stared for several seconds before finally stepping inside. The Muscle moved behind him, but not before he took a last long look of the street himself. He looked older than me, but not by more than a decade.

Chapter 18

Once Schacter and his bodyguard had disappeared inside the building, I got out of the Ru and hurried up to the front entrance. As they had done, I turned around to stare back down the street, but nothing seemed extraordinary or offered a reason to wonder. I then stepped inside and was not hoping for trouble. I was there in person now, not on the phone, and the quickest way for Schacter to be rid of me would be to answer a few questions.

"May I help you?" I was unsure if the voice was the woman on the phone, but it was the woman who had opened up the premises and her tone was peppered with inveterate suspicion—nothing friendly about it. Up close, she looked even more like a wrestler and someone you'd think twice about tangling with, pugilistically or sexually.

"I need to talk with Mr. Schacter. It's extremely important."

"Mr. Schacter can't see you."

"Sure he can," I said and raised my arm and pointed a finger. "Look for yourself. He's right there at the back of the room in that fish tank of an office."

"You need to leave," she said.

I picked up the i.d. plaque at the front of her desk. I

examined it while she kept her eyes glued. They were that rare set of eyes that can follow another person without the head ever having to arc. All the plaque said was "Receptionist." No name of who the woman sitting before me was. I set it back down, tweaked it to the exact position it had been, and smiled.

She jerked a stiff finger at the door.

Then, as swiftly as the strike of a snake's head, I darted beyond her desk and moved toward the rear of the office. She swore a loud profane objection that swept across the room like a crack of thunder and it brought the attention of the Muscle my way, as well as every other body that was busy in some manner of employment. On my entrance I had observed that he was transferring numerous boxes from one location in the office to another that looked more remote and easily forgotten. Which figured, I thought—the menial work. How much of a threat could Schacter possibly be under that he required his bodyguard to be on duty full time? No, this dude was required to do a second job if he was expecting to receive a satisfactory paycheck.

"Hold it right there!" he shouted. He was already posturing like some mean mother as he stepped into my path. Schacter remained at the very back of the room inside his glass confines and I could see him shift his attention in our direction.

I raised my hands at chest level, palms outward. "Easy. I just need to ask Mr. Schacter a few questions. After that, I'll leave and you can get back to your boxes."

"I don't think so," the Muscle said with a self-admiring smile and a bully's emphasis, and he reached out to poke a javelin-like finger against my chest.

Who knew ol' Grandfather would be in my ear!

As though it were entirely on its own, my left arm

circled with the velocity of a horsefly and hit this big fellow squarely between his wrist and elbow, and then up rolled the right as smooth as ball bearings, and my knuckles slammed into his nose so hard that his blood flew onto the breast pocket of a yellow shirt dressing a young fellow at a nearby desk. He went down, the Muscle did, like I'd wager he never once thought he would.

"WHAT THE HELL IS GOING ON HERE!"

It was Schacter. Already on his feet, he was yelling from the doorway of his office. He came rushing out of it at a clip and to where I was standing in the aisle amid several desks and staring down at his now recumbent bodyguard. "WHAT THE HELL IS GOING ON HERE?" he shouted a second time. He dropped a stiff hand on my shoulder and spun me around so that we were facing each other. "WHAT DO YOU WANT, SONNY?"

"My name—"

"—I KNOW WHO THE HELL YOU ARE! I ASKED WHAT IS IT YOU WANT?"

"My girlfriend Patsy Lukehart recently spoke with you," I said, making sure not to stammer. "What did the two of you talk about?"

"What are you? The FBI? It's none of your goddamn business what we talked about. Now get the hell out of this building!"

The Muscle was getting to his feet, and I continued to keep one eye on him in case he wanted more of the fast *riken*, but he was already aiming for the men's room to clean himself up. Schacter scowled in his direction.

"You want his job?" he said to me with an obvious disdain for his employee.

"All I want—"

"—Get out of here!" he repeated.

I pressed, not moving an inch. "She hasn't been in contact. I'm worried and I need to find her. Did she say anything to you that might help my search?"

"I can't help you," he said, turning away.

"I think you can," I said, this time putting one of my hands to his shoulder.

He looked at it as though it were dirt, then said, "You intending to haul off and hit a cop if I call one?"

I saw him glance at the front desk and the woman occupying it, and then he started to walk away.

"Mr. Schacter, please."

He hesitated, turned, and grinned. It was a grin that said he considered me to be a genuine fool. It endured for two, three seconds, and then he swung back and moved away toward his office.

For my effort I'd gotten nothing and all that was left was to leave. But I was truly in a despondent turmoil now because what was I to do next? Where should I go?

I took a final look behind me before walking out the door. On several computer screens were paragraphs of copy undergoing formatting. On others there were cover photos undergoing manipulation. Something told me the photos weren't original art created for each book, that they were stock and free for anyone's use. The Muscle was just coming out of the restroom with a cloth stuck to his nose and Schacter was right there in his face with a blast of ridicule. The Muscle wasn't happy with me, but I had the feeling he would have throttled his boss then and there if he'd thought he could get away with it.

Outside as I slogged back to the car, I glimpsed a figure come out from behind the rear of the Quotidian building. She moved halfway up the nearest alley and waved for my attention. I recognized her as the second employee who earlier had entered the front door. She couldn't have been more than nineteen.

"Mr. Falkner, I've something that might help you," she said and held out a sheet of paper. "Take it. It was Ms. Lukehart's. As she was leaving, Rick, the one wearing the yellow shirt? Well, he noticed some papers hanging out of her portfolio, and when she crossed by his desk, he reached around without her knowing and withdrew one. Everyone kind of silently laughed, and then Rick, after a quick look at the paper, tossed it into his waste basket. But I didn't think it was right, and I thought the paper might even be important to her and she would come back for it. And so the next time he left his desk, I went and pulled it from the rest of the trash. I think it'll be of use to you, Mr. Falkner."

"Thank you," I said.

"I really hope everything is okay and you find her."

"What's it like to work for Schacter?" I couldn't refrain from asking.

"It's terrible," she said.

"How long have you been an employee?"

"Just four weeks," she answered, "and I won't stay much longer. There's a lot of turnover. Most of us who work here were thrilled at first because we thought we had accepted a job with a real publisher and would gain some great experience in the area of editing and overall book marketing. But all most of us really learned was how to run some simple software that checks spelling and grammar. I watched some who didn't know any better change an author's deliberate fragment into a sentence. Rick and most of the others you saw in there are new and so they're eager to take Mr. Schacter's side on anything. Only the woman at the front desk isn't new. She's been here from the start. Her name is Mona Fowler, and although there's an age difference, I think she and Mr. Schacter go back a long ways and have a special relationship. She's who you spoke to on the phone yesterday. Both times. Mr. Falkner, I hate to tell you this, but your book isn't going anywhere."

"They'll honor online sales, won't they?"

"Yes, but they won't be in any hurry to fulfill the orders. Many will even get cancelled. They're interested in orders only from you, the author; and they won't be filling them either in any timely manner because they get your money first. That's what it's about. Money. I'm not even twenty-one, but I was able to figure that out."

"Wish that I had," I said.

"If you'd worked here, you would have, Mr. Falkner. They take advantage of the best in people, and I think it's a crime."

She was younger than me, but she was also smarter and even more passionate.

I wagged the sheet of paper at her. "Thanks again," I said.

Chapter 19

Once inside the car, I gave a closer look to the legal-size sheet of paper of which the yellow-shirted Rick had relieved my Patsy. It was crammed with her scribbles and mini-notes, but here and there appeared quite a few names. Patsy sought efficiency whenever possible, and one area of the greatest benefit to her was in the taking of notes, especially during interviews. She habitually omitted an unneeded vowel in thousands of words and even extended it to names long before the popularity of texting. If I could interpret the scribble, I had a shot at the word.

Overall, the sheet had a history. There were more than a dozen names in a perfectly aligned column, plus the penmanship approached elegant. These she undoubtedly had copied down at home before leaving Valley Camp. A handful of other names had been added afterward along the edges and they were not in any order. Then there were her copious notes. These most likely had been written in a half-fever during an interview. Either that or she had opened the portfolio to the sheet while driving and had jotted something down so that it wouldn't pass out of mind and run the risk of never again surfacing.

I took my time sitting there behind the steering wheel

of my car to digest what I had in front of me and what it might lead me to do next. Most of the notes were indecipherable, but one near the bottom had an arrow extending from a single word, mimicking an old-time directional signal. It pointed at a name that was circled not once, not twice, but three times. The name meant nothing to me. I'd never seen it on any of the boards, or anywhere in fact. And it was absent of an address and phone number, whereas most of the remaining did have one or the other, or both. One of the names, which had no address or number, had a time: a small 6:00 beneath it. I considered whether this had significance, and it came to mind this was likely the rescheduling of her appointment to the evening (Who would agree to an interview at 6 in the morning?) and the reason she couldn't talk long. She had to get out of Philly and on her way to New York.

It was all I had and I went with it. I turned over the Ru's engine and pulled away.

An hour into the journey, which was about halfway to New York, I exited hellish I-95, braked to a stop amid a tight neighborhood of small businesses inside a dilapidated New Jersey town, and booted my laptop. Wireless was ubiquitous and I piggybacked on the first network to display that wasn't locked.

As odd a surname as it was, there were three of the same in the Metro area and I was lucky with my opening call.

"And who are you?" the woman asked in a challenging voice after I inquired about Patsy.

"I'm her boyfriend."

A long silence followed, and because I had an idea of what she was thinking, I said, "Please. I'm not intending to hurt her. I'm just worried for her safety. She hasn't called, and that's unlike her."

After some reflection the woman said, "I pray I'm not fooling myself, but I believe I hear the concern in your voice. It's true I had to reschedule our morning meeting to the evening before with Ms. Lukehart. Only she telephoned about an hour before we were to sit down together and apologized because she said she had to cancel."

"Did she provide a reason?"

"No, I'm afraid she didn't, and I didn't ask. I didn't think it was any of my business."

It's the most horrible feeling to know that you must do something, yet you have no idea what the next step is that must be taken to begin to get there.

I sat in the car after the call, mentally numb and totally immobile. If ever I had thought I was a really smart dude, at that moment I considered myself to be equally stupid.

After a time, I again took out the sheet of paper. It was all I had. I stared at it, hoping Patsy's feral jottings would speak to me, tell me something about where to go next to find her.

The arrow extending from the lone word and pointing at a name again caught my attention as it seemed to be the only thing with possible promise. But try as I did to discover its import, the word remained a mystery and would not surrender itself. On the other hand, Patsy's rapid circling of the name—one, two, three times—suggested emphatically that this item was very significant and something she wanted to make certain she did not overlook or forget. And the longer I thought on it, the more it seemed the name could have been offered up to her by Schacter during the interview. Except he might not have provided any details. Perhaps it was even a mistake, a slip off a too casual tongue and one he realized he'd made as soon as it was out of his mouth. And Patsy would have noticed the signs of that slip, too, signs that would have been manifested in his tone and facial expression. And then just like I was going online to learn what I could uncover, that's what she had done after leaving the offices of Quotidian Release. And what she found was a whopper of a revelation so that she had no choice but to cancel her rescheduled appointment and set out in a new direction.

I was aware that my thinking was nothing but speculation, yet in spite of that I was beginning to sense I knew what that direction was. Patsy, with her questions, had come onto some pivotal information regarding the murders.

About then my cell sounded, and the name "Dempsey" lit up the display.

"Mr. Falkner?... Detective Harley Dempsey.... My partner informed me of your earlier call. Here's what I can tell you. We telephoned Ms. Lukehart's publisher in New York. There's been no contact. We also inquired of the various hospitals there. Nobody was recently admitted by her name. Nor is there anyone who fits her age and description which, I suppose, could be good news. We also contacted the rental car company. Her vehicle remains out and we have the information regarding it."

"Thank you, Detective," I said. "I appreciate it."

"If we learn anything, I'll be in touch. Try not to worry."

After closing my phone, I sat a while in a sort of balancing trance: relieved there was no news on Patsy; yet it was not the relief I wanted.

A semi roared by and blew its air horn to a gray-haired man in a motorized wheelchair waiting at a crosswalk. The man waved at the truck that was already by him. I blinked myself back into the reality of the moment and stared at the thrice-circled name Koldren on the yellow paper.

Had Patsy gone to see this person? It's what I was thinking, sitting alone in my car, although I had only the most general idea why she would, and that was a connection to the killings. I next flipped open my laptop and went to the online white pages a second time. Koldren was all I had and it wasn't much. I narrowed the search and up came dozens of names. I started with those Koldrens who had addresses that weren't in towns a hundred miles away. When the Intelius search ended for one of these names, a Dan Koldren aged 38, I scrolled down and there on the right under the "related to" column was the name Spectra Suter. Just to be on the safe side, I started an identical search with Suter's name. It produced Dan Koldren in the column. Husband and wife, it had to be. Plus, they had been living under the same roof.

Before shutting down and moving off, I checked my email.

Still no message from my Patsy.

I love you, girl. C'mon, talk to me.

Chapter 20

It was a tiresome slice of pavement the Ru had to eat up to reach the Suter-Koldren residence, some of it in traffic that challenged my waning concentration from an excessive amount of earlier tedious driving. The route turned me around and rolled me back inside the Pennsylvania line and the final miles were on tortuous county roads with too many squirrels and rabbits appearing suddenly so that I was braking and accelerating with an unnerving frequency. Fatigue was fast setting in, but I fought it and was relieved of its accompanying anxiety when the Suter-Koldren home at last came into view.

The two-story house sat at the apex of a long semicircular drive and was a stylish exemplar of architecture as several roofing lines effortlessly slipped in and out of those adjacent, reminding me of a well-managed, animated, now frozen matrix. It was not the kind of structure that was likely to appear in an old industrial town like Valley Camp. Three shades of a soothing aquamarine dressed the house and this made the glass-enclosed pool at the upper side appear integrated and not the usual extra item to enhance personal living. A four-car garage, also in three shades of the comfort color, pushed against a slope settled in tight, squared-off shrubbery. Throughout the property there were trees from generations long ago and each sported a thick trunk and full crown, all properly pruned years in the past, all beginning to sprout their spring foliage. Yet despite the beauty of the place, a lonesomeness loomed pervasive and I did not think it had developed since the murders.

Before setting off to reach the home, I'd considered using the phone number that was alongside the online entry for Dan Koldren. Only I was afraid that, in his grief over the death of his wife, the man wouldn't have any tolerance for questions from a complete stranger. As it was, I wasn't entirely comfortable that I was doing the right thing. However, my motivation was Patsy. That meant I could be intrusive at the same time I was sympathetic to his loss.

I parked in the empty drive at the front of the house, got out, looked well enough around to see if anybody was watching, then walked to the door, a solid structure of dark oak with small glass panels, some frosted with floral design, running up along each side of the jamb. I rang the bell and could hear the muted tones unfold inside with automated restraint.

No one came to the door. I rang the bell a second time, waited, and got the same result.

Stepping away a moment, I gazed down one end of the neighborhood and then up the other. It wasn't a development where one house was closely situated to another. Considerable space separated all the residences and each had a cornucopia of trees and shrubbery. Their frontal exteriors barely presented themselves to the eye at any angle except straight on. Not a man, woman, or child was in sight. Only a dog, a black and brown mutt, took notice, and for less than a full pause in his stutter-step gait.

I stepped back up to the door, made a hood of my

hands, and peered through the glass squares at the side.

And at that moment a strange feeling of apprehension flooded my consciousness. It was of the kind that overcomes a person who notices that the morning newspaper is piling up outside the house across the street. Automatically he reminds himself the subscribers are his neighbors, which means he knows something about them, and they most likely decided on the spur to get away for a few days, probably to visit their children, or weren't they just talking about how they hadn't been to the shore for God knows how long? So this person, this homeowner, he takes a pass on his curiosity and works the optimism until he can't any longer. Finally he summons the police, whereupon it's discovered that husband and wife died of carbon monoxide poisoning, or maybe were gagged, bound, and shot through the head; and if the latter, this person, this homeowner, he tells the cops he's sorry and that he regrets that he mistook the sounds of gunshots for the explosions of firecrackers, which is perfectly understandable to the police because they know that although a celebration of the day of the nation's independence was weeks, maybe months before, somewhere along the way the country's adults had usurped upon the kids' prerogative for setting off cherry bombs and other explosives.

But if they aren't his neighbors and he doesn't know them—as I knew nothing of Spectra Suter's husband—and the feeling of apprehension takes hold, he will forgo the police and enter the house by himself, and he will do so with a reluctant immediacy because this is America and every night when he watches the local news on his television, he knows there is murder after murder being committed, some routine, others abhorrently brutal, and from what he can tell by the reports, all senseless. And even if it isn't the news,

God knows the man loves his thrillers and murder mysteries, seems he can't get enough of them, so that when he eventually sets that first shoe down inside this house of someone he knows nothing about, he does so expecting the worst, because choosing the other will result in his feeling like a fool.

I gripped the doorknob and turned it clockwise. The door was unlocked.

Pushing it away, I paused yet a long moment because of uncertainty and then stepped inside the beautiful home. And there my apprehension morphed into a terrible reality of which I was in no way familiar.

Off to my right and hanging from the room's large center wood beam was Koldren. At least I assumed it was him.

I stood planted and stared with disbelief at the lifeless body that had a brown leather belt wound around its neck. How long he had been hanging there I couldn't say, but the floor below him had dried, and there was a lingering stench, not so overpowering that it was already outside the building, but trending in that direction. I continued to stand where I was, not wanting to touch anything, but not wanting to miss anything either.

On a secretary in the far corner my eyes spied a note. It was so perfectly forty-five degrees crooked to the desk lines that I was moved to cross the room and look at its contents. *"I'm sorry,"* it read. *"I'm sorry for them all."*

I suppose the words might have meant something altogether different to a family member or someone who actually knew the man, but I at once understood them to be a confession for the recent murders of his wife and the others. So much then, I thought, for the drama on the boards. The sex allegation was not a lie. There was no underhanded fabrication by a prankster.

About this time a breeze stole itself into the house as I had left open the door. Faint, it was strong enough to turn Koldren's body on its axis, sparking both a jump from me and a frightened stride away from the desk since I wasn't anticipating movement from anyone but myself. For the following minute I remained motionless to allow my nerves to steady. Once the breathing slowed, I tugged a handkerchief from a rear pocket and pressed it to my nose.

Koldren was not what I would have expected if I had ever thought of Spectra Suter's husband. Her photos on the Web showed a very alluring woman, whose looks could only have helped her writing career. I would have presumed that her mate would have matched her in appearance and physique. But Dan Koldren, I could see, had been hardly an impressive man to lay eyes on even when he was alive, and a framed studio photograph of the couple on the wall was proof. Of course, that was the sort of item that could provide a motive: he knew he'd gotten better than he deserved; she eventually realized she hadn't. He learned she was having sex with others and killed her along with her sordid partners: believing then he had nothing to live for, he soon snuffed out his own life.

Yet for all that simple, logical plotting that was engaging me, I couldn't but wonder why he had chosen hanging. Why hadn't he put the gun to himself as he had done with the others?

Time was slipping by and I was anxious to leave the premises because I couldn't ignore the possibility that a neighbor, unseen by me, had witnessed my arrival, and too much time could be construed as just the right amount to commit a crime, particularly if Koldren's final breath was closer to my arrival than the odor implied. The suicide note might offer protection against incrimination, but it wasn't something to count on. Even so, I pushed the moment. Removing a white lace doily from underneath a table lamp, I raced about the house opening drawers and cupboards in the various rooms. I was expecting to find a gun, but I found none, and so I returned to the secretary where I again read the note several times— *"I'm sorry. I'm sorry for them all"*— while I slid out the desk's numerous drawers, even the smaller ones that couldn't possibly hold a gun but could easily house a box of shells. I fingered the nubs of several pencils, opened the cap of an old Zippo lighter, turned over a pocket-sized, promotional tape measure showing an investment firm's logo, did everything with the doily to prevent the leaving of a fingerprint because I was already unsure whether or not I was going to inform the police, and not even sure on why I was unsure. In the smallest drawer was a torn page of stamps with only one removed. There were unmarked keys in another, plus a batch of unused postcards. I pulled out a checkbook and thumbed through the numerous carbons before returning it to its assigned place. Their writing was different from that of the note. I searched the bigger drawers beneath. There wasn't any gun and there weren't any shells.

The inquisitive nature of a writer was the motivation for my search, but Patsy herself, her book, and a lot more were also a part. Had she been here like I'd been thinking while sitting in the Ru and studying the sheet of paper? Had she seen Koldren's hanging corpse? Or was he alive at the time?

I grew dangerously concerned about my dawdling and realized it was time to get the hell out of the house and off the property. I took one last look around at everything in the room before me to see if there was any sign at all that Patsy had visited. I gave a last look at Koldren, too, and this time with a sadness because no family, no friend, not even a neighbor had thought to contact him since his death.

Chapter 21

I slipped out of the neighborhood, mindful not to exceed the 35 mile-per-hour speed limit. I stared at the pavement in front of me at the same time my eyes tugged at the periphery to see if any resident was watching from the sidelines. Reaching new territory a minute later, I let out a breath and sucked in a bigger. I'd not found relief; I was simply in need of it. The fact was, Patsy remained missing and I continued to have nothing on where she was or what might have befallen her.

There was something else, too, that was now on my mind and it was quickly eating away at it. Circumstances that had one side saying *Yes, inform the authorities that Koldren is dead* and the other side countering with *No, fool, don't do it.* Would it be prudent, I argued with myself, to inform Dempsey and Maines of what I'd come upon? To do so was suggesting several unknowns and together they warned against my involvement. I won't deny it seemed morally wrong, except at the time morals were not a concern.

With this dilemma set aside, though it hardly mollified my insides, I searched out somewhere to eat. Tired as my mind and body were from all the driving, hunger was trumping sleep.

A sign inside a weed patch advertised a diner and I followed its simple directions. The place was more a richly decorated shack than a shiny diner and was mostly empty of customers when I got there. I settled into a booth and a waitress came by right after to take my order. She looked a lot like my sister and I would have been ashamed of my mistrust of a stranger if the feeling had endured for longer than an instant. After she left, an old man wearing a John Deere cap and broken eyeglasses swiveled about on one of the nearby counter stools and held up a newspaper. "Any interest?"

He reached across and handed me the local rag.

"There's not much in it," he said.

"There never is," said a hatless man beside him

"That's okay," I responded. I meant it, too. A few minutes surrendering my attention to other things, no matter how mundane and trivial, was what I needed.

Wasn't to be.

Woman Survives Crash Over Embankment

It was Patsy, all right. I read the account twice and the old man was correct. There wasn't much in the report, not even the mention of a hospital.

I reached out and touched his backside as the waitress delivered my club. "Excuse me. The police station, how do I get there?"

He gave a questionable look to my finger before answering.

I thanked him, then wolfed down the club sandwich as though it were a pill, along with the chips that came with it.

Leaving the tip on the table, I stood up and offered the paper back to him, which he said to keep. At the register I paid the bill, and then moved out to ask the local police of Patsy's whereabouts.

I was there under two minutes and hurried inside. Two officers were behind the front desk and the older one stepped forward.

"Can I help you?"

"The young woman who was in an accident. Where was she taken? What hospital? And how do I get there?"

"Are you family?"

"No, but Patsy and I have been together a long time," I replied. "We're not married. But that's only because I haven't yet popped the question."

It was sufficient to satisfy him.

"Would you care to know what happened?" he asked.

"There wasn't much in the paper," I said. "Please."

He told me that Patsy's car had careered off the pavement in an isolated, inauspicious location. The rental ended up a hundred feet below the road grade in a shallow creek hidden by heavy brush and wild vines with no nearby homes. Luck was with her, he said, a lot of it, and she wasn't seriously injured. But the collapse of interior parts of the car had pinned her body and she was unable to extricate herself. The horn had ceased working and her cell phone catapulted out of her reach so that she was unable to call for help and its battery soon drained to nothing. There was an empty wrapper to a package of cheese crackers on the floor and they were all she had to eat during the ordeal. She would have died if the car hadn't come to rest at an angle in the creek. This permitted water to seep through to the inside of where she was held fast, and she was able to cup some in her hands and drink.

"Who found her?"

"A bicyclist discovered her," he said. "The young man had stopped to make an adjustment on his chain derailleur at the exact spot where she had left the road. He'd glimpsed the vehicle below and saw the fresh broken timber leading to it. Descending, he saw that a woman was in the car and she was either unconscious or dead. He did a couple of the necessary things, he told us, to determine which and was relieved it was not the latter. Then he called for help."

"The hospital?"

He turned to the other officer. "The young woman... where'd they take her?"

The second officer threw out an arm and extended a finger to the south.

"Make a left out front. It's three miles, no further. You can't miss it."

He was true to his word on both counts and I was there in minutes. The hospital was indisputably in line with the wealth of the community. Its façade boasted huge magnificent stone, long strips of bright copper, and several ornate carvings of men and women who had influenced the region. There was no driving by it with a blind eye.

I pulled into a slot adjacent to those reserved for the physicians and administrators and hastened inside. At the front desk I asked for Patsy's room number and was informed that visiting hours for the afternoon had ended.

I imagine an obviously disappointed expression flooded my face because the woman manning the space behind the glass window then asked, "Are you her husband, sir?"

"No," I said. "We're not married."

"Family?"

"No," I answered.

"Well then, do you work with her?"

I shook my head again. "We don't work together. What I mean is, we're not co-workers or colleagues. Nothing like that."

"Young man?"

"Yes?"

She regarded me for an extended moment and in a softened voice said, "Can't you see that I'm trying to find some leeway for you. Till now she's had no visitors. No one has even asked about her. But I'm not going to let just anybody walk into her room. Not in this crazy world we live in today."

"Is it enough for you when I say I love her?" I said plainly. "And that she loves me?"

After another lengthy moment of staring into my face, the woman permitted her smile to show. "Two floors up. Room 71."

"Thank you," I said.

Patsy was in the hospital's southern wing and on my way to see her, a funny moment from a year earlier came to mind. We had just returned from a dinner with some of her friends and their husbands, and I questioned Pats about how she answered others when they asked of our relationship. How did she describe us? What word did she apply to me? Just as *girlfriend* reeked of adolescence, so *boyfriend* did the same for her. And while we threw these out on occasion along with *my woman* and *my man*, none of them became habit. *My squeeze* didn't cut it either.

"How do you refer to me? I want to know," I'd asked.

"Oh, that's easy. I tell others you are my *in-ti-mate*," she said with an articulation of its parts.

I repeated the word a few times, mincing the syllables as she did.

"That's pretty good," I said. "I like it. I'm your *intimate*.

You're my *intimate*."

"That was my response soon after we met. I don't say that anymore, Wyatt."

"You don't?"

"No. Not any more."

"Well, why not? We're closer today, aren't we?"

"Oh sure. I didn't mean to say we weren't."

"So then, if you were asked the same question today, how would you refer to me? What would you tell that person who wanted to know?"

"Oh now, Wyatt," she said with a devilishly delicious look, "now I tell them that you are my *con-sum-mate*."

It had taken me a moment to understand what she was getting at. Then I'd shaken a naughty finger in her face, which she would playfully nip. After that, I pulled her to me and held her tight. And as always, she was warm and wonderful to hold.

The doctor attending to Patsy was leaving her room just as I located it. Looking over his shoulder, I could see that she was asleep. I introduced myself and inquired of her condition. He remarked that he was confident that she would recover and be fine. She was in and out of consciousness but this, he assured me, was only because of the unintentional fasting she had experienced.

"Besides that, she's young," he added. "And it's evident she takes great care of herself. Park yourself in a chair. When she wakes up, she'll recognize your face, I'm sure of it. She's a very lucky woman, you know."

"Yes," I said. "The police filled me in."

He reached out and squeezed my shoulder, then disappeared into the corridor. I stepped inside the room and settled into a cushioned chair at the side of Patsy's bed. There was a second bed in the room, but it was empty.

An array of bruises marred her face and arms. Open cuts and lacerations that would have required stitching and excessive bandaging, there were none of these visible to my eye. No broken bones either, the doctor had said.

Lucky, for sure, I thought as I sat there staring at my Pats. And blessed. And not only for surviving the crash without severe injury. Lucky and blessed for the crackers. Lucky and blessed for coming to rest in a shallow creek. Lucky a bicycle's derailleur jammed when and where it had.

Relieved and grateful that I had found her, fatigue had no further barrier to struggle against and my eyes soon became too heavy to function. When they again opened, there was a nurse standing before me.

"I've been on the road a lot," I said, feeling the need to explain.

"Now that isn't necessary," she said. "Your friend has been doing what she's been doing since they brought her in. But all her signs are on the plus side and stable. She'll come around before you know it. So it's good you're kind of resting together."

"It's a relief to hear everyone is so optimistic," I said.

"Sure. And you know we wouldn't say it if it weren't so." She was holding a newspaper and now extended it. It was the same edition as the one I'd left in the car. "I thought you might want to have a look. There's a picture of her car being dragged out of the creek and there's a story too. She might want to have a look herself when she's able. Can I get you anything? Something to drink perhaps? Some juice? Maybe ginger ale?"

"Thank you, but I'm okay."

"Very well then. I'll leave you be."

She was a middle-aged nurse with a silver cross displayed on her neck, and her expression was one of genuine kindness.

I read the story yet again, still amazed by how little reporting it contained. But of course, no one could talk to Patsy, so I probably was expecting too much. Two photos butted against each other and accompanied the copy. I examined them closely now. One revealed the serpentine section of roadway where the accident occurred. It must have been shot after all police and rescue vehicles had cleared out and gone home. The second photo had been taken from somewhere on the slope. A long steel cable stretched from a bottom corner of the photograph down to the bumper and rear undercarriage of the car. Several men stood in the vicinity of the creek and watched as the vehicle was drawn out of the water and through the brush on its way to the macadam above.

I folded the paper and set it aside on the stand beside Patsy's bed. Then I pulled my chair closer and rested my hand on one of hers.

"Pats?" I said it quietly.

Although there was warmth in her hand, there wasn't any response. Still, I preserved the connection. In a little while the warmth intensified and spread to my own. I said her name again. This time her eyes opened. First, they rolled left like a ball in water, slowly and languidly, then right. After much of a minute, they stopped on my face.

"Wyatt?"

Thank you. Thank you so much.

I rose out of the chair and bent over her. She lifted her arms and I embraced her with the greatest of care.

"How long have I been here?" she asked, her voice tired and weak.

"An ambulance delivered you before noon, Babes. Do you remember anything of what happened? The police said you had an accident. They said your car slipped off the road and traveled down a steep embankment. It broke through some brush and mid-size saplings before coming to rest in the bed of a creek."

There was only the faintest recognition of what I'd described.

"How do you feel?"

"Wyatt, why are you here? If I wasn't.... They wouldn't have notified you in any case."

"I became worried," I said. "When you failed to get in touch with me, I became really worried. So I took off work and went searching for you. You must have fallen asleep at the wheel."

She had been pushing it ever since leaving Valley Camp, so it seemed reasonable that fatigue had taken its due.

Except I was wrong. She bolted upright. Her eyes widened and she gripped my arm. The weakness was gone.

"What is it, Babes?"

"Wyatt, I was forced off that road!"

"Forced? You mean like someone out to get his kicks?"

"I'm not sure! But I was run off that road intentionally. Someone forced me over that embankment." Suddenly, she was remarkably awake and alert. "Wyatt, do me a favor. Find a nurse and get me something cold to drink. I need to clear my head. I need to clear my head and remember all that I can. I want to think this out. And I want to do it without any interruptions."

"All right," I said, patting her hand. "Only it'll have to be juice, mind you. I'm pretty sure they don't serve beer."

I got a smile from her, not a big one but a smile nonetheless, and again gave a thanks skyward.

I left her alone with her thoughts and went out into the

corridor and back to the nurses' station. On the way I greeted those patients who were out of their beds and standing at their room's entrance. They all appeared bored and to want someone to occupy their time. Patsy's doctor stood at the station examining charts. I informed him that she had come awake. He notched the air with a thumb. Then I grabbed a nurse's attention and passed on Patsy's request.

Ten minutes passed before the nurse reappeared at the floor station and she carried a tall glass of orange juice. I took the beverage from her and went back to Patsy's room, hoping I had allowed her sufficient time. The doctor was there and the newspaper carrying the story with the accompanying photos lay across her midsection.

"Wyatt, he says I might be able to get out of here today."

"Now that you're awake, we've one or two more things I want to look at," the doctor cautioned. "If all is well, and I suspect it will be, I'll discharge you. In the meantime, let's get some additional nourishment into that resilient body of yours."

He left the room seconds later to make the arrangements with the others for whatever it was he wanted to check out.

Alone now with Patsy, I waited patiently until the footsteps outside the room diminished to nothing. A curious thought had been hugging my mind ever since leaving the Suter-Koldren house.

I drew close. "Babes," I whispered. "I have to know. Where you at the home of Dan Koldren?"

Even though she was recumbent, I could see that my question startled her. I placed my hand on hers for immediate reassurance and tossed out the lifeline. With one eye glued to the corridor and continuing to speak softly, I said, "I need to know, Babes, because when I was there the man was hanging from a beam."

My words were all she needed. She glanced toward the corridor herself to make certain no one was loitering near the entrance to the room, then patted my hand one, two, three times,

"He was dead," she whispered back.

Chapter 22

The doctor released Patsy late in the day. I drove her to the police station so that she could retrieve her belongings and interview materials. On the way two enforcement vehicles raced by us in the opposite direction, their blue lights flashing. I followed them in the rearview mirror to see if they might turn off in the direction of the Suter-Koldren house.

At the station's front desk Patsy was required to sign a receipt ticket for everything the police returned. I wondered if she would correct the law's interpretation of what had occurred out on the roadway. Whether she was going to inform these local cops that someone had run her over the embankment. I wondered, too, if they might have a question or two for her. But then I reminded myself that it was a small town. The explanation for the accident appeared obvious. There wasn't a need for interrogation.

Patsy, however, had a question for them.

"Am I going to be cited?" she asked.

The officer who carried out her possessions smiled and said, "No, Miss. It doesn't appear you were speeding or driving recklessly. There was no sign of alcohol on your breath, nothing of drugs, plus one of the tires blew out.

Now maybe that occurred after you went over the hill or maybe before. There's no way of telling and it's probably not important anyway. But like I said, you hadn't been drinking, weren't high, and so we're happy to leave it at that. I think your rental car agency will be happy as well, if that's a concern."

"Thanks," she said. "Thank you for everything."

Patsy returned a smile to the officer and gathered her materials in her arms. "Oh, and could you give me the name and address of the young man who found me? I'd like him to know how grateful I am."

"I'll write it down for you," he said.

Patsy accepted the card from him carrying the information on the bicyclist and thanked him again."

"You're welcome," the policeman said warmly. "We're glad you're still with us."

We were all set to leave, except there was a hunch I wanted to explore.

"Officer, as we were driving in, two of your police cars were hightailing it the other way. Now we're headed back in that direction. Has there been an accident? Should we change our route? I don't want to be forced to wait in traffic if it's avoidable."

"No accident," the officer said, shaking his head.

And the second officer, much older, at the other end of the room confirmed my hunch. "One of our residents was found dead in his home," he spoke up, and the expression on his face was sufficient to realize that he knew Dan Koldren as more than just a resident under his protection. "He lost his wife a short time ago. She was an accomplished writer and was senselessly murdered, along with three others. If you pay attention to the news, then you know what I'm talking about. Because it was all over the news when it happened. Anyway, it seems her death became too much for him and he took his own life."

I waited with the passing of a few seconds before offering a sympathetic response. I was curious if he would allude to the note and the confession by Koldren that he had killed not only his wife, but three others. When he did not, I said, "That's terrible. Both terrible and sad." Patsy nodded with a solemn expression of her own. And although my words were truly meant, I'll admit they contained a dose of cover for both Patsy and myself.

We left the police station without any further exchanges with the officers. Seated inside the car again, I pulled out my cell before starting the engine.

"Who are you calling?" Patsy wanted to know.

"Dempsey," I answered. "When you went missing, I got in touch with the detectives. I'm just letting them know that you've been located and are in one piece."

I punched in the numbers for the police station, but found my finger hesitating at the detective's extension. I didn't want to waste his time, it's true, but I also didn't want him to start asking me a lot of questions. I wanted to leave a message, was all. Which is what I did. I refrained from stating the extension and instead gave my name to the desk sergeant who answered and asked him to inform both Dempsey and Maines that my friend Patsy Lukehart had been located and was okay following a fender-bender with some trees and brush.

Then, while turning the key in the ignition, I looked over at Pats and asked what she wanted to do.

"Why don't you decide," she said.

"Well, Babes, I've been on the road far longer than is healthy for anyone. I really have to close my eyes for more than a catnap. Still, I need to know. Are you intending to continue with your itinerary?"

"I haven't decided," she said with a tilt of her head. "I really don't know."

"I'm asking because there's a Hampton Inn midway between here and the Jersey Pike."

"In that case, head for the Hampton. Get the shut-eye you need. I can make up mind later whether or not to continue with the interviews."

On that instruction I slipped the car into gear. A mile later Patsy laid her head back on the seat's headrest and shut her eyes. She was asleep in seconds.

I drove the highways at a moderate speed, letting others pass me as they pleased. I cracked my window. The sun was well over the horizon behind us and the air was cool on my face. On the radio I searched out a station with music that countered fatigue and the darkening evening in a satisfyingly restrained way. I kept the volume low so it wouldn't disturb Patsy.

An hour passed before the Hampton Inn came into view. I swung the Ru to a stop in front of the entrance and left Patsy in the car while I shuffled inside. I asked the desk for a room far away from those that were occupied.

Chapter 23

The next morning, with my face smashed in the pillow, I glimpsed that Patsy was up. She was sitting at the room's corner desk in front of her laptop and her fingers were dancing like spider legs across its keyboard. Light from the world outside had yet to make its way under the hem of the drawn window curtain. I raised my head to check the time on my cell phone beside the bed. Several minutes before 6. I let my morning's eyes swallow all of her before getting to my feet. Waking up to a beautiful woman is a wonderful thing.

"Coffeemaker's in the bathroom."

"Thanks," I mumbled.

I cleared the grit from my eyes and peered over her shoulder. What she was doing, I realized, was entering her now unscrambled thoughts into a computer file before they faded out of existence.

I kissed her on the neck without saying anything further, then went into the bathroom to pursue the necessary things. When I re-emerged sipping away at a cup of the motel's in-room coffee, she was wrapping up.

"I want you to look at what I've written, Wyatt."

I came closer and slipped into the chair as she stood up.

"How are you feeling?" I asked. The bruises on her face

had darkened.

"Both legs ache below the knee. They ache a lot. Of course, they were jammed under the dash, so that's to be expected. What about you? Did you manage to rest any?"

I was glad we'd called it a day and said the same.

"Will you read what I've written?"

"Just as soon as the caffeine kicks in," I said. I then jerked my head at the four corners of the room in an attempt at some early-morning, inane humor. She offered a brief smile of appreciation and left for the bathroom. I dropped into the chair before the screen.

Her story began with Jan Sherman, a.k.a. Nine Lives, but this I rapidly scanned as it wasn't new. I slowed when the name Mona Fowler appeared on the page. Sherman had told Patsy this woman ran the show at Quotidian Release as much as Schacter, and when it came to dealing with the requests and complaints of authors, particularly younger men who had gone to college and whom she regarded across the board as stupid and arrogant, she ran it almost entirely. Sherman said you wouldn't find the woman's name on her desk at Quotidian Release, something I had observed. The reason for the absence of that detail, Sherman went on, was that Fowler feared some young author, who wasn't centered too well and was "full of himself," might search her out and try to kill her. Might actually walk into the facility one day with a gun and open fire. Sherman suspected Fowler had a loaded gun of her own sitting inside her desk to prevent that.

Patsy left Jan Sherman's home and arrived at the publisher's place of business soon after. She immediately ran into Fowler who attempted to turn her away, the same as she would attempt to do with me, days later

"I'm not here to dig up dirt on Quotidian Release,"

Patsy had responded to the testy woman. "Besides, hasn't that been worked to exhaustion?"

"Then what are you after?" Fowler demanded.

"If Mr. Schacter has a sense of humor, he'll be included in my book."

"What book? With us?"

"I'll be happy to explain my work to Mr. Schacter," said Patsy.

About this time the president of Quotidian Release had stepped outside his glass office at the rear of the building, and Patsy wrote that she shifted her attention from Fowler and smiled, which caused Fowler to swing about in her chair and when she did, Schacter waved Patsy on back.

According to Pats, he ushered her into his office without any show of reservation or fanfare. She took a seat that faced the rear wall, which was lined with shelves from floor to ceiling and plugged with single copies of the more than 10,000 titles the company had put out. She then began to tell him about the book she had planned, wisely omitting any mention of her editor's suggestion that involved the murders of four writers.

"Are you going to have us do it?" he asked her.

Patsy wrote that she once more smiled and said, "That, Mr. Schacter, would require I return the advance I've received from another publisher. It's considerably larger than what Quotidian Release routinely sends out."

Patsy noted that the publishing head had laughed to himself.

"So why do you want me in your book, young lady? What have I done to deserve this special consideration?"

"Depending on how you answer my first question," she replied, while thinking that his own questions were reminiscent of a chunk of dialogue from *The Godfather*, "you might not be included at all. And if that turns out to be the case, then I simply toss the name of Tor Schacter into the trash."

Patsy observed that his eyes shrank as he regarded her a long moment to determine if her remark was just an offhand utterance relevant to the computer and not to actual trash.

"Why don't we get to your questions," he finally said.

Opening her tote, she withdrew the digital recorder and asked his permission. She described the expression on his face as one of governed coolness set atop a backdrop of uninterrupted calculation. He motioned with the slight flick of a hand his approval to be recorded.

Patsy began: "Mr. Schacter, I've read thousands of postings on the writer message boards of Pixel-to-Paper and AuthorsRetreat. Never have I come across one that was signed 'Tor Schacter.' Never one as 'President, Quotidian Release.' Yet quite a few of these posts did appear under several pseudonyms, which the regulars on those sites have accused you of writing."

"They fancy the 'troll' designation, there's no disputing that."

"Did you write them?"

"On occasion. When things were slow around this office and I was in need of a laugh. It's quite easy to rile them, as I'm sure you know. Mona, however, handles most of the replies to postings and emails."

Without mentioning my name and that Quotidian had published my work, Patsy said, "I've a friend who's argued with some of those same people who despise you. Yet in spite of that, he's of a mind that if he were ever to meet them in person, they would get along just fine. He thinks they might even enjoy a drink together. What do you think?"

"Inform your friend he's a fool. They'd eat him for a

Happy Meal."

Patsy put down that she had laughed at that.

"It sounds like you harbor ill feelings for these people, Mr. Schacter."

"Lukehart, is it?"

"Yes, Pats Lukehart."

"Miss Lukehart, just so you know, I'm an unapologetic practitioner of schadenfreude. So it's not ill feelings that I harbor for these people; it's ill wishes. Now let me ask you a question. Before you ever accessed those boards, had you heard of even one of those writers?"

"Are you're referring to those who were murdered?"

"Any of them," he'd said. "Dead ones, live ones. The whole nauseating bunch."

"No, I can't say they were familiar names," Patsy replied.

"And now that you have been to the boards, have you read even a single work by any one of them?"

"No."

"What about your friend? Had he heard of them or read their writings?"

"He's read some. What's your point?"

"You know what the point is, Miss Lukehart. You're an intelligent woman. I don't believe it requires me to explain."

Patsy impulsively punched off the recorder.

"Ah, let me guess. You're switching gears," he said with a sardonic smile. "Now you want to know if I arranged the killings of four of my major critics, and turning off that device is your good-faith gesture designed to elicit a truthful response."

"It wasn't going to be my first question," Patsy replied.

"Maybe it shouldn't be a question at all, young lady."

"Why's that?"

"Perhaps I did order their deaths."

(Later, I would ask Patsy about the bodyguard. She replied that there wasn't any bodyguard on the premises while she was there, at least no one who fit the description of the dude to whom I'd delivered my fast *riken*.)

I re-read Schacter's words, "Perhaps I did order their deaths," but this was all the farther I got in her recap because Patsy at that moment emerged from the bathroom. She closed the laptop in front of me and slid it from the desk.

"Wyatt, let's go."

Something that was absent only minutes before was now distressing her. I didn't ask for an explanation. Rather, I gathered my things from the bed and one of the chairs and stood at the door. I opened it when she was ready and followed her from the room.

The Hampton Inn offered a continental breakfast for its customers out near the lobby. We poured ourselves coffee to go, grabbed hold of some favorite fruit, along with a couple of pastries that weren't showing age, and went to the front desk to check out.

As soon as we settled inside the car, I started the engine, but stayed out of gear.

"What is it, Babes?"

"Somebody wants me dead," she said somberly. "I thought I'd remembered everything. I thought I'd gotten it all down and worked out in my head this morning. But I was wrong. The car that forced me off the road and into that ravine, it had followed me at a distance."

Her point eluded me.

"He could have run me off the road anywhere, Wyatt! But he didn't. Instead, he waited until I was riding alongside that long embankment. He wanted me dead and that was his best chance to kill me and have it look like an accident."

"But why would somebody want to kill you, Pats? That's what I don't understand."

"He must think I know something that he'd prefer I didn't."

"But you don't, do you?"

"Isn't that the final Jeopardy question? Wyatt, I don't mind telling you I'm a little scared."

"All right. Well, try your best not to be. We'll figure it out. Whatever it is, we'll figure it out."

I plunged the shifter into gear and rolled us out of the Hampton Inn parking lot and onto the road that would take us back to Valley Camp.

Ten minutes, maybe it was a half hour, passed without either of us uttering another sound, and I realized my woman, scared as she was, was rehashing in her mind yet again her ordeal in an effort to discover what it was she might be in possession of that could be threatening to someone else, so threatening that the person would want her dead.

"Anything?" I asked.

"It's got to connect to my visit at Koldren's! But from what you described to me as your movements when you were there—except that I used a pencil where you borrowed a doily from an end table—our actions weren't any different. So why isn't someone after you?"

Before the hospital released her, with both our voices at a surreptitious level, Patsy and I had exchanged our stories, and everything I witnessed and whatever I did during my visit had been a replication of her own a few days earlier. Even when she had discovered the suicide note on the secretary, her immediate thought was a parallel of my own: why had Koldren not taken his life in the same manner as he had murdered the others? Unlike me, however, Patsy had intended right along to inform the police of Koldren from a pay phone, if she could locate one, only she had been run off the highway before she had the chance.

I swung the car off into a gravel patch next to the road and shut off the engine.

"Let's go over this again," I said.

"So you think I'm right?"

"We'll eliminate it if you're not. Start at the beginning. Don't leave anything out."

She inhaled, then brought her hands together beneath her jaw and let her thumbnail tap her teeth as her eyes focused inward to mind and memory. "All right. After getting out of the car I walked up to the front entrance where I pressed the button for the doorbell. While waiting for someone to answer, I gazed around at the landscape and up and down the street. There weren't any cars in my view from either direction and I don't recall seeing anyone. No one ever came to open the door and I waited for an entire minute, maybe longer. Eventually I squinted and looked through the small panes at the left. There wasn't any life inside that I could see and I didn't hear any sounds. So that's when I tried the door. Out of curiosity, nothing more. Had it been locked, I would have turned around and left. But as it wasn't locked and opened freely, I called aloud to the inside. There wasn't a response. After that is when a feeling overtook me that motivated me to enter uninvited. And there was a man—Koldren, I assumed, although I couldn't be sure because I had never laid eyes on him before —hanging from a beam. And it was obvious that he was dead. Well, after that, which stunned me to no end as it must have done to you, and following my inspection of the note and a search for a weapon, both of which I already told you about, I left. I shut the door behind me, careful not to leave my fingerprints on the doorknob. I looked around again to see if any of the neighbors were about, then got in the car, hurriedly backed out of the driveway, and drove off, intending, as I said to you at the hospital, to hopefully find a pay telephone somewhere and call the authorities. The police could trace my cell, and I wanted to do the right thing without getting my name recorded. I didn't think it would be a good move at this time with regards to the book.

A few ticks went off the clock before I smacked the yellow bulb.

"It was a semicircular driveway, Babes. Each end intersected with the street out front. Why did you back out?"

"I would have been forced to drive on the lawn and it appeared rather soft. I didn't want to take a chance and find myself stuck with the wheels spinning."

"That's it."

"What is?"

"There wasn't any car parked in the driveway when I was there. You're telling me there was when you were there."

"Yes."

"You must have taken it for granted that it was Koldren's."

"That's exactly what I thought."

I paused as another revelation flashed to mind. "Babes, whoever's car that was, they were inside the house at the same time you were moving about." I paused to let that sink in. And it did, rather quickly I could tell, but she didn't say anything. "Think. Do you remember anything about the car?"

"Wyatt, once I was out of the house, my concern was to get away without anyone seeing me."

"Something must have registered. Was it an older model or relatively new?"

"I don't know."

"Did you recognize the make?"

"Too many cars look alike to me. But it was a car, not an SUV. That much I'm certain of."

"Sporty?"

"No."

"Two doors? Four doors?"

"Two. It was two."

"Was it a domestic car or foreign?"

"It wasn't foreign."

"You're certain?"

She shook her head. "It wasn't foreign. I'm always surprised when I see a foreign car," she repeated. "I don't know why that is."

"Do you remember the color?"

"The day was overcast. It's hard to say exactly what the color was. Silver.... Gray.... Blue gray.... Something like that."

"What about the license plate?"

"Wyatt..."

"Not the number, Pats. The design of it. The state that issued it. Was there a slogan that you noticed? Maybe a word that stood out like 'enchantment' does in those New Mexico license plates."

"Sorry.... You know, I once turned down an assignment from a car magazine. I was never sure why I did that. Now I think I know."

"It's all right. Look, I'll stop with the questions. Only for the next minute or so, concentrate on that car. See if something remarkable about it didn't stick in your mind. I'll get us back on the road and headed home."

I restarted the engine and eased back onto the highway.

A mile down the road she said, "There is something. I remember glancing at the passenger-side window as I walked around the car and up to the front entrance. I couldn't make out anything inside."

"You mean the glass was tinted?"

"Like a mobster's."

"That's good. Anything else?"

"I was trying to recall if I'd observed any decals on the bumper or any blemishes to the exterior, but nothing comes to mind. That car was awfully clean."

"Well now, I have another question."

"Was it the same car that forced me off the road?"

"Was it?"

"I can't be certain because that car had maintained a distance behind me and it was such a surprise when it pulled alongside. Before I understood what was happening, my own car was off the road and crashing through trees. But it could have been. What I'm saying is, I remember looking at it for only a fraction of a second when it was mere inches from my door. I could barely see the driver's outline. It too was heavily tinted."

"Male or female?"

"Male. I'd swear to it. Wyatt, turn around. I want to go back to the house."

"Koldren's? The police will have tape all around it. It'll be locked up tight."

"I wouldn't think so. If Koldren hanged himself, where's the crime?"

"But why? What do you expect to find by going back there?"

"Answers. Hopefully, ones that will keep me alive."

"Look, if the man who forced you off the road is the

same man who was in the house, it's because he's afraid you can describe his car to the police. Except you can't. Not much anyway."

"But he doesn't know that. And he can't count on something coming to my mind later that isn't there now."

"I still don't understand what you hope to find at the house."

"Wyatt, maybe we'll discover something that will lead us to who this person is. Now that's something that would be useful for me to know, don't you think?"

It began to rain and the day soon sopped from overcast into downright dreary. That turned out to our advantage because there was no one to be seen in the neighborhood when we approached. A small sign enclosed in a large rock of granite identifying this wealthy residential community as Capers told us we were back.

As Patsy had predicted, there was no yellow tape anywhere on the grounds, and although I expected that we might run into a family relative of either Suter or Koldren, the doors were locked up, the windows shut, and no vehicles were parked in the driveway. Patsy wanted in and I was waiting to see how far she would go to access the house. She tried the doors, all of them, front and back, east side, west side, and the windows too, but not a one was welcoming.

"So what now?" I asked.

"Let's go back to the door by the pool. There was a gap separating it from the jamb."

"You're intending to bust in?" I said, not hiding my incredulity.

"Not exactly," she responded.

She led the way back to the rear of the house and where the pool was attached. She opened the storm and pointed at the entry door, at the gap. It was sizable.

She feigned a sheepish look, then took hold of the knob and jolted it as though she'd been subjected to a surprise muscle spasm. The door opened, barely resisting. The strike plate remained intact.

"After you," she said with an extended hand. I hesitated, because along with the invitation, I detected a grin. It was a kind of joke, I understood, this pre-empting of the protective gentleman's line, 'Let me go first,' but I saw it also as a healthy sign. Patsy was already re-shaping her new fear of being murdered from disabling worry to positive control.

"Thanks a lot," I muttered in a tone of voice that matched her touch of levity.

Nevertheless, when I stepped inside and stood in front of Patsy, I paused and gave both my eyes and ears to the house interior. It was as still and soundless as it was on my first visit. I was hoping I might hear the poignant sound of a hungry cat who had been overlooked by the police and any others who might have come to the house after Koldren's death, the poor critter grateful that someone had come along to give it food and water. But there wasn't even the familiar buzz from a solitary fly.

Patsy came around and stood next to me. Off to our right was the pool. It was unlit and the pump was off, yet the clean, insistent odor of chlorine permeated the air.

Together we went through the rear of the house and this was where Patsy took over. She moved us to the front room where we'd both discovered Koldren's breathless body hanging from an overhead beam. She did not switch on any lights and even went to a window to see if anything had changed out by the street, whether a person or two were there when they weren't just minutes ago.

She next turned back and approached the secretary that

had displayed the suicide note. She started sliding out the many tiny drawers, closing the one that contained a smoker's pipe and an old Zippo lighter, and another with a small tape measure and several pencil nubs. When she found the checkbook, she removed it from the desk and opened the register.

"You said you looked at these carbons?"

I nodded.

"Do you remember any details about the suicide note? The penmanship, in particular."

"I remember the cross on every t was separated and off to the right. That was quite unusual and it stood out."

"I noticed that too," she said thoughtfully.

She searched through the many carbons, pausing at those on which a t had been scribbled and showed each to me. In every instance the horizontal line crossed the vertical.

She slipped the checkbook back into the drawer where she'd found it and went to the much larger drawers below. Nothing in them proved of interest and she appeared to be disappointed.

"Just what are you looking for, Babes? Maybe I can help."

She held up a finger as a sign I should be patient with my question, then dropped to her knees and felt the floor underneath the desk. After several seconds she slid out a sheet of paper and got to her feet.

I watched as she read what was scribbled on the sheet. Then she held it out so I could read it as well.

Each *t* in the message had its cross-tie to the right, barely touching the vertical line.

"It's Suter's hand," she explained. "Her name isn't anywhere to be found and what it says could have been stated by anyone. I'm guessing this paper was probably sitting on the desk and it's what the writer of the note immediately saw. But because everything else suggests it's the workplace of a man, he assumed this was part of the same. Except how did it end up on the floor?"

That was easy for me to answer. I told her about the breeze that had come through the open door and spun the hanging Koldren, scaring the hell out of me. Something similar must have occurred at her presence, I said, lifting the paper from the desk and depositing it on the floor out of sight.

"How do you know the handwriting is Spectra Suter's?" I asked.

"A book jacket to one of her novels," she explained. "It included a personal paragraph in her own hand, along with a signature."

"So someone was really wanting it to look like Koldren wrote the suicide note."

"And whoever it was who wrote it, that's who murdered the others. And he won't be wanting to leave a certain stone unturned."

"And you're that certain stone?"

"Unfortunately I am," she said.

Chapter 24

We fled the Suter-Koldren residence, scurrying like mischievous mice through the shaky door we'd entered, although Patsy made certain it was shut and "securely" locked. Still, before moving off, I had a question wanting addressed. Why had she gone to Koldren's in the first place?

"Schacter tossed out his name as the interview was winding down," she said hurriedly. "Only he refused to say anything more when I pressed him. So then I thought he was playing with me. You know, having an inside laugh at my expense because I had a few on him during the interview and he knew it. I was on the verge of dismissing what he said, except the Fowler woman, who midway through the interview had left her post at the front of the office and stood directly behind me—I'm sure she was trying to see what I had written down on my tablet. She chimed in with a word of her own. 'Sicko,' she blurted out.'"

"Is that what you scribbled next to Koldren's name on that sheet of paper I returned?"

"Wyatt, let's not sit here in front of the dead man's house. Let's get moving."

I shut up and took her advice. I slapped the shifter into gear and the car rolled out of the half-circle driveway and onto the main road. I looked to see if anyone was around, but the neighborhood seemed to be contagiously quiet.

Once we were clear of the place, Patsy went on to answer my question, only in a slower delivery. "I asked Fowler to explain who Koldren was and why she was calling him a sicko and she said he wasn't all there. I asked her to elaborate, what did she mean that he wasn't all there? She said, 'Do I have to spell it out for you? Something isn't right upstairs.' So then I asked how Schacter knew this—he'd already walked away in the direction of his office—and she said smugly, as though it were a slice of information that very few people had possession of, that he had been known to show up at a writers' conference or two."

"Schacter?"

"Yes, Tor Schacter. I asked her again who Koldren was, but she remained mum on that, which is what Schacter must have wanted. Anyway, I left the building after that, still thinking the pair of them might be jerking me around for their own bizarre amusement, till in the car I recalled the handful of posters on WritersUp who had accused Schacter of inventing the group sex allegation. At the time I read those posts I considered it to be nothing more than the same old blame game. But sitting at the wheel with the car key in hand I began to think that perhaps things were getting a little too close for his comfort and he was, in fact, looking to hurl a wrench into the matter to take the heat off himself. And a face-to-face meeting with an unstable Koldren would be to his benefit."

"Is that when you circled Koldren's name a few times?"

"Wyatt. Do some thinking. I had to have circled his name before that. Anyway, I decided to pay a visit to Spectra Suter's husband."

"You'd figured that already?"

"The only thing to make any sense was that Schacter must have heard about his mental instability when he was at one of those writer conferences. At first, I thought Koldren was himself a writer and some kind of incident involving him and the others had occurred. But then I also considered that he wasn't a writer at all and was instead related to one of the dead. Perhaps Schacter had eavesdropped on a gossip session that had Spectra Suter as the subject and a difficult husband had been mentioned. And Lillian Purvis, I already knew, was a divorcee. All I had to do was crosscheck Koldren and Suter on the Web and that's how I found the common address. And that's where I headed."

I looked at her askance while keeping one eye on the road.

"What now?" she said somewhat peevishly.

"Babes, I went to Koldren's with the mindset that he was just another man who happened to be Spectra Suter's husband. You drove there already informed that he was unstable and that he might have murdered four people. It didn't cross your mind that Schacter and Mona Fowler might not have been covering for themselves. That they actually knew what they were talking about and that you could have become victim number five?"

"Easy, Truman. It occurred to me, all right. But as much of a bastard we consider Schacter to be, I couldn't imagine he would send me off to become yet another murder victim. And if you consider this minor after-the-fact ingredient—namely, that he did not tell you about Koldren when you stopped by—doesn't it suggest he was attempting to use me because I am the one writing a book?"

Patsy's reference did not escape me. Her interview of a disturbed, unbalanced spouse would have sullied the investigative waters and spread some suspicions beyond

Schacter. And that was something he would have wanted, guilty or not.

I drove the entire distance back to Valley Camp, allowing Pats more opportunity to rest. After unloading her bags from the car and carrying them inside her house, I offered to stay the night.

"I'll make myself invisible," I promised.

"Don't you have to get back to the market?" she asked.

For sure, I did. Stocking shelves and putting up displays in the aisles is what paid the mortgage and kept me from starving. It wasn't writing.

"I'm good yet," I assured her.

"Wyatt, I know you're worried for me, but I'm okay. I really am. Now I've collected a ton of material from all those interviews, and I want to get at them. I want to get at them and I want to keep at them while everything is fresh in the mind. You know how that works, don't you?"

I did, indeed. There wasn't any reason for her to spell it out. "Okay," I said, "but once I learn of my new schedule, I'll call you."

She nodded her approval and I started to go so that she could be left alone.

"Wait a second."

She disappeared into her kitchen and returned seconds later with a key to the front door. She placed it in my palm.

"I intend to keep it locked."

"Very wise," I said and pocketed the key.

The following day I resumed work at the market and my boss informed me that I would be working a few evening hours until he could hire two additional workers. Each night after punching out on my card, I took the long way home and cruised by Patsy's house. The lights were always extinguished and I was happy that she was taking the time to rest and renew herself. During the day I sometimes stopped, poked my head in, and asked if she wanted to break for lunch, maybe run over to the Welcomian for a fish sandwich. But she was immersed in her work and wanted to stay at it, as she had warned would be the case. She had some puff pieces too, she said, that needed to get out to meet approaching deadlines. These were short magazine articles that didn't pay much and were on a variety of subjects, but Patsy was quite efficient at putting them together. For a byline, they carried either a male or a female pseudonym, and collectively they helped pay her day-to-day expenses.

Our separation stretched into the weekend, and I'm not sure why, but I was beginning to question if the self-control I had witnessed earlier in Patsy wasn't actually a form of self-imposed bluster. Had it eventually lost its air as all bluster does, and was she afraid to admit that she was fearing for her life? I confronted her on the matter the next time I popped in to invite her out for something to eat and drink.

"Pats," I blurted out at what I thought was the proper time, a moment when her eyes were turned away from me and were examining several papers she was holding, "whoever it is, he isn't going to find you."

It was a mistake, I realized at once, as every sign of movement of her flesh froze instantly like a digital image. Seconds passed. Three. Four. Five. Dead seconds, every one of them.

"What?"

It was a word of disbelief from her, not really a question, not an exclamation. Her eyes slipped from the papers and onto me where they crawled over my person like they hadn't done for a very long time. She was studying me as she had when we'd first met, ruminating if something inside me was altogether new, or had she all this time in our relationship missed something significant in her assessment of Wyatt Falkner.

"He isn't going to find you," I repeated in a softer voice.

"You mean he'll be like your sodbuster from Omaha? Zebulon Something or Other?"

"His name was Jeb," I corrected her.

That she recalled this story at all surprised me. What she was referring to was a long delayed work-in-progress. A Nebraska man waiting to switch planes at an East Coast airport finds a satchel in the men's room containing a large cache of money. Thrilled, he nevertheless becomes uneasy because he fears the money is drug money and that its owners will hunt him down and kill him. Yet he cannot resist the instant wealth. The story was intended to illustrate that his fears were foolish, that it was unlikely the criminals would ever track him to Nebraska, more than a thousand miles away. Patsy hadn't bought in, and now I was hearing that nothing had changed her mind.

I defended my tale. "Like I've said before, that sort of thing happens in the movies. It's plain foolishness to think it could happen here in Valley Camp."

She shook her head almost involuntarily as a prologue to her counter. A short laugh she couldn't contain accompanied it. "Wyatt, I'm a researcher, and you know me to be a very capable researcher. But this person who ran me off the road and wants me dead, all he has to do is look at the front page of that weekly newspaper for that small town of Capers. Once he does that, he'll have everything he needs to find me. Or did you forget that minor detail?"

Shut up, Wyatt. The foolishness was with my thinking! What the hell! Had I been thinking at all?

Several awkward seconds passed. I apologized.

"It's all right," she said. "I can't say I've become entirely at ease about all this, so in a manner of speaking it's nice to know that you haven't either."

"I am sorry," I said again. "What do you want to do?"

"We have to figure out who the killer is."

"You mean the police have to figure it out."

"If they can, all the better. But not for a moment am I removing myself from the process. You're a developer of plots. How do you explain what we're dealing with?"

"I believe he traveled there to kill Koldren," I said. "Didn't we already conclude this?"

"New words on the matter won't hurt. Run with it."

"Well, killing Koldren while making it appear to be a suicide would probably end the search, especially since there was an incriminating note left behind. The person would have gotten away with a fifth murder without having to pay for any of them."

Once the letter on the floor under the secretary had come to light and we understood the significance of the *t*, this became the only plot to make sense.

"Then it is Schacter," she muttered after a time.

"I don't follow."

"Remember when you asked if that bodyguard you encountered was on the premises while I was there for the interview? Why did you ask that?"

"I suppose I was wondering—"

"—You were thinking that Schacter might have sent him to kill Koldren, that's the reason you asked. And I think you could be right. This is all falling into place."

"Not for me it isn't."

"The bodyguard was in the office when you were there. He wasn't on hand a few days earlier during my visit. I think he's more than a bodyguard. I think he's a hired assassin and

Schacter sent him to kill the unstable Koldren. He would have forced him to write the suicide note before shooting him. Except it turned out Koldren was more unstable than Schacter had figured on, and by the time his hit man arrived, the poor widower had already killed himself by hanging. Still, that didn't scuttle the plan, and the killer now had to write the suicide note himself and leave it on the desk to be discovered."

"Pats, would an unstable man like Koldren leave a suicide note?"

"In a lucid moment he might. It's a point that at worst is debatable."

"There's something else," I said.

"Let me finish. Schacter and Fowler gave me Koldren's name and the 'sicko' remark because they knew I would go there and discover the dead Koldren. And he calculated a writer would immediately make something of it. That way, attention would turn away from himself and in another direction. The pair of us were in that house together, and didn't you get the feeling it wasn't a home that attracted many people? Hardly any framed photos of husband and wife. None that I saw of children or parents or even grandparents. I don't know if there was even a photo of a cherished dog or a cat. In other words, there was nobody coming and going on the premises. If I hadn't gone there, Koldren might not have been discovered until the stench of decay made it out of that house and into the neighborhood, and that might have required another week. Schacter must have known this and so he needed someone to find the body and that turned out to be me, although he never considered that the police might not learn of it as quickly as he'd assumed."

"But what about the gun?" I said. "Neither of us

discovered it and even though this dude I've been calling the Muscle missed his opportunity to put a bullet in Koldren's brain, he still would have left the gun in the house for the police to find because it would have been the same gun used to kill the others."

"My search wasn't exhaustive. I can't imagine you weren't just as anxious to get out of that house and away from the property."

We ceased talking and stood staring at one another. A small smile of satisfaction formed in our faces. Mine soon faded.

"You've discovered a fly in our ointment," said Patsy, interpreting my expression.

"Now there's a phrase you don't hear nowadays."

"Wyatt?"

"Well, if it was Schacter's man, why was he still there at the house?"

She pondered a long moment. "I don't know," she said, shrugging. "Perhaps I arrived there soon after he did. Or perhaps he panicked. After all, he wasn't intending to be the one who wrote the suicide note, so maybe it slipped his mind and he had to go back to take care of the matter. Or maybe he forgot to leave the gun. Maybe he had to return."

I shook my head, puzzled. It seemed to Patsy and me both that we were onto the truth. And yet there were still questions in demand of answers.

Chapter 25

When I left the abbreviated message for Detectives Dempsey and Maines, stating that Patsy had been located and was okay and which omitted about everything else, I did so first of all because Patsy had refrained from telling the Capers Police that she had discovered the dead Koldren and also that someone had run her off the road intentionally. Why, then, would she want me revealing the truth? But however indefensible a reason it was, I had another. A certain sense had been creeping into my consciousness that both Dempsey and Maines, ever since I'd informed them that Pats was to interview Tor Schacter, might be wishing we would stay the hell out of the investigation. We hadn't done the murders, so why were we so goddamn interested? It was a fair point, and certainly that would have been the case—that we would have exempted ourselves—if the editor for Patsy's book had not pitched the idea to delve into Tor Schacter and his possible connection to the crimes. She wasn't about to pass up the opportunity and a substantial sum of royalties awaiting her if the killings connected, however remotely, to the president of Quotidian, and who could blame her. Moreover, with Patsy going to see Koldren and with me going to see Koldren, and with Koldren ending up dead... suddenly I was envisioning law enforcement—Dempsey and Maines, especially when they learned of all this—taking a step back and saying "Perhaps we ought to take a closer look at this couple." And if that became the new mindset of the investigating authorities... well, I was never the optimist who believes that truth will always win out. Plus, I'm a writer, a novelist. I understand how plots work. If it were discovered that Patsy and I had been to Koldren's, some smart prosecutor might just weave a tale before a grand jury that could bring us up on murder charges. In other words, an indictment of us would become the latest version of that familiar ham sandwich.

Over the next week, Patsy remained chained to her desk and I began working the daylight hours at the market. It was a relief granted by the new schedule that I could step out and have a few beers in the evening and not worry about heading to work at midnight. On occasion I tried to persuade her to join me—there were always laughs at the Welcomian was my argument and I thought she could use a few—but she remained steadfast with her diligence, which I was wrongly thinking was because she was still afraid. I brought the matter up again with a bit more delicacy than the previous time. I asked if she wasn't losing some control of her life.

"That's not it," she responded. "What's happened, Wyatt, is my editor called. He wants me to push harder to complete the manuscript and get it into his hands as soon as possible. He met with some of the other editors and his marketing people and they are in agreement that the book could be entirely worthless if the murders are solved too quickly. And if that turns out to be the case, then all my time and effort will have been for naught."

So there it was. Patsy would continue her work without

interruption and there was nothing to negotiate. Nevertheless, I would phone or text her, but always in the morning before she was at her desk or late in the evening when she routinely abandoned it to sit down to eat and watch the news, as she was a dedicated current-events junkie. I stopped by briefly, too, to check if she was in need of anything, for the fridge or cupboards or whatever. But it was clear the task she had before her was huge, and so I did not press to make her time my time.

Unlike the preparation I engaged in for the crafting of a novel in which everything—dossiers for major and minor characters, plot and subplot outlines, storyboard, generous pix of a particular location intended for use as a setting—was confined to a computer file, Patsy's preparation was in the form of paper, and sheets of it were everywhere throughout her office: stacks on her desk and on a metal table in a corner, a few ragged piles on the floor, dozens pinned to several corkboards hanging on the walls. Often these were multiple-paged, stapled and paper-clipped transcripts from her interviews, scores of screenshots from the message boards, and countless copies of emails that her interviewees had offered to her in support of what they'd said in-person. Many of these papers were marked up for possible use in the book. Now I was not sifting and snooping through Patsy's material when at her house for those few minutes to look in on her, but neither could I keep myself from perusing the copy in some of these emails that were at the top of a pile. And it was eye-catching because these emails were replete with threats, and these threats had been sent by Quotidian to its own complaining authors, many of them signed by Schacter, still more by his right-hand front woman Mona Fowler.

Observing my expression while reading one of these

appalling messages during a brief visit, Patsy had said, "Something, isn't it?"

"How many are there like this?" I inquired, shaking my head in disbelief.

"More than anyone would think."

"They're not moved at all by that constant chatter about them on the boards, are they?"

"That name calling by Metheny, Ellis, Thalia Dunne and all the rest? That's kids' stuff to them. Their hides are tough. They laugh at it."

"Now that you've had some time to study on this, Babes," I asked with a change of tone, "do you still believe it's Schacter who's behind the murders?"

"I really don't know," she said. "But they're capable, Schacter and Fowler both, I believe that. I believe they've gotten away with a lot in their lives that crossed the line, and I believe they're confident they can get away with even more and no one will be the wiser."

There was much that I missed from our diminished time together. For one, Patsy and I would talk frequently about writing itself, problems we had encountered during the development of a narrative and solutions invented or "stolen" from others who had confronted similar stagnation. In this way we were no different from a couple who enjoy their employment so much that they talk of it at length and even ad nauseam when they return home in the evening. I was trying to develop a plot and a structure for my third novel, but none of it was forthcoming, and I wanted Patsy's input. Without it, I decided to take a breather.

Working daylight at the market was a big change for me and I was glad to have the evenings to myself. I left Patsy to her own endeavors as I've already said and made my way over to the Welcomian where one could still get a draft for under a dollar. The bar was never empty and as mentioned previously, the clientele covered all types of the human species, and for a novelist like myself, they were deserving of study, if only for the discovery of a personal quality that might fit with a character already a part of my imagination.

On my third visit of the week as I made my entrance, the bartender, a young woman with a sleek ponytail and who was only a few years older than myself and whom I dated a time or two before meeting Patsy, cried out, "Here he is now." She said this to a somewhat slovenly man sitting on a stool at the side of the bar that faced the door. I actually looked behind me to see if someone was following, because the face was that of a stranger. Charlotte, the bartender, then started to wave me over but stopped just as quickly because the stranger was doing it himself. I again glanced behind me and even pointed at myself. He nodded confirmation and so I moseyed his way.

"Wyatt," Charlotte began, and then instantly switched to her customer, "I forgot your name already, but this is Wyatt and he's the writer I was telling you about yesterday when you were here in the afternoon. He's a writer, too, Wyatt."

"Can I buy you a beer?" the man said. "Or whatever it is you drink?"

"Beer's fine," I said dryly, not entirely denying myself a standard suspicion.

He patted the empty stool to his right, patted it several times which struck me as odd, but I settled into the one at the left as it offered an extra foot of separation. The first thing I noticed looking at him straight-on was his crooked nose and something about it said the result was genetic and not the result of an accident or fight. He was wearing jeans the same as me, but they were too roomy and the brass button at the front was wrenched above his belt in a careless fashion. His hair, prematurely gray, had been styled over the ears to make him appear younger, yet they lacked a neatness.

"I'm told that you write novels," he said.

"I have one out there now in the world, and another that's getting shipped around in search of a publisher. What about you? What do you write?"

Charlotte placed a familiar draft before me and he signaled that he would have another.

"I don't write so much anymore," he said. "Nowadays I'm an editor."

"An editor... for a publishing house?"

He cut low air with his hand. All his movements, even the smallest, demonstrated a quick energy.

"The Dideron Corporation. Ever hear of it?"

In fact, I had, but couldn't recall a single thing about it.

"They own thirty-seven newspapers throughout the country, most of them weeklies that serve small rural communities. But they strive to maintain a uniformity in their op-ed pages, which is mostly political. That's where I come in. I'm their Op-Ed editor."

"Op-Ed editor...huh..."

He must have thought I didn't know what that was because he then said, "Op-Ed? Opinion, editorial?"

"Oh, I get it," I said. "I just never figured an editor would be assigned wholly to that section."

"Normally, that would be true. However, like I said, the owners are looking to have some kind of uniformity across that section of their papers. Besides the political element, there's also some cost considerations because, of course, they can print that section off for all of their papers at one time."

Well, it made sense to the short extent I knew what was

required to run several newspapers.

"But that's enough about me," he said. "It's not often I run into other writers, at least not one who actually has a novel that's been published. Tell me what it's about."

I gave him a brief synopsis of *As I Lay Dreaming* and followed with a run of the shameless self-promotion that is necessary if you have hopes of moving your book into the hands of readers. I thought, too, that maybe he might plug my story in the paper.

"Did your agent wangle a contract for you with one of the publishing giants?" he asked when I finished my spiel.

"I wish," I said.

"Hey, nothing wrong with the smaller independent presses," he said. "People, you know, trust them more. Less celebrity, more true writers."

I wasn't going to mention that I did not have an agent, of which I was still of a mixed mind anyway.

"Who did publish it?" he asked.

"Quotidian Release," I said.

He briskly shook his head. "Must be one of the new independents. The digital revolution has introduced quite a few new faces."

What a relief, I thought, that he had not heard of Quotidian, which meant he was unacquainted with the war that was raging between the publisher and its scores of authors.

I took a slug from my beer and turned the questioning around to him. I wanted to know what it was that he had written before his current stint as an editor. Was it short fiction, long fiction? Was it fiction at all? Was it possibly biography?   What was his main involvement with the English word?

"Come on," I urged him. "It's always of interest to me to

come in contact face-to-face with others who pound the keyboard. That doesn't happen often. Certainly not here in Valley Camp."

He kind of smiled at my blast of questions before raising his hands that I should stop. Then he looked over at Charlotte who at the moment was paying attention to us, and the hands shook like a stop sign blasted by severe winds. "I'm not going to get into that," he eventually said. "That's all history, and it's going to stay history." And to make certain it did, he laughed, then said he had to make a pit stop, whereupon he quickly excused himself, rose off his stool, and wound his way through several tables en route to the men's room at the rear of the building. That left Charlotte and me to look at one another and exchange a shrug.

Chapter 26

As far as I know, Patsy never identified herself to others as an investigative reporter. Had she, anyone who called her out on such a claim would have suffered an embarrassment. She knew enough to recognize when a matter of a sinister nature was before her eyes and was equally astute to see that it was layered, even if she could not tell immediately what those layers defined or how the information they contained should be configured.

On Friday she phoned and said she wanted me to come over. I took to heart that she was missing my company, and she said this was so. Of course this was a response that was both perfunctory and genuine: Patsy had discovered something and she wanted to share.

I've written that among the countless papers she had collected from all those she interviewed were scores of emails, messages that the recipients had printed out to make certain they weren't lost in cyberspace or the cloud. These emails were often sent from Quotidian because AuthorsRetreat, in its war against Schacter, had time and again advised its posters to save copies in the event they wished to take legal steps in the future, whether alone or perhaps as a member of a class-action suit, although this advice was part disingenuousness, part ignorance, as Schacter's contract included an arbitration clause that would prevent a disgruntled author from ever going to court.

In most instances the interviewees had picked through their papers and culled out only those that had obvious relevance to Patsy's questions. But in several others the interviewees had pushed the entire file at her, thick Manila folders, several so bloated they resembled a sling that might better have held a fireplace log or even a mending forearm rather than a ream of paper.

"There's nothing in there I'm ashamed of, though I suppose I oughta be," some of the presenters had said to Pats as they nodded at the file they were turning over to a woman they had met less than an hour before. "And forget about returning them. I've neither the money nor the energy to go after Schacter. This is an experience I'll have to eat."

This was a curious thing, although it would not have been for Patsy's editor who had understood the value of a book of interviews that approached the murders. All those she had sat down with to ask her questions, the first of which dealt with the heated exchanges on the message boards, were cooperative and pleasant, Patsy had reported. However, once she had asked her lead-in question about the killings, it was as if that's what these writers and wannabe authors had been waiting for, had been banking on—this is what the book is really going to be about—and they became complicit, not to the crime, but to Patsy's efforts, which they believed was to uncover the truth and put that bastard of a publisher in prison for the rest of his life.

And so it was nothing short of great astonishment I experienced when, upon entering Patsy's work area after my time away, I saw that the accumulation of paper had grown to a most prodigious quantity. Observing my speechlessness, she would later explain that many of her interviewees had passed along the word that she was digging into Schacter's possible involvement in the quadruple murders, more exaggeration on their behalf than process by her, and that they networked with one another more than she had guessed. The results were that upwards of several hundred forwarded emails soon appeared in her inbox, each with the writer's letter to Quotidian, each followed by the company's response, all of which she then printed out for ready access. At the time, I did not know what I was looking at, and Patsy was online, Skypeing with a female writer I recognized because she was fighting cancer at age 23 and was so completely bald on the monitor as she was in her thumbnail on the boards.

I loitered out of the field of view of the computer's pinhole camera, but I glanced upward momentarily and Patsy, taking note of my expression that was equal parts stupefaction and wonderment, stretched her arm below the desktop. She indicated the paper askew at the top of a nearby stack. I slipped it off to read the contents. It was from the young woman with whom she was Skypeing and was addressed to Quotidian. In it the woman complained that they had made a fool of her because the one hundred books she'd ordered for a signing at her local bookstore had never arrived, even though she had paid for them with a credit card in the amount of $1200 and was promised, even assured, they would be there on time. The manager of the bookstore had worked with her, she wrote, and even placed an ad in the local paper at his own expense, publicizing herself, the book, and the upcoming signing. He had commissioned the printing of a hundred fliers as well, plus a large poster for the bookstore's street window. But now, he wanted nothing to do with her and the same went for her book.

The words in the complaint were assertive and determined, but they were not appreciated as Schacter, or possibly Mona Fowler writing under a false name, replied that she should refrain from addressing them with a menacing tone and act as the professional to which "Quotidian expects its authors to aspire." I so thought that was galling enough, but the final paragraph proved otherwise:

"And one other thing, Ms. Redmond. Get yourself a wig. If you haven't the money to purchase one, then use a crayon to draw one. But do SOMETHING! No one enjoys looking at a bald woman, whatever the reason."

I laughed, but it was only because an oddball thought had occurred to me. It didn't matter whether Mona Fowler had a gun hidden inside her desk. That off-center writer she feared was more likely to just open the door and hurl a bomb into the joint.

My eyes continued to wander about the papers and their words while Patsy Skyped. It seemed Quotidian spent an exorbitant amount of time responding to the emails of complaining writers when it would have been easier for Schacter and Fowler to have fulfilled the company's contractual and implied obligations.

The image of Ms. Redmond started to break up on the monitor and Patsy steered the conversation to an end.

"That is one courageous human being," she remarked after the screen went blank. And then, a few seconds later, pretending coyness, she said, "We've met, haven't we?"

"Wyatt Falkner," I said, playing along and using my best

theatrical voice.

"Like the famous southern novelist?"

"No *u*," I said, and slipped my arms around her waist.

"I was asking if you write like him."

"He wouldn't sell."

"More of the dumbing-down theory?"

"Readers hate forty words in a sentence. A comma here, a comma there—"

"—Not to mention a semicolon planted somewhere for the fun of it."

"Then you understand. You must be a very smart young woman."

We held the embrace awhile, knowing that each was smiling over the other's shoulder, and followed with a true but unimpassioned kiss. Business pervaded the air. Still, I managed to grab her buns, to which she responded by grabbing hold of mine much harder.

"Ouch! Easy on the goods."

"Wyatt, I'm sufficiently along on this project so that you no longer have to stay away," she said. "In fact, I think you'll be helpful."

She stepped aside and went to the other end of the room and over to the metal table where she retrieved a folder. She opened it, briefly studied several of the sheets inside, then extended them to me.

"Read these."

"These" were emails, a half-inch of them. I rapidly glanced through the pages, just out of habit. Some were marked up heavily with the highlighter, others a line or two.

"Key me in what I'm supposed to look for."

She shook her head without saying anything.

I thought this a bit unusual, but of course Patsy always had her reasons, and my guess was that she was wondering if I would be of a mind similar to hers after I had gone through the messages.

I took my time and read them all. They were from members of the Nemesis Nine—the four murdered members.

"Where did you get these?" I inquired. "I would think each of their computers is in the hands of the police. I would think Dempsey and Maines are going through their emails looking for motive." My curiosity went from seed to sprout and I repeated my question. "Really, Babes, where did you get these?"

"I didn't need their computers, Mister Gardner. All I needed were their webmail addresses."

"And a password."

"Well of course. The Purvis daughters were more than willing to tell me what their mother's was. Underwood's brother—he gave me three and said he was certain one would get me in. Smmith's mother, she wasn't aware of her son's password, but her name is Delphinia and I played a hunch."

"And Spectra Suter?"

"At the house when I was searching on the floor. A small rectangle of paper was taped to the underside of the bottom drawer and it had four easily recalled passwords scribbled on it."

I started to ask why these people had so willingly cooperated with her in divulging personal information, but shut myself down in mid-sentence. It was obvious they were hoping to assist in having the killer arrested and convicted.

I looked again at the papers in my hand.

"What about the others? Warner, Cotton, Metheny...."

She again shook her head. "I got in touch with each and informed them of my endeavor and then asked for their emails that had any reference to Quotidian. The trio you mentioned plus Montgomery wanted nothing to do with it. The mysterious Grimalkin wouldn't respond. John Warner said that I might be making myself into a target and he wasn't going to be responsible, and Metheny scolded me for trying to capitalize and make money out of the whole affair."

"Why did you show me these? What am I supposed to be looking for?"

"I wanted to see if you see what I saw."

"Pats, you've been at this a while. I've read them, but I can't say that anything jumped out at me."

"Look again."

She did not want to tell me what she saw. She wanted me to discover it on my own because if I did, it would corroborate her observation, her own lighting of the bulb.

I read the emails again as she wanted, read them slowly, read them and compared them to see where there might be similarities in what was written. I looked at the information at the top—addressee, subject, CCs and BCCs. I checked to see if there were attachments.

"I'm sorry."

There was the minutest shake of her head. I was a disappointment.

She reached out to retake the papers but I pulled them back to look once more. What had she taken note of that I was missing? Any one of the papers written by a victim included the other victims. Underwood had written to Suter and CCed it to Smmith and Purvis. Smmith had written to Underwood and CCed it to Purvis and Suter.

I went to the table and spread out the messages so that I could view them all at the same time. And that was when it became so obviously clear. The remaining members of the Nemesis Nine weren't in the loop. Nothing had been CCed to any of the five who remained alive.

"I got it," I said, and was sure that I did. I presented my finding to Pats, which she rewarded with another kiss.

"Babes, are you thinking this has something to do with their being murdered?"

"You went to the boards. You read their posts, the glut of exchanges among the Nemesis Nine. On the boards you couldn't help but come away thinking they formed a solid block that was mutually respectful of one another's opinions and talents. But what you read just now suggests there may have been a big strain of disingenuousness among four of them."

"What's to account for it?"

"They're successful writers."

"Purvis wasn't."

"No, but during our meeting Schacter kind of challenged me to read some of these people. Lillian Purvis wrote extremely well. If she were alive today, she certainly would have found a reputable publisher."

"That still leaves John Warner out. He's the one remaining who calls himself a 'pro.'"

"Except he isn't, and the others knew it. A few of his short stories were serialized in his hometown newspaper. Nothing more."

I shook my head out of appreciation. My Patsy. The Researcher.

Chapter 27

It was easy to understand why we liked Schacter for the crimes. The motive was a snap to decipher. The four victims had been hammering his business and himself relentlessly and he was determined to put a stop to it before it cost him great sums of money. And as for the brutality expressed in each of the killings, that wasn't hard to understand either. My few minutes with him at his business had informed me that he didn't care an ounce for helping someone in dreadful need.

But what Patsy had stumbled upon concerning the Nemesis Nine was teasing my authorial compass in another direction as it suggested there could be another motive that had yet to surface. And this possibility of another motive further suggested there might be someone besides Schacter and the Muscle to look at for the murders.

As soon as I left Patsy and returned home, I settled into my office and booted up the Mac.

Keeping five people out of a loop—a loop these five people of the Nemesis Nine must have believed they were always a part of—naturally brought up the question *Why?* Especially since the postings on the boards had implied that everything was copacetic among them. I decided to go back to earlier times on the message board and see if there were any stirrings of trouble.

By far the favorite message board for the Nine had been AuthorsRetreat, although, to be clear, they were hardly negligent about making timely visits to the others. Its home page came up and I went to the section devoted to Quotidian. The number of subsections it contained stretched well below my monitor's screen, but the most popular bannered there at the top and it indexed at more than a thousand pages and ten times that number for posts.

I clicked on the most recent thread out of curiosity. A rapid scan of the entries showed them to be brief reassurances and obvious agreements *(Were you expecting anything but, Wyatt?)* to a post further up, which belonged to someone who called himself Growler and who would post damaging remarks on a half-dozen of the most recent Quotidian offerings. He'd used a thumbnail photo of himself to accompany his criticism until one of his targets responded with some threatening language. His next post showed the selfie replaced with a picture of a dog's muzzle. This time around in his criticism, he'd decided to include *As I Lay Dreaming*. Here's a partial of his so-called "review."

Growler	... with a plot so convoluted that Sherlock Holmes and Columbo working together couldn't unravel it. As for real characters, not a one. Altogether, *As I Lay Dreaming* is just more drivel from the presses of Daily Release.

I won't deny this was an irritant, and it was the sort of thing that had enraged the writer at the Statler who then squeezed the neck of a fellow writer and slammed his body into a wall. Yet there was an upside because Growler's targets were always books that were gaining an attraction, evidenced by sales on Amazon and elsewhere. He hadn't read any of the offerings, it would have been apparent to the proverbial duck, but in spite of that there were lesser forms of life frequenting the boards who believed his cocksure broadside and took the scripture as honest. I made a mental post-it note to check the sales numbers of my novel at the online booksellers.

And at the same time I was thinking this, something else began to beat on my brain and it sprouted from Growler's use of the word convoluted. Although I was confident that the plot of *Dreaming* was not tortuous and confusing, that had not always been the case. Early drafts had me confident, certainly, until the very end when I checked and double-checked to see if there were any loose ends that remained untied, if there were questions unanswered. The shocking fact was, there were both. And it wasn't just one or two I discovered; there were several. And each time I went back and fixed one, another opened up. Eventually, I was forced to pull out all the elements of the plot and make some big changes to many of them. Well, that's how I was slowly beginning to think of Schacter and the Muscle regarding their responsibility for the murders. Each time Patsy and I had answered a question as to how, why, or what, yet another question was born, and you couldn't help but wonder if there might not be an end to it. You couldn't help but wonder if all of it was too convoluted to be real, too convoluted to have actually taken place.

I paged to the start of the section devoted to Quotidian.

The criticisms of the P O D publishing house were already present because this section of the message board would not have been created were that not the case. However, the recent levels of intensity were missing from the earlier posts. To the contrary, interspersed throughout the opening pages were tenuous salutes to the new Quotidian Release, and aligned with this kid-glove approach was the noticeable lack of baptismal names for the posters. This I understood was to reflect the writer's insecurity. At the time a verdict on Quotidian Release was still a long time away, and the wise writer would not want to be on the wrong side if the publisher emerged victorious. Even Schacter and Mona Fowler at this early point had yet to be identified. Still, there were a few writers who did sign on without the fear of reprisal at the inception—Dalton Ellis among them, who complained because his complimentary copies had fallen apart within weeks of their arrival; and Thalia Dunne, who lashed out at an unnamed company president with a barrage of invective and standard obscenity because pages were missing in her memoir. Like them, Underwood and Suter were already convinced that Quotidian was not what it was saying it was, but unlike them, they were the wiser. Neither at the time was releasing their governors on the individual statements of concern.

And there was yet another familiar name that appeared and it was Oliver Metheny. While his appearance on the board was late, it was Metheny and his Rottwriter website the others credited for bringing this dedicated section of AuthorsRetreat into existence. A handful of writers who had signed early with the Quotidian makeover of an out-in-the-open vanity press complained to Rottwriter, and so the warning to others was out there for all to see. Trouble was, Metheny's site was not dynamic. In fact, it could have been described as stagnant because writers consulted its pages solely to learn if the agent or publisher to whom they were thinking of sending a manuscript was present on its blacklist. Soon the complaints multiplied and the matter transferred to a message board, and that board was AuthorsRetreat where voices were plentiful and demanding to be heard.

I continued to read the early posts and soon came upon some that fired a potshot at Metheny himself for the unpolished appearance of his website. I chuckled because Rottwriter today, even after a recent makeover, still imparted a suspicion that an underage family member who liked to draw was behind the design—it still looked anything but professional. And while the site may have emboldened a few writers to hold their ground and keep away from those persons and outfits on Metheny's list, it was at the same time hard for me to imagine that its elementary look could ever threaten a publisher or literary agent with any kind of standing.

I kept at my task of wading through various threads and cruising from one post to another well into the evening. So much of it was boring stuff, plus a pop-up ad frequently stalled my reading by blocking out a paragraph. Eventually, the tedium took its toll on my concentration and I blackened the screen. Beer is what you need, I told myself. Beer and barroom distraction. So out the door and into the night I went.

Chapter 28

I was off work the next day yet woke up early all the same. The beer had slid down the gullet more like 10W-30 than it did alcohol and reminded me throughout the night that sleep would not endure.

While at the bar, I'd run into four classmates from my high school days who were in town for a wedding. One had signed on to be the best man. They'd heard of *Dreaming* from some other classmates and two said they'd ordered copies from the bookstores in their communities and read it without putting it down. A third fellow said he was going to buy a copy. Which I didn't buy because I remembered him as a student who promised to do many things, yet never fulfilled a one. I thanked them all and told Charlotte to pour them a pitcher of Iron City, on me.

Feeling upbeat so early in the day, I decided to surprise Patsy and take her out for breakfast before she started in on her own endeavors. Only the clock said it was too early, first light remained dim, and she wasn't likely to be on her feet for another hour.

So into the kitchen I went and brewed a half-pot of coffee, then took a mug with me to the Mac. I did a quick scan of the news, world and local. After that, I pulled up my third novel, the biggest of my WIPs. Only the problem with structure had yet to find a solution, and so I was journeying to a destination with a poorly marked road map to get me there. Still, I tickled the qwerty for twenty minutes. It was all tripe. I selected the entire mess, deleted, and brought up Pixel-to-Paper.

One look at the page and I found myself squinting and muttering "What's all this about?" LOLs and LMAOs punctuated the screen from top to bottom like a spread from a shotgun blast. Even the immutably sober Snollygoster was having a fit. I paged back to the post of provenance, yet what was generating the frolics wasn't clear. AuthorsRetreat, I thought. They were the usual instigators, and I switched over to its message board. But I discovered the same thing when its website came up. LOLs, as if they were guffaws, in every post and at least a dozen ROTFLMAOs, which I thought would make a great YouTube video if acted out. Again I paged back, and I had to go through several as board members I'd never heard of were driven to post their excitement of the wondrous news, whatever it was.

More than a dozen screens later, the stimulant behind all the written comedy appeared at last and, sonovabitch, if I didn't laugh as well. No rolling on the floor and my ass remained attached, but it was a backslapper all right, notwithstanding that it would be yet another strike against my novel going anywhere.

A little history first.

About the time I received my acceptance letter from Quotidian for *As I Lay Dreaming*, a post had appeared on an obscure website that dissed a group of writers on AuthorsRetreat who wrote in the fantasy genre. The genre itself was belittled as well and the message was that anyone except an idiot could write the stuff. Whoever had authored the message obviously had never heard of Tolkien and probably wouldn't have had any respect for Bugs Bunny either. No one, the message warned, should put much stock in the criticism of these so-called "writers," who obviously were persistent critics of Quotidian Release. Schacter never took responsibility for the post, but that didn't matter to the critics. They were convinced he had authored it.

However, the response at AuthorsRetreat wasn't one of defense and explanation, as might have been expected. Much to the contrary, they held their fiery breath and counterpunched by secretly compiling a piece of shit fiction with a plethora of hideous mistakes. This included missing chapters, repeated chapters, dead characters who suddenly and inexplicably returned to life, pages of *lorem ipsum*, pages with absolutely nothing on them, and worse. They submitted it to Daily Release under a fake name. The point of their exercise, in which more than thirty writers had contributed, was to show that DR was in actuality a vanity press in a new suit and not a traditional publishing house as it advertised itself, and that it would accept and publish anything. They intended to show the world that its "editors" didn't bother even to read the manuscripts that came to them as digital documents.

And not at all to their surprise, the fake author of *Talladega Tremors* received his letter of acceptance with the promise that the two-dollar bill advance would be mailed to him as soon as Quotidian received his signature on the contract.

Like I said, I laughed. But after awhile, I ceased laughing and could only shake my head. What had I gotten myself into by signing with Quotidian Release?

I shut down the Mac after that but only because I glanced out a window and saw the sun was an inch above the horizon and climbing fast. If I didn't catch Patsy before she immersed herself in her work, my effort to persuade her to go out for breakfast would be futile. I snatched up my keys and wallet and hurriedly left the house.

Ten minutes later I pulled up to hers and saw the nondescript car with the moonlike hubcaps parked out front. The detectives were in Valley Camp for a second visit. Maines opened Patsy's front door as I stepped onto the porch.

"Good morning, Detective."

"Mr. Falkner."

"You're up early," I said.

Inside, in the front room of the house, Patsy stood off to the rear. She'd been letting her hair grow since the last cut and she had it pulled back behind her so it wouldn't always be dropping and interfering with her work. She looked beautiful as always. Off to the right was her office and the door was open. Paper filled the frame so that one unfamiliar with her activities might have thought this was a supply closet or a space for recyclables. Dempsey stood near the center of the room, straight as any block of stone, and his eyes set upon me as I entered.

"What's up?" I asked, upbeat.

"We had some questions for Ms. Lukehart," he replied tonelessly as his eyes took me in from head to toe. "We have some for you as well."

"Fire away," I said, "'cause I'm hungry and I hope Patsy is too. I'm treating her to breakfast."

"Mr. Falkner," he said curiously, "have you ever been arrested?"

"Not a once," I answered, grinning.

"Fingerprinted?"

"Not that I remember. I was a goody two-shoe as a kid

and have stayed that way into adulthood. Pretty sad, huh? I mean, a writer should have at minimum one black mark against him so that he has something to reckon with throughout his life. Don't you agree?"

"We found fingerprints at Koldren's. They weren't his and they weren't made by his wife, Spectra Suter. In fact, we're certain they belong to a male. We're waiting for you to tell us they're yours."

He had ignored my friendly smile, reacting as though we hadn't once shared a breakfast table and exchanged a little friendly dialogue.

"Were they yours, Mr. Falkner?"

"Who's Koldren?" I said.

"Do us all a favor and cut the crap," he said with stern impatience.

"Wyatt, they know," Patsy whispered under raised eyebrows.

"I repeat. Were they yours?"

"Okay. I was there, sure," I replied with a thick strand of huffiness. "But I doubt it was my fingerprints you discovered." I winked at my woman.

In a voice not hiding his exasperation, Dempsey said, "Detective Maines can tell you that I'm not normally in the business of giving advice to others, but I'll make an exception in your case because you're sorely in need of it. The next time you go snaking through another person's belongings and you don't want others to know, select some item beside a doily made of lace. Our forensic man had an easy time of filling in the gaps."

This detail amused Patsy. Maines, too, was restraining a laugh.

"Now Miss Lukehart informed us of your visits and has sworn she left nothing out. Do you have anything that you would like to add, Mr. Falkner?"

"Well then," I said, "you must already know that neither one of us were able to find a gun."

"We have the gun," he said firmly.

"Do you now!" Hell, I was sounding flip even to myself, although that didn't put a stop to it. "And are Koldren's prints all over it? I'm betting they are, Detective. I'm also betting it's the same gun that was used to kill the others." I darted a look from Dempsey to Maines to Patsy and then came back and settled it on Dempsey. "Well? Am I right?"

For the first time I saw that skyscraper posture of the man slightly buckle and the expression that accompanied it told me he was undecided whether he should laugh or haul off and swipe me a good one across the face.

"Why don't you do us all a favor and lose the attitude, Mr. Falkner. What do you think?"

He stood in place and stared into me. I took a deep breath and raised my palm.

"All right," I said. "I'll reel in the flippancy."

"That would be appreciated."

"But I have a reason for asking what I did," I said. "If the answer to my questions is yes, then it would be easy to conclude that Koldren murdered the others and killed himself. And that would close the book on the case."

"And you're wondering if that's what the detective and I will do. Are we the kind of cops who eagerly want to close the book on a case and if what we uncover during our investigation fills in a script, then that's what we do?"

"You have it right," I said. "That's what I'm wondering."

"Well, we're not, Mr. Falkner. And as for your curiosity, yes, Koldren's fingerprints were all over the gun and yes, it is the same gun that killed the others."

"Then you haven't—"

"—We haven't concluded anything."

I nodded. It was one of those things about a person that was nice to know.

"Now why don't you tell us how your stop at Koldren's differed from Ms. Lukehart's."

"Well, if Patsy told you everything, then you're aware a car was parked out front of Koldren's that wasn't there when I arrived. As far as we can tell, that's the only thing that differed in our visits, and we've gone over this a couple of times."

"While you were there, did you observe any vehicles on the street near the Koldren home? Did anyone pass you in a car, in a van, in a pickup on your way in or out? Was there anyone sitting next to the curb in a parked car?"

"Nothing like that," I answered. "While I was there, the entire neighborhood could have passed for a cemetery."

Dempsey regarded me a long moment after that. Then he nodded. He turned back and addressed Patsy. "Ms. Lukehart, thank you. You've been very helpful."

Maines offered her thanks as well and they stepped toward the door.

Patsy interrupted their departure.

"Before you leave, I hope you'll answer a question of mine. Have you found any of the writers you spoke with during this investigation to be of any benefit?"

"A few provided information to which we gave a closer look," answered Maines.

"Why do you ask, Ms. Lukehart?"

Patsy shrugged. "I'm not really sure."

"There's been nothing like a Deep Throat," said Dempsey, "if that's what you're asking. No one from inside of Quotidian Release spilling significant bits of information that could lead to an arrest."

Patsy nodded. "All right. Thanks." She knew, as did I, they wouldn't be telling her more.

As they moved to step across the threshold, it was my turn with a question.

"Detective, I'm a writer and because of that I'm curious."

"What is it, Mr. Falkner?"

"What inspired Detective Maines and you to drive out from the city to little Valley Camp this morning?"

"What caused us to drive out here?" He seemed surprised by the question.

"Yes. It's not like Valley Camp is just around the corner from your precinct."

The detective's face constricted. Then it suddenly morphed into a humoring slyness, and I again considered that he might be laughing at me.

"Like you, Mr. Falkner, the detective and I read our share of fiction when we have the opportunity."

The strange reply caused me to jerk back my head an inch and my brow must have furrowed before I finished with a wide spread of the hands. It made no sense. I even looked to Patsy to see if she understood what he was talking about.

"What am I supposed to take away from that?" I finally asked.

"When you're writing, aren't their passages where you want to make certain that you aren't prematurely giving too much away to your reader?"

"Of course. Better to pepper than to flood. Any writer worth a dollar knows that."

"Yet am I correct in saying that you also want to avoid giving away too little?"

And on that I got it at once and grinned. Grinned because I understood where he was coming from. Too little in a novel and your story gets tossed. Too little to the detectives, which described my phone message to them, and they wanted to know why. They'd obviously delved into Patsy's accident and once they discovered it occurred in the vicinity of Koldren's home and learned that he had taken his life, they had suspicions with questions attached.

"Anything else?"

"No, that's all," I said with a genuine inflection of amicability that I hoped would make them forget my earlier impertinence. Dempsey turned away without further response, but Maines minced a smile as she left the house.

Patsy shut the door behind them and loosened her hair.

"So. Now to more important matters, big boy. Did I hear you tell them you're taking me out for breakfast?"

"My dime," I said. "Where would you prefer to go?" I rattled off a few of the restaurants to which I knew she was partial.

"None of them," she said. "Let's just walk. I've some pieces to mail and their deadlines are two and three days away. I'd like them on the truck before noon. Afterwards, we can eat at Delbert's."

"Delbert's works for me," I said. It was a small restaurant with a great reputation and was just up the street and over a block.

Patsy's post office sat under a magnificent oak tree at the south end of Grant Avenue. Though small, it displayed a contemporary design built from some unexpected pork won by the area's aging congressman. Much of it was glass, large thick panes, and as she and I approached, the sun was rising at an angle behind us that permitted the frame at the entrance to mirror our image. We looked great as a couple—strong, proud, energetic, and full of the young life we felt every day. I pointed out our reflection to Pats. She stopped in her tracks and curled her arm around mine.

"Hmmm," she muttered, pushing her body tightly to my own, tilting her head one way and then the other, finally tipping it onto my shoulder. "We look like we belong together, don't we? Just what do you think is behind that, Wyatt?" she asked with comic suspicion.

"You don't know?"

"Tell me."

I wrapped my arms about her waist.

"Well?"

"We have in common a love for the long sentence," I said solemnly. "Or at least we don't object to it."

"Already, romance is lost," she said drily, while pretending to swoon from despair.

We gave a mutual peck to each other and stepped inside. Patsy went up to the window and dropped off her manila envelopes addressed to those magazine publishers who still would accept only a manuscript on paper. We then continued our walk to Delbert's where we claimed a table in a corner. The small restaurant framed its unchanging menu on the wall.

Once we ordered and our beverages were delivered, I asked Pats about what she had told the detectives. At the house I was unsure if she had informed them that the car parked in Koldren's driveway was likely the same car that had run her off the road and tried to kill her. She hadn't mentioned it to the Capers authorities, so it was a fair question.

"Wyatt, do you know they picked up on the identical thing we'd observed concerning the note and those odd ts that weren't crossed?"

"They're a couple of sharp detectives," I said. "Babes, what all did you tell them?"

"I told them what was important."

"Dempsey said you swore that you left nothing out. That's not the same as putting everything in. So how did they respond after you informed them the car that ran you off the road was the same car that was at the house?'"

"I didn't tell them about that."

"You what?"

"I didn't tell them."

"Why did you leave that out? Don't you think that's important?"

"Because I've come around to your way of thinking, much as I hate to admit it."

"What are you talking about? What's my way of thinking?"

"Maybe you've been right all along. Maybe no one is after me."

"Hold on now, Babes," I said and my tone took on a more serious note. "Are you now of the mind that you weren't forced off that road? That no one is looking to kill you?"

"Yes and no."

I placed a hand on one of hers. "Look, it's not a good idea to begin doubting yourself."

"I'm trying not to. Yet I find myself thinking like you were thinking. Why hasn't he made an attempt on my life? It's been weeks."

"Are you sure that's something you want hurried-up?"

"I'll allow it kept me alert," she said. "The past few days that's not been how it is."

"Yeah, I noticed."

"What do you mean by that? What did you notice?"

"Babes, it's three blocks from your house to the post office. And yet, as we were walking, I didn't see you check your back or cast an eye to the vehicles that were driving past us. Not even once."

"Then you understand what I'm getting at. Wyatt, you're the novelist, and a novelist is attentive to the failures and excuses of individuals. He dwells on their motives. Tell me why we haven't seen him? Why hasn't this man shown his face? Tell me. I really want to know."

"I'll think on it," I said, patting her hand. "I promise. I'll think on it real hard. But just so you understand, Babes. In my novels, he would never just up and go away."

Chapter 29

I thought on it, you can be sure. Even as we ate our eggs and sipped our juice, I pondered the question, and when Patsy started to introduce some other matter I held up a hand to cut her short, then directed a finger at my temple. I wasn't sure if my small attempt at humor would be recognized because of her troubled mind, but she did manage to release the faintest grin.

And I was continuing to think on it after I walked her back to the house. Because I knew she wanted to get back to working on her book, I kissed her at the porch, told her again how much I loved her, then spun a one-eighty and strolled back to the car. But after another half-dozen steps, I spun a second one-eighty.

"Hold up, Babes!" I yelled back while smacking myself upside the head. "I almost forgot. There's something you have to see."

I led her inside and to her office profuse with paper. Patsy's computer never slept, she never powered off. I touched a button to bring light to the monitor and stepped away.

"What do you want to show me?"

"Have you visited any of the boards in the past twenty-four hours?"

"No."

"Then pull up AuthorsRetreat."

The homepage was quick to emerge and was shotgunned with still more of the acronyms indicating laughter unhinged, a veritable cyber orgy with asses moving about on the carpets and linoleum floors all across the continent.

I watched my Pats as she read what was before her. "Just wait," I said and paged back until I found the post that had generated all the other posts.

I watched again as she read its contents. She didn't laugh a note.

"I know you're a little upset, Babes, but you don't find that somewhat funny?" I said when she turned away and looked at me.

"One of the posts states they didn't sign the contract."

"Yeah. So?"

"They turned down the offer."

"Okay."

"Wyatt, this group is claiming that Daily Release will publish anything." The emphasis was for my edification. With their ruse they might legitimately claim that DR would accept anything, but to claim the other?

"Even so, Pats, isn't the jump too logical and obvious not to swallow?"

"Wyatt, before leaving the Quotidian offices I asked the Fowler woman if anyone from the various websites had ever got in touch to arrange an interview with Schacter. She said she had always expected Oliver Metheny would be the one to call, but it was Garnet Underwood who phoned and presented himself. Only Schacter was out of town at the time and Underwood declined to speak at length with her. She said he never called back."

"So what are you saying?"

"They wrote him off as a crook a long time ago."

"That appears to be the truth, doesn't it? Babes, are you defending Daily Release on this?"

"Please, the man isn't stupid. He'll have this covered as best he can, if he hasn't already."

No sooner had she said this, the page refreshed with new posts and there at the top was Schacter's.

Tor Schacter	A recent entry on this message board reports that a manuscript with the title *Talladega Tremors* was accepted by Quotidian Release and a contract offered to its author. The report states also that the submission of *Talladega Tremors* was not in good faith. That, quite the contrary, it was a manuscript deliberately crafted with errors by upwards of thirty men and women from the AuthorsRetreat board and with the underhanded but explicit intention to discredit and embarrass Quotidian Release and its many satisfied authors. We at Quotidian Release regret this unfortunate incident. We regret that the antagonists present on this board saw fit to go to such extraordinarily unprofessional measures in an attempt to prove a point, which exists in their minds and nowhere else. For our own part, we deeply regret that one title was wrongly substituted for another when it came time to send out our letters of rejection and acceptance. For this we at Quotidian Release take full responsibility and will make every effort to see that it does not happen again.

After Patsy and I read it, all she said was, "Told ya."

I was forced to admit that it was Schacter who came off as the adult while the others brought to mind a group of middle-schoolers who secretly attach an insulting sign to the back of their teacher and then run about giggling to one another.

Chapter 30

Little Jake Kotecki's father stood in his driveway chatting with the cable man as I was leaving the neighborhood. When he saw me, he waved. Rather than return the wave I again pointed my index finger at my temple as I'd done at Delbert's. I'm thinking, I telegraphed. Can't be disturbed. He upped his head to say he understood the code.

Put simply, it didn't make a bit of sense that someone—the Muscle or anyone, who was hiding at the Suter-Koldren residence when Patsy was padding through its rooms and opening cupboards and closets—would allow more than a week to pass if he intended to kill her to protect himself and avoid arrest.

Why would he wait? I kept asking myself, and the answer was always the same: He wouldn't! But if Patsy was now having doubts about herself, I didn't think it put anything in our favor if the two of us were of the same mind. That could get her killed faster than anything. I continued to muse on the matter, trying to discover any reason a killer might wait, but nothing was coming to mind that made any sense. Best, I figured, to give the matter a rest. That often worked in the development of a stalled plot.

And so on this day off from the market, I cleared my head as best I could of my anxiety and struck out to the back of the house to where I'd stacked some lumber from a friend who had dismantled an old shed. I was intending to use the boards to construct a small lean-to inside of which a few items, like the Cub Cadet and my ten-speed, could find rescue from the rain and other inclement weather. I grabbed a hammer as I thought I might get started on its construction and yanked out several rusty nails that could wreck a saw blade. But after a half-hour's work, it was clear that I wasn't ready to get immersed in the project. I put away the hammer and returned to my office.

Never the kind of writer who dedicates himself to one effort before moving on to another, I booted the Mac and pulled up six windows, each with a short story, none of which was anywhere near completion. I read all there was in each and selected one that I found still exciting. I stuck with it for the rest of the morning, using placeholder words for the right words that wouldn't come readily to mind.

About mid-afternoon I glanced out a window and saw the postal vehicle start up the street to make its deliveries. In my neighborhood the boxes are at the curb and I watched the carrier as she inserted a few business-size envelopes into mine. Most writers, I believe, are optimistic until the letter of rejection arrives, and even though it's a matter of fact that a submission is unlikely to bring a response inside a month, nevertheless, it was in my head that the acquisition editor in Manhattan, a colleague of Patsy's roomie from the past, had jumped out of his chair after reading my manuscript and screamed, "Quick! Get a contract to this Falkner fellow toot sweet. This story is FANTASTIC!"

I sauntered out to the box and withdrew the envelopes. I didn't have to open them to know they were junk. I paused before returning to the house and looked up and down the street. As usual my neighborhood was quiet, even dormant. There was no one sitting on a porch or lingering in a window, and nothing was moving except for the Llewellin Setter, the only sign of life other than myself. He was crossing a lawn several lots down and suddenly looking a little older since our photo session. I saw him pause and glance my way and I woofed at him in greeting. Then I turned and walked back to the house. But at the stoop I hesitated and swung back around. I took just a few steps and again surveyed my neighborhood where every window in every house was covered by a shade or a curtain. And in that moment I got to thinking of Patsy and me as husband and wife and wondered if we would live together in her house or find contentment in mine. The homes themselves were not so very different, but their neighborhoods were sharply defined opposites. Mine was always silent like an empty church, withdrawn and introverted. Some might even describe it as dead. Hers was active. It routinely manifested an attention, as well as a caution, to daily living.

I spent the remainder of the day at home, choosing a seat in front of the TV, rather than a swinging stool at the Welcomian. I alternated between watching one of the many shows from the past and reading a book.

On the following day I returned to the market and my boss informed the others and myself that he needed us to work a large part of a double shift. Earlier in the week, a semi en route for the store was involved in an accident on I-80 and its cargo of canned goods had flown from the box. Another truck was later sent out and it was arriving today along with the normal deliveries.

While at work in the aisles I usually carried my cell along, but on this particular day I mindlessly had left it sitting on the shelf inside the locker and didn't return for it. At the lunch break I checked to see if there was a text or call from Patsy, but there wasn't. At the end of the extra shift I checked again, having still left it in the locker, and this time there was a voicemail, and her words seemed colored by fear.

I drove away from the market's parking lot in a rush and headed for her house. When I arrived at her neighborhood, the sky was already dark and the lights were going out, but of the houses on Grant Avenue very few were black. I gave a simple knock of two beats on her front door before inserting the key she had given me, then stepped inside. All the rooms were unlit, just as was the porch. Even so, I was able to make out her form sitting on the sofa. On the stand to the right loomed a bottle of beer and her right hand was closed around it. Her left hand, resting on a small revolver that I'd seen only once before, was limply holding a disc. The house itself was giving off a fresh fragrance, like she had recently taken a long shower.

"You all right?" I asked as I snapped on a lamp.

She held out the disc. "This arrived in the afternoon mail."

I took it from her and examined one side, then the other. There were no markings on either.

"What's on it?" I asked while glancing at the gun.

"Pictures."

"What sort of pictures?"

"Pictures of me."

"Are you all right, Babes?" I asked again.

"Slip it into the Mac. See for yourself."

She got up, leaving the beer behind, but brought along the revolver. I followed her into her office and sat down before her computer. I inserted the disc into its slot.

Up quickly came four photos, and it was immediately apparent that she had been unaware that she was the subject at the time of their taking. The first picture showed her standing in the open front door and withdrawing her mail from the box at the side. In the second one she was crossing the street to a neighbor's. The third photo showed her removing her garbage from the rear of the house. And in the fourth capture she was a few steps away from entering the post office. Except for this last, each of the photos had been shot probably with a mid-range telephoto.

"Well...?"

"No message? No hint of who it's from?"

"No. Nothing."

I took a closer inspection of the first three photos, then stepped away and returned to the front room and a window, which offered a view of the street. Despite the darkness of the night, it was easy to determine where the photographer had positioned himself. In each case he had stood just outside the neighborhood. And with this knowledge came the answer to the question I'd been pondering.

"He's been waiting because he had to," I muttered to myself.

I turned around and looked Patsy in the eye.

"The man hasn't made an attempt on your life, Babes, because he hasn't had the opportunity. Leastways, not one that would allow him to do you in and get away unseen."

I took her hand in mine and pulled her up alongside. "Take a look out there. What do you see?"

"It's a new moon. Nothing much," she said. "Which, if you're wondering, is the reason I pulled this .38 from the back of the closet."

"Is that thing loaded?" I asked.

"Wouldn't be much good if it wasn't. Isn't that what they

always say?"

The revolver had come with the house. I didn't know if she knew how to use it, but she had once said that her aunt had been quite proficient in hitting her target.

"Are you sure you're okay, Babes?"

"That's the third time you've asked, Wyatt."

"Yes, and you have yet to answer me."

"What do you think? Would you be feeling all right if you received photos of yourself in the mail? This guy is stalking me, for chrissakes."

"No, I guess I wouldn't be okay," I said. I shook my head in apology and squeezed her hand awhile. Then I turned my attention back to what was outside the window. "What time is it? About 10?"

"Closer to 11. Why?"

I pulled her closer. "Babes, there's never a time in the day that a face or two isn't available in your neighborhood. Even now, if you look up and down the street, most of the houses have their lights on and you can see people passing by the window. Your neighbors like to look out their windows to see if anything is going on. What's more, they look out them quite often. There's no possible way this man could have sat inside a car for more than a few minutes in your neck of the woods. Someone surely would have noticed him and been suspicious enough to notify the police. He must have realized that. And since you haven't left your neighborhood in recent days, there's been no opportunity elsewhere to put an end to you."

My explanation buoyed her and she took her hand away. "Let's look at the photos again," she said.

"There's nothing to them," I said, thinking to ponder them further would only cause more fear and discouragement. They're intended to intimidate. He's been unable to murder you, but he's making sure you haven't forgotten him. The pictures are his reminder of that fact."

"Humor the researcher," she said. "Sometimes the obvious gets overlooked."

We slipped back into her office.

"You're making me a little nervous with that gun." I said. "Set it down somewhere."

She reached and placed it on a shelf above the computer.

We paged through the four photos again, one by one, and I tried to be helpful. The photo of Pats retrieving her mail from the box on her porch—"Are you sure you didn't throw away a card or a letter that might have been connected to the pictures? Something containing a warning and a threat?"

"I didn't throw out anything."

"I don't mean a sheet that was inserted with the disc," I explained. "He photographed you getting your mail. Was there something else in the mail that day, perhaps a postcard or something in an envelope from him and he wanted to capture your expression when your set eyes upon it?"

"No, Wyatt. There was nothing like that."

"Can you tell me if these photos were taken on the same day?"

"I take my cans to the curb on Tuesday, but I'm not sure when I mailed out those first puff pieces for the month."

"You don't maintain a record of when you send out your work?" It surprised me that she didn't know.

"For those pieces that go by snail mail I record only the week, not the day," she explained. "It's on the wall calendar behind us."

I next brought up the snapshot of her entering the post office to full-screen. I didn't want to tell her that her stalker had captured this photo when he was less than twenty feet at her back.

"Close the window," she said, turning away. "I thought a second inspection of these might reveal something that I didn't see at first because I was shaken. But there's nothing there. Let's go back into the other room. I'll get you a beer."

"How many have you had, if you don't mind my asking?"

"Do you want a beer?"

"No."

"Wyatt, I want to strangle this man and I just needed something to put my hands around, okay? The revolver satisfied one, the beer the other."

She started to walk out of the office and return to the living room, but stopped when she noticed that I wasn't following, that I hadn't moved. That I hadn't even closed the window on the computer screen like she had directed.

"What's wrong?"

"I'm thinking your bonehead friends might have secretly slipped me an important note," I said behind a smile that was losing its reluctance.

She winced. "What are you talking about?"

"I might have to send them a thank-you card, Pats."

She winced more deeply out of befuddlement and I pulled up the iPhoto sliders to the side of the picture. At the same time her doorbell sounded.

"Watch," I said.

"Now who could that possibly be at this late hour?"

She left the room as I moved the slider for contrast to the left and the one for shadow to the right.

"Is Wyatt Falkner here?"

I redirected my attention from the computer screen to the outer room. It was a male voice from the other side of the front door.

"I'm looking for Wyatt Falkner."

"Who are you?" I heard Patsy ask suspiciously.

"I need to see Mr. Falkner. It's urgent. I was told at the Welcomian that I might find him here."

"This isn't the Welcomian," she said in a scolding tone.

"Yes, I know that. But I was told by its bartender that he often comes to this address."

"Who are you?" I heard Patsy ask a second time and with a much stronger suspicion. "And what's so urgent?"

"If you'll unlock your door, Miss, and just let me step inside, I'll be glad to explain my coming to your home at this late hour. I know how odd it must strike you and I apologize. But I assure you there is nothing underhanded or sinister about my presence. And, believe me, it is urgent!"

The voice was too familiar to me, in fact it was recently familiar, and yet I couldn't connect a face or a name to it. At least not until I glanced at the computer monitor. And there in the large windowpane of the post office magically appeared the image of the person who had photographed Pats.

They were a match, voice and image. "NO, BABES!" I screamed. "DON'T LET HIM IN!"

I shot out of the chair like a frightened cat, snatched the revolver off the shelf, and rushed to where Patsy was standing behind the door.

"You scared him!" she exclaimed. "He's ran off."

The chain remained extended on the door. She was peering through the crack.

I nudged her aside and freed the slide with my empty hand. I opened the door and rushed onto the porch, Patsy behind me. The man was racing up the sidewalk to the end of the curb where a car was parked. We dashed off the porch and into the street where we saw him glance over his shoulder at us before the car door opened. When it did, the courtesy lights came on to reveal tinted windows all around. The car roared to life a second later, made a screeching U-turn on the pavement, and beat its way out of the neighborhood.

"So much for your reasoning," I heard Patsy say.

"He must have decided he couldn't wait any longer."

We stood in the middle of the street for a time and listened till the sound of the motor diminished and mixed in with the others sounds of a Valley Camp night. Once it was gone, we looked around and discovered that the event had not gone unnoticed. Several houses on the block had come further alive with more lights, and in a few the front door was open and the occupants were in its frame staring out. Even young Jake Kotecki was peering through a window. I was still holding the gun and several eyes appeared to be lasered on it.

"Who is he?" Pats asked. "He's nobody I've seen before."

"Come along. I'll show you." I took her hand in mine and led her off the street and back to the house and into her office. I set the gun on the shelf and pointed at the monitor.

She was stunned by the image it displayed. She bent to the screen for a closer study. "Do you recognize him? Is it Schacter's bodyguard, the man you refer to as the Muscle?"

"No, that man isn't the Muscle," I said.

"What about Dalton Ellis from the Pixel-to-Paper board? Is it him?"

"Ellis? Why would you think of him?"

"He's had trouble with Schacter and from what you said about his behavior at the conference, he's upset with his fellow writers. Recall what Detective Dempsey said at the Statler? Hatred toward both sides was prevalent in more than a few of Quotidian's authors."

"Well, that isn't Ellis in that reflection," I said, comprehending the motivation for her question.

"Yet you're staring at the image of this man as though you do know who it is."

"You've been so busy with your book, I forgot to tell you.

"Tell me what, Wyatt."

"I met an editor one night at the Welcomian."

"What's that have to do with anything?"

"This looks like the same man," I said, snapping a finger at the screen.

Patsy stretched her brow and took another look at the image on the monitor. "Tell me about this meeting," she said. "Was he a book editor for a publishing house?"

"No. He said he worked for a newspaper chain that owns numerous weeklies across the country. He mentioned that he was in town visiting a friend. I plugged *Dreaming* to him and I plugged it pretty shamelessly so that maybe he'll plug it himself in the weeklies. Wouldn't that be a bit of a boon?"

My woman tossed me a look that said I had a screw in need of serious tightening. Of course I realized at once that she was correct. I put a full turn on it.

"That's better," she said. "Is he a book reviewer for the chain?"

"No, no. Nothing like that. He's an editor, but it's the Op-Ed page that he's responsible for."

Her brow stretched further and shrank.

"Op-Ed. Opinion-Editorial? C'mon on, Pats. That can't be new to you."

"Is that what he said?"

"Yeah, but only because he thought I was ignorant of its meaning."

The brow remained shrunken. The furrows deepened.

"What's the matter?"

"Wyatt, it wouldn't surprise me if everyone on Grant Avenue doesn't know what it means. But it does surprise me to learn that you don't know what it means."

"What are you getting at?"

"It's a common mistake. Op-Ed refers to the page opposite the editorial page. And anyone working a desk job at a newspaper would know that. And any person claiming to edit the contents of that page would absolutely know it. Had you ever seen this man before?"

"It isn't short for Opinion-Editorial?"

"No."

"Well don't I feel stupid."

"Had you ever seen this man before?"

I shook my head

"Did you ask him where he was from?"

The truth was, I had. After he returned from his "pit stop," I'd hit him with a small battery of personal questions, but he parried them one after another with more questions directed about *As I Lay Dreaming*. How could I object to that? An editor interested in my novel! Forget the common courtesy to shove one's ego aside and show a mutual interest. I related this to Patsy in so many words. This, she understood, was not another loose screw. Any author would have done the same.

"How old would you make him out to be? And what did he look like?"

"I'd place him in his early to mid-forties. He had a crooked nose and not the kind that would prompt you to ask how he got it."

"I thought something was wrong with that nose when I saw him jump from the porch. Did he give a name? It wouldn't matter. It was most likely a fake. Did he ask if you were married?"

"He didn't have to. He noticed that I wasn't wearing a ring."

"So he must have asked if you had a girlfriend. Did he?"

"Did he what?"

"Did he ask about a girlfriend?"

"I mentioned you, although not by name."

"But you told him I was a writer?"

"I didn't have to. He'd figured that out."

"How did he figure that out?"

"He said he hoped you like to read because I was probably asking for your feedback and reaction to the stories I was working on. I responded by saying that you were an extensive reader of all subjects, to which he then said that you must be a writer too."

Patsy shook her head in a worrisome way.

"For what it's worth, Pats, he'd never heard of Quotidian."

"And I'm a virgin. Anything else about him?"

"He was forceful with everything he said and with every action no matter how small. When he lifted his glass of beer, he didn't sip from it; he gulped it. Yet when he rose off his stool to leave and I offered my hand, he just stared at it. Like why would he ever want to shake my hand. And yet he did take hold of it, but the grip was soft, void of energy, and not at all in line with any of his earlier movements."

"That's because he was done with you," Patsy said sharply. "He'd gotten what he wanted."

"And what is it that he wanted? I'm missing something here."

"He must have seen you and me together."

"So?"

"He already knows he needs to get rid of me, Wyatt, because I might recognize his car. He was trying to decide if he needs to kill you as well."

"And why would he want to kill me?"

"Because, my love, he's unsure if you're just a casual friend in whom I would not confide, or someone much closer in whom I would tell all my secrets. From what you just told me about your time with him at the Welcomian, he now knows the answer. He didn't show up at my door tonight just for me. He was intending to take you out as well."

Chapter 31

I didn't mistrust Patsy when she'd stated that my life was in danger, but I was undergoing a difficult time getting past the humiliation. There I'd been tossing down cold beers at a bar while shamelessly pitching my book to a man whose sole interest in me was whether or not he would reward me with a bullet. Worse, I was feeling like a featherbrained amateur.

Furthermore, although I wasn't doubting Patsy in any way this time around, it wasn't clear to me how she had arrived at her conclusion and I was wondering if she was entirely clear on it herself. What if I had said that night at the Welcomian that my woman doesn't ever open a newspaper or a book? Would that have been the end of it? Would he have crossed me off his hit list? The fact that his question had started with the given that my woman was a reader suggested he already was in possession of a significant fact.

I stayed the night at Patsy's and while sex wasn't far from either of our minds, we reluctantly refrained because we weren't sure our visitor wouldn't return, and it was the most horrible image presenting itself when we thought he could sneak into the bedroom while we were in a heated consumption of each other and kill us both. Consequently, we remained awake for much of the night, one of us dozing, the other thinking. At about 4 a.m. I tested the silence.

"Babes, are you awake?"

"Lying here with my head on the pillow, eyes open. What's on your mind?"

"I'm puzzled. Why were you concerned as to whether or not he knew you were a writer?"

"I'm not sure I understand your question," she said.

"You want me to switch on your reading lamp?"

"No. Just say your question again"

"At Koldren's, he was unaware you were a writer."

Silence.

"Okay. Turn on the lamp."

I reached over to her vanity and fumbled on the switch to the small reading lamp.

"Once more."

"He didn't know who you were at Koldren's."

She raised herself from the prone position and leaned against the pillow and headboard.

"I'm actually wide awake," she said. "Let's just get up and I'll make us some coffee. I've some African beans I can grind."

We slid out our sides of the bed. Pats put on her robe, and I reinserted myself into the sweats I'd been wearing. In the kitchen I pulled out a chair from the table and sat down while she prepared the coffeemaker.

"Are you thinking about what I asked?"

"Give me your opinion on something," she said. "Do you consider it a mark of a good researcher if she asks a question without knowing exactly why she asked it?"

"You're not a lawyer," I answered. "Isn't it lawyers we always hear about who are cautioned against posing a question to which the answer isn't already known?"

"Research isn't the same as lawyering. While it's an unknown that we seek to uncover, a qualified researcher should at least be able to tell you the reason she asked the question."

"What are you getting at?"

"At the door, when the detectives were leaving, do you recall why I stopped them?"

"They most likely had talked with some of the same people you interviewed. I'd figured you asked what you did because you wanted to measure your abilities with theirs. I'm sure you were hoping to get more out of Dempsey and Maines, but I knew that wasn't going to happen. I don't believe you thought it would happen either"

Patsy switched on the grinder. Once it finished several seconds later, she looked over at me with squinted eyes and all I heard was "Hmmm."

I left Patsy's house for my own once the sky began to light up. I did not think this person who was seeking to kill us would return during daylight hours, even though Spectra Suter had been shot while the sun was up. Yet even with that specific detail the location had been a dark underground parking facility. I showered at my house and hurried to work.

How odd it sometimes is when a thing enters a person's mind and he doesn't realize immediately that it has. It's like passing by a collection of items on the edge of one's property and there's something suddenly confronting the eyes that is a little different from previous days. All of a sudden you take note of the discarded snakeskin. Funny, you think to yourself, that you never noticed the snake itself, which must have been hanging out there on the rocks and working its way out of an old suit for quite some time.

In this case what floated to the top of my head while I'd been in the shower that morning was the name Grimalkin. Right along I had been thinking the secrecy surrounding this member of the Nemesis Nine was to his or her credit. That is, if the killer were intending to silence all nine of the parties, he would have a difficult time tracking down and meeting up with this one. But suddenly the name established a firmer root and I considered for a long moment if Grimalkin could actually be the killer and whatever was attached to the name on the message boards was no more than a fabrication and a ruse, a cover for who and what Grimalkin actually was. Had we all, the detectives along with Patsy and myself, overlooked this person? And was there a way to learn about whoever he or she was? Much as I pondered this on the drive to work, I did not think so. I didn't think even Patsy, a very shrewd and thorough researcher, would be able to dig up much on Grimalkin

And it was then that I understood a distinguishing feature of the message boards. Everything about a person in any posting was already cherry-picked. And it was done by the poster himself. Even with the most prolific of contributors there wasn't much to go on. On the other hand, one could read a three hundred-page memoir or an autobiography of a famous figure and afterwards pull out a phrase or a passage that would place the author in the whitest of light. Or if the reader was of another mind, the cherry-picked passage would cause embarrassment. But on the boards, even for those who had posted a thousand times, the words still did not cover a lot of their life. Typically, their statements were directed at the same issue, the same person, the same whatever. Anybody who thought a person's personality sheet and typical behaviors could be filled in strictly from the posts alone was fooling themselves.

While at work I phoned Pats to see if everything was all right.

"Just so you know, Wyatt, I decided to call the detectives. And this time I told them everything. I didn't let anything out."

"You made a wise decision," I said. I then changed the subject. "Babes, this man who came to your house last night, he knows where you live now. My address might be a mystery to him. Come over and stay at my place for the night."

"I can't," she answered.

"Why not?"

"My editor got in touch. He wants the manuscript."

"You're not finished, are you?"

"It's in the process of my own editing. But he said he would take care of that. That I was just to get it to him as quickly as possible and in whatever shape."

Patsy had informed me the finished piece would run to 100,000 words and it was the reason I didn't think she could be finished, despite her being the facile writer she is. But then I remembered that she had said a large portion of the book were the transcriptions of the recordings from her face-to-face interviews, and another portion, though smaller, were the actual posts that had appeared on the message boards.

"Aren't you curious, Wyatt, as to why the rush?"

"The murders have been solved?"

"Schacter's disappeared. No one knows where he is. Or if they do, they're not talking."

"How did your editor come to discover this?" I asked, curious.

"Detective Maines," she said.

Of course, I thought. When Patsy had gone missing, I'd spoken with the detective on my cell and she had said that she would contact the publisher. The smart editor had kept that channel open.

"There's more, Wyatt. Schacter's bodyguard, the one you call the Muscle, he's disappeared as well. When I spoke with Detective Maines this morning, although she didn't come out and say it, I sensed that she and her partner are inclined to think this pair might be good for the murders after all and the two split because they felt a tightening of the noose. Anyway, I'm planning to get everything together and the manuscript to the post office first thing in the morning."

"Is there anything I can do to help? Maybe I should come over and stay the night again," I said.

"No."

"You won't hear a word out of me, I promise. I'll bring along a book to read."

"Not tonight. Besides, our Valley Camp boys in blue have been alerted. There's been a patrol car rolling up and down the neighborhood every hour. I think I'm covered."

After we ended our call I got to wondering where could Schacter have disappeared to. Posts that appeared on AuthorsRetreat claimed he had three homes, each on a different continent, but I was never persuaded that this was true.

I got to wondering, too, about the Muscle. Wondering if he wasn't already dead. He could point the finger back to his employer, so why wouldn't Schacter have gotten rid of him?

My head, I soon realized, was shaking. Here I was back to thinking that Schacter was responsible for the murders and yet a short time ago, I had given him up.

But as the day wore on and evening came, I was giving him up again.

And the reason was hardly a reason at all. It was more a writer's intuition: I was unable to put the slovenly man, who lied about being a newspaper editor, together with Tor Schacter. For starters he was too old. All those I had seen employed by Schacter while visiting the Quotidian offices were young men and women. This included the Muscle who I'd placed in his early 30s. Mona Fowler was the exception, but the young woman who had helped me find Patsy had explained her presence. This man I had met in the bar, whoever he would turn out to be, he was not the type of man with whom Schacter would affiliate. He simply and clearly did not fit the goddamn bill. So who was he? I had no answer. I didn't have even the smallest amount of information to entertain a conjecture.

Much later in the day after darkness had fallen, I shut off each of the lights inside the house, then walked through the rear door into the yard out back. Spring was continuing to develop and the air carried with it a chill. In the summer I would often park myself in a chair and stare at the woodlot —soothing moments for a writer trying to collect his thoughts. Peepers were often in abundance in the spring and early summer, and so long as the weather was warm a squirrel or two were always leaping from one tree to another. A real surprise was a nearby repetitive whippoorwill. But on this night I forgot the chair and stood in place with my ears more attuned to the surroundings than my eyes. There was nothing of significance behind the woodlot except an unmaintained dirt road that led into several acres of undeveloped land and if, in fact, he had learned my address and were coming after me, this, I thought, would be his approach: park off the road on the far end of the woodlot and make his way inside its perimeter and onto my property.

I remained outdoors for most of an hour, standing all the while, and listening. Two cars had gone up the road on the far side of the woodlot and I could see the extended glow of their headlights, and then the second one extinguished its own. I tensed and listened carefully and was relieved when the sound renewed and the engine was lost in the distance.

Afterwards, I returned to the house as the chill began to penetrate my clothing. I thought of Patsy and the revolver and wondered if maybe I should get a gun. But buying a gun and knowing how to use it for personal protection were miles apart. The advice to myself was immediate: Don't fool yourself.

I entered the kitchen with that thought and was about to switch on the light over the sink, except a familiar sound of danger broke the still air. It belonged to that category of sounds that you need hear only once and when you hear it again it is instantly recognizable: such as a cat sneezing, or the sharp click of a circuit breaker, or the metallic snap of a canning lid on a Mason jar. In this case it was the slow pullback of the steel hammer on a hefty revolver. I didn't move except to swing myself around in its direction. It had not come from the room I was in but I sensed that footsteps were heading toward me, none of which were audible. I would likely and foolishly have said "Who's there?" if I hadn't remembered that all of his victims had been shot at extremely close range, which signaled to me the killer was a man of practiced stealth and comfort. A man who would tap you on the shoulder and when you turned about, he would fire the bullet dead-center into your forehead. I told myself that I could not be surprised when I saw him. If I were, if surprised for only a fraction of a second, Wyatt Falkner would end up dead like the others.

And then a fortunate sliver of light from a car turning at the near corner of the street out front briefly and faintly illuminated the barrel, and the *riken* responded, even though it was forced to reach higher than normal because the black hole was already pointed at my forehead. My left hand plunged down like the blade of a guillotine and the gun fired and a slug smashed into the floor. Shattered pieces of porcelain tile were sent flying into the air and at my ankles. The right fist then followed as if released from a tautened spring with every pound of my body behind it and struck my attacker in the face. He staggered greatly, collided with a wall, swept the processor and the toaster to the floor, went thrusting into the refrigerator, even sliding it several inches away from the wall. Still, the move failed to put him down, and he immediately made for the rear door to escape, his every step fighting to recapture his balance.

I sped after him, only not to stop him. The karate move had failed to relieve him of the gun, although his left hand, I could see, had a wrenching grip on the wrist of his shooting arm. All I wanted was another look, and as he skirted the woodlot's perimeter, the second house south of mine switched on its backyard light and by it rays, however weak, I could see it was unmistakably the same man with whom I'd shared a beer at the Welcomian and who had run from Patsy's house the night before.

I turned about and darted back inside and picked up my cell. It sounded in my hands before I punched a button.

"Wyatt?"

"Babes, I was just about to call. Are you all right?"

"I'm fine."

"Are you sure?"

"I'm fine. I finished," she said gleefully. "The manuscript will be in the express mail tomorrow morning. Wyatt, is something wrong? You sound out of breath."

"He was here," I blurted out. "Just minutes ago. I was one second away from becoming his next victim. If I'm sounding frazzled, that's the reason."

"Oh, Wyatt."

"Babes, we've got to get our heads together on this. We have to discover the identity of this person. This has gone beyond his worry that you might remember something about his car. There's something dreadfully wrong with this man."

"Wyatt, it's the reason I called. Are you going to be okay?"

"I'm settling. Give me a few seconds." I took several slow, deep breaths while Patsy waited silently. "What do you have?" I finally asked.

"Do you still have the paper? The Capers weekly?"

"It's amid a pile of things on the filing cabinet in my office."

"Get it and look at the photo of the car being pulled from the creek below. We missed something."

"Please, Babes. I don't need any mysteries right now. Just tell me what this is about."

"The bumper sticker I made for *As I Lay Dreaming*? It's missing."

"Someone removed it?"

"That bastard got out of his own car after running me off the road and scrambled down that embankment to see if I were dead. He apparently thought I was. Before he climbed his way back to the highway, he took a moment to scratch away the sticker. Who would do that, Wyatt?"

"How do you know it was him? Anyone could have ripped off that sticker. Including the bicyclist who discovered you."

"No."

"But how do you know?"

"I stopped for gas for that rental less than five miles from Koldren's."

"And?"

"An old man on the other side of the pump, he read the sticker. He asked, 'Yours?'"

I thought about what she was telling me. And I didn't seriously think the youth who found her had removed it.

"Wyatt, I can come over."

"No, stay where you are and get yourself to bed. You must be beat. Anyway, he won't be coming back any time soon. I'm sure I injured his wrist. With any luck I broke it. And Babes? Congratulations on completing your book. I'm really proud of you."

After punching off, I found the broom and returned to the kitchen to sweep up the shards of broken tile. When I finished, I took a knife and dug the slug from the underlayment. I had no idea what its caliber was. I set it aside and finally called the police.

Chapter 32

The next morning, with my first step away from the bed, I realized that every piece of the shattered floor tile had not been swept into the dustpan. A sliver had become embedded in the flesh below my right ankle and overnight the surrounding tissue had swollen. I was in trouble the moment my weight set upon it. I called the market and left a message for the boss who always opened, informing him of my problem, and said he shouldn't expect me. Afterwards, I located a needle and tweezers from the medicine cabinet, found a bottle of alcohol and, like a jeweler, set to work to extract the sliver.

Outside, the wind was picking up, even at this early hour. The long wisps of the willows in the lawns across the street were beginning to dance and the huge white oak of my neighbor was giving sway up top. A few tornadoes, including a terribly destructive EF4, had struck in states to the west and severe weather was the call of the day for our region as warmer air was continuing to push northward from the Gulf to meet the chill.

Around ten o'clock, Patsy's car drew up at the front of the house. She carried her larger tote bag, a red one she'd received at the writers' conference. From the car to the house the wind morphed her hair into a gorgeous mess.

"What happened to you?" she asked as I hobbled to the door to greet her.

I got her inside and again told her the story of last evening. Only this time I mentioned every detail, including the scrap of tile that had spiked my flesh.

"It didn't begin to hurt until this morning," I said. I raised my foot and picked at the spot to reassure myself I had withdrawn the entire sliver.

"Try to stay off it as best you can," she said. "And when you're sitting down, remember to raise it up." She set the tote on an end table.

"I dialed 9-1-1, Babes," I said. "When it was over."

"Were you thinking you shouldn't?"

"No, not really. It's just that after it happened, I felt drained. All that adrenaline left me as quickly as it came. The last thing I wanted at midnight was to answer a battery of questions from the police."

"Well, it's best that you did call them."

She reached into the tote and withdrew two twelve-ounce bottles of a dark amber brew. "I brought these along to kind of celebrate the completion of my book and its sendoff. But you're not looking all that great this morning, so forget it. We can do it some other time. Or not at all."

"Thanks."

"Wyatt, I've been thinking about what you said on the phone last night and you're absolutely right. We've got to put our heads together and identify this man who's looking to kill us. This can't go on. If it does, neither one of us may be around to hear the news on our books. Which reminds me—"

"Nothing to date," I informed her.

"I wouldn't worry," she said. "It could be the first editor

loved your story and wants the opinions of others to see if they match his own."

She took the longnecks of beer and went into the kitchen and set them in the fridge.

"So where do you suggest we start to discover who this person is, looking to kill Pats Lukehart and Wyatt Falkner?"

"With that bumper sticker I created," she replied, returning.

"Why there?"

"Because it mentioned the book title and your name. It made no mention of Quotidian. And that tells me whoever removed it is from the boards. He might not have even recognized the title. But your name, that's a different story."

"So then you want to know who isn't a fan of Wyatt Falkner?"

"Every one of them."

"Babes, there are many people on the board who have no love for me. I couldn't tell you the names of but a few."

"We'll work with what we got. Maybe we'll get lucky. Now Oliver Metheny doesn't have any use for you. You conveyed that information to me in a prior conversation. Who are some of others you can point to?"

Growler came immediately to mind and so too did Disheveled. "Ned Cottrell is another," I said. "I don't think Thalia Dunne holds any pleasant thoughts of me either, although I guess we've ruled out women."

"She could be a man passing for a woman. That's not unheard of on the Internet. Anyone else? Growler, Disheveled, Cottrell, and Dunne? That's the best you can do?"

"It's an online message board, not the Sons of Columbus."

"Okay, if that's all we have, then that's all we have. Let's get started. Fire up the Songbird, Penny."

"What?"

She waved off the question with a speedy answer. "It's an old TV show that's been resurrected. My aunt used to watch it, and when I was a little girl and wanted to help her do something, that's what she would say to me."

"What's a Songbird?"

"An airplane."

"Your nickname was Penny?"

"Of course not. Didn't your folks ever watch TV?"

"How old was your aunt?"

I turned away in the direction of my office to boot up the Mac with Patsy right behind. I pulled a chair up for her and sat down in my own. There was no strategy to follow as we hit the message boards of PtP and AuthorRetreat. We simply scrolled and searched for posts by the names I'd cited as well as other posts that mentioned me either by name or innuendo. It was slow-going and I wasn't expecting to find anything incriminating. But Patsy was the researcher and so I wasn't thinking that our abilities in this matter were a match. If there was something in any of the posts, however negligible, that could point a finger, however remotely, at a possible killer, while I might not see it, Patsy probably would.

We kept at it for more than an hour when her cell sounded inside the tote. She removed it and accepted the call, smiling as she did, which meant the screen was identifying the caller.

"Hello, Douglas."

She mouthed "Atherton" to me.

"It's done and is on its way to my publisher," I heard her say. "Yes, I pulled a few lines from the interview and so those who read it will learn that you actually possess a pleasant side."

Whatever Atherton said in response to this, it made Patsy raise her head and laugh. And then she lost the mirthful expression and listened for several seconds.

"There's no need for that," she said. "He's with me now. Let me put you on speaker and you can tell him yourself."

I grew instantly suspicious of what this could be about and grimaced at Patsy, but she didn't return a response as she placed the phone on my desk.

"Mr. Falkner, this is Rexford Atherton. I was just telling Ms. Lukehart that I read your novel *As I Lay Dreaming* and found it to be an extremely satisfying read and a well-done piece of writing."

"Thank you," I said, surprised. A compliment from the man was the last thing I was expecting.

"Unfortunately, as you've no doubt already discovered, because your book was published by Quotidian Release, all efforts at promotion is on the author, and history proves, because of that, the book is likely to die a quick death."

This I did not want to hear.

"So I can't help you there. However, do you have another book?"

"I'm waiting to hear on my second and working on a third," I said with some volume.

"Not with Quotidian, I hope."

"No, I'm finished with them."

"That's wise. So here's my offer, Mr. Falkner. If you send your work to my publisher, I'll endorse it. It's not a guarantee, of course, but I've made sufficient money for them over several years that they won't automatically dismiss my word."

I saw Patsy light up with approval.

"So when you're ready, let me know. Ms. Lukehart has

my phone number and address."

"Thank you again," I said. "That's very generous."

Patsy picked up the phone from the desk and was about to turn off the speaker except I shot out a hand to stop her. She had forgotten; I hadn't.

"Mr. Atherton."

"You might as well call me Doug," he said.

"Patsy had me listen to the tapes of her interviews. In yours you said the words 'riding shotgun.'" Patsy tossed back her head in remembrance. "What did you mean by that? Was the phrase in reference to your traveling parrot?"

We heard him laugh to himself. "Yes, I suspect I was talking about Moses. He sits perfectly erect in his seat when we're on the road and gives off the impression that he's taking in everything there is to take in on the outside, when the truth is he's too much of a pipsqueak to see out of the window." He laughed again. He so obviously loves his parrot, I thought. But then, after a couple of silent seconds, he said rather straightforwardly, "Of course I might also have been referring to a new website that was soon to come online."

"What sort of website?" Patsy asked.

"A watchdog. For writers."

And on his words the connection began for Patsy and me both. She wagged a finger in my direction.

"Can you tell us anything about that website?" she asked.

"I only know what I heard from Spectra Suter."

"You knew her?" I said.

"I wouldn't make that claim," he said. "I met her only once. About a year ago when we both participated at a Chicago book fair. We talked for much of an hour. She said she and some others were developing a website where authors could air their complaints against unscrupulous agents and publishers. She was quite aware that with the ditching of typewriters, whiteout, and carbon paper and with the spread of computers and the software for word-processing, countless men and women would be trying their hand at crafting a story. But more importantly, I remember her stressing, was that publishing scams, like Quotidian Release, were certain to proliferate. I asked her if there wasn't already a site to warn others."

"Rottwriter," I said.

"Yes, that was the name she mentioned," he said. "However, she didn't have too high an opinion of it or of its webmaster. I'd never accessed it because I had no reason to, but she described the pages as juvenile and remarkably unappealing."

"Did she provide any details on how this website of hers and the others would differ?" Patsy asked.

"Oh yes," he said and his tone was that Spectra Suter had surrendered more than a little. "She told me that they had already hired Tony Clausen. Do you know who that is?"

"No," I said.

"He's a top web designer," said Pats.

"How do you know that?" I mouthed my astonishment.

"He's considered one of the best," said Atherton. "In fact, she said his name on their project had already attracted dozens of advertisers. So while the site was to be informative to writers, they were also intending to make it profitable for themselves."

"Did she name any of the others involved with the project?" Patsy asked.

"No, I don't recall that she mentioned her partners."

When the call was finished and the connection broken, Patsy looked at me and smiled. "How did we miss it?" she said. "They're all puns. Writers Up, Rottwriter, even Pixel-to-Paper. It's Writing Shotgun....Why am I the only one laughing? What's wrong, Wyatt?"

I related to her what I'd found when I was sifting through the old posts on AuthorsRetreat, the putdowns of Metheny and his website.

"Really!" she said with great interest. "Show me."

We went back to the Mac. I pulled up AuthorsRetreat and paged to the older posts. I found those I'd discovered that criticized Metheny and his Rottwriter website. Patsy read the posts, then took over the keyboard. She went searching for more criticism. At least, that was my thought. What she was really looking for, however, was a rebuttal post by Metheny. She found two.

"He's definitely honed his invective in recent years," she remarked after reading them.

"They're still nasty," I said, reading them for myself.

Pats minimized the page and turned to me. My woman's gears were shifting to high.

"He knew me," she finally said. Her eyes, though pointed in my direction, were moving all about as if they were doing a fast search of her brain.

"What?"

"I now know the reason behind my question to the detectives as they were leaving the house." She paused because her thinking was racing ahead of her expression.

"Would you care to share?"

"Metheny's email to his listserv," she said. "The one in your box. Remember? He wanted any information from the workshops in Philadelphia sent to him. He was offering himself as a liaison to the police."

"Yeah. So?"

"Dempsey said there wasn't any Deep Throat."

"He said at Quotidian there wasn't."

"That's immaterial. What isn't is the fact that no one was providing the detective with a flow of information."

"I'm sorry, Babes, but I'm not seeing the dots you're connecting."

"Metheny offered himself as a repository and said he would pass on all information to the police."

"Well, isn't it obvious he didn't collect any? No one passed him anything."

"You're not seeing it, Wyatt. It's Metheny who was at Koldren's and he recognized me. He recognized me because he'd seen me before. Despite the erroneous spelling, it was his name that was on my editor's list at the conference. He was there to push a book for himself and it was going to be about Quotidian and Schacter. He certainly was passed information. I can't say what it amounted to or what value was attached, but he obviously thought he could make a book from it."

I took the keyboard away from her. "There's an online photo collection from the conference," I said with new enthusiasm. I tickled several keys and up they came. "There."

Patsy drew her chair nearer to the screen, tickled a few keys of her own to increase the brightness, and scrutinized each of the photos.

"Just to get this straight, Babes, are you now thinking that Oliver Metheny is responsible for all five murders and that he's the same person who is after us?"

"Isn't he all of a sudden looking like our man to you?"

"Well, yeah, if we could confirm it."

We studied the conference photos, searching for a facial figure with a distinctive crooked nose. Although I appeared in none of them, we found two in which Patsy was included, and the second of these showed her talking with several other attendees near the table where she had pitched her idea to an editor. In the shadows outside the flash area of light stood several more figures and one whom we thought could be Metheny and the same person who was after us.

"I wish we had a closer look of his face," she said.

I zoomed in, but the picture became too pixilated.

"I have an idea," I said.

I closed the window and hit the bookmark for Amazon.

"What do you have in mind?" she asked.

"I'm downloading his book. Maybe it will tell us something."

The main page came up, I found the title, did a couple clicks, okayed the credit card information from my last purchase, and in seconds Metheny's tale appeared in the app on the Mac.

We began a read of it at once.

As with his many words on the boards, the writing sometimes bordered on childish, metaphors implied weird comparisons, and the diction and grammar were not what you would expect to find in a polished novel, even if it turned out to be a story that was not to your liking. What was crystal clear was this: Metheny was no writer of fiction. He was fooling himself.

The main character was a Tarzan-like individual as anticipated. And likewise expected, all the action unfolded on a small planet in distant space light years away, except it was not inhabited by lions and tigers and crocodiles and cape buffalo and elephants and apes. It was inhabited by numerous prehistoric creatures of magnificent dimensions and two tribes of men who hated each other. The first convincing evidence that Metheny was our man came on page ten when he described that one of the tribes dispatched their enemies by sneaking up on them and striking them in the middle of their foreheads with an *"iron malleta."*

When Patsy and I read this we turned and stared at one another and our mouths dropped open. Suddenly, we were sure Oliver Metheny was our man. Further proof appeared when Patsy paged to the story's end. There along with his bio was a black-and-white photo. He was much younger in it, but it was him, the same person who wanted to kill us. Yet I couldn't pass it off so quickly because there was something else about the picture. I'd seen it before.

"What is it?" Patsy asked, noting my expression.

"It's Growler," I said.

"Who?"

"Growler. The guy on the boards who criticizes every Quotidian book that shows a chance of success."

"Oliver Metheny and this Growler are the same person?"

"Looks like it."

"Do you know what that's about?"

"Haven't a clue."

Patsy puzzled this revelation herself for several seconds. "I'll have to think on that," she said. "But for now it appears the murdered members of the Nemesis Nine got wind of his story, read it, and realized how awful it was and said the same among themselves. Then Metheny somehow learned of their real regard for him, both his writing and his website, and decided he would teach them all a lesson."

"I can see it happening," I said. "Not sure exactly how, but I can see it. God knows I've responded to a particular individual in an email and mistakenly hit reply-to-all, which was embarrassing and required an apology and some cleanup. A mistake like that could have triggered this entire thing."

"So what do you think we should do now?"

"Now I think you should get hold of the detectives again and let them in on what we've discovered."

"Why not you?" she asked.

"They respect you, Babes. They'll act on what you tell them."

I could see that Patsy regarded my statement as an odd admission.

"Why do you say that, Wyatt? I've never heard anything coming out of the mouths of either Dempsey or Maines that would suggest a disrespect for you."

"They might not show me disrespect, but take it from me that a word from you will mean more to them."

Patsy again dug into the tote for her cell phone. Her quizzical expression told me she was continuing to turn over what I'd said, that it was a thing that had not occurred to her. Frankly, I wasn't sure why it had occurred to me.

Chapter 33

It was Dempsey who took the call. Patsy identified herself and informed the detective that I was in the room with her.

"I'm placing the phone on speaker," she further informed him. Although not entirely convinced of what I'd expressed to her, if there was any truth in it, she was letting him know that she and I were in this together.

In the minutes to follow I listened as she told Dempsey everything in the orderly fashion Patsy could be counted on to always do. This included the previous night's murder attempt on me. When it came to describing how I had defended myself, she omitted mention of my fast *riken*. It was a phrase which, when I'd first introduced it to her, had prompted an amusing smile. My guess was that she thought Dempsey would explode in laughter if she relayed it to him. Instead, she related that I'd simply struck Metheny on his wrist and face. Which produced a smile of my own. (She at least could have used uppercut or roundhouse, I thought, however inaccurate either would have been.) Somewhat strangely, the detective listened to her account with few interruptions or even a question about my near occurrence with death. Perhaps Metheny was on his radar all along, I thought.

"They'll find him," Patsy remarked after the call had ended and she'd set the phone aside.

We were in the afternoon now and the weather was beginning to look like it would honor the predictions of our TV meteorologists, as the rain had started to sound on the metal roof. Settling back on the sofa with my laptop, I continued to read Metheny's novel. It was a drudgery and were the author anyone else, I would have closed the file for good and dumped it from my hard drive. But as it was Metheny's creation, my curiosity remained alive. And on page forty the story elicited a special curiosity because it's where the reader learns that the victims of the *iron malleta* have access to audio and visual technologies that could save them from the menacing tribe, except they have no knowledge, much less an inquiring mind, concerning how to use either. It was a strange anachronism, if it can be loosely labeled that, because no explanation was provided on where the technology came from, who the inventors were, and even what it looked like in its three-dimensions.

It was not a small book at more than four hundred pages and it was no better at the end than at the beginning. Metheny, I thought, must at some point have received criticism of his efforts, as all writers receive whether they want it or not. And yet he must have rejected every observation, every recommendation whether from a friend or an editor. That alone was telling me he was not a man given to compromise or collaboration. Rather, he was a man who more than believed he was right—he knew he was right. And such men are often dangerous.

Nearing the end of the book, I noticed that Patsy, who had brought out a book of her own from the tote, was barely through a third of it. This was unlike her because when it came to the perusal of just about anything, including tortuous research studies, legal agreements, and government documents, she was hardly a plodder.

"What are you thinking about?" I asked, interrupting myself.

She closed the book's cover and crunched her lips. "Oliver Metheny might not be much of a writer," she said, "but he certainly exhibits an active imagination."

"Why do you say that?"

"Remove us from this entire matter, Wyatt, and consider what remains. First off, he murdered four people. That started everything—men and women who were disingenuous in their friendships and who, with regard to the writingshotgun website, were about to destroy his own website and his part of protecting writers against the dishonest agents and publishers. All along Rottwriter has been his claim to fame, and killing them was his revenge. However, that still left Quotidian with whom he wanted to strike some kind of a blow, and doing away with four of Schacter's most effective critics meant that he was now alone on dealing with him. Forget the remaining others of the Nemesis Nine. They're noisy creatures, nothing more. Their remarks lacked the force you often read in the broadsides of Underwood and the others. And so when Metheny asked those who had attended the workshops in Philly to pass along whatever information and pictures they had of Schacter's enforcers, his intention, as I earlier said, wasn't to inform the police. His plan was to write a book about the murders, except that its main intention was to smear Schacter. He would have done whatever he could to make it appear that Schacter was a bastard and was getting away with murder."

"And Koldren was his way of bringing an end to the

entire matter?"

"Except here, too, he would have implied that Schacter was the cause of the man's suicide."

"Babes, do you think he felt any relief when he realized he wouldn't have to kill Koldren because the man had already hanged himself?"

"Now, bring the two of us into things and it's where his lunacy explodes. That conference photo you dug up? It's got to be him. He must have heard every word of my pitch to the editor and every word that came back."

"Then he must have realized he didn't stand a chance. Because not only is he a terrible writer, asking others to send him information tells me that he hadn't much of an idea as to how to go about it. Would you agree he wasn't a researcher?"

"He was clueless."

"Yet it sounds to me—correct me if I'm wrong—as though you're feeling just a little bit sorry for Oliver Metheny. Just a bit. Are you?"

"Please! He murdered four people in cold blood. How could I ever feel sorry for him? However, that doesn't deny the fact that he dreamt of becoming a writer."

"Maybe so, only he couldn't have been much of a reader," I said with a condemning headshake. "Read widely and you know as well as I do that you learn to write. Maybe you won't be the author of a bestseller. Chances are you'll still have to keep your day job. But you will learn to put down words better than what I was treated to in that worthless tripe of his."

Until that very moment the rain had been unaccompanied by frightening punctuation, but then a bit of hell broke loose as a bolt of lightning with its explosive thunder only a nanosecond behind rattled the entire house like an earthquake too close for comfort.

"Whoa," I said in shaky but reverential awe. I closed my laptop immediately and got to my feet. I tried the foot that had harbored the sliver. It seemed to be loosening up nicely.

Patsy, grinning because of the vibration, set her book aside and rose from the chair. She stepped over to a window and stared out at the menacing sky. "Once this quiets down, let's go out for a pizza."

"This weather making you hungry, Babes?"

I left her gazing through the window and went into the office. I set the laptop on the desk and unplugged the router and a few other cords because I didn't trust the power strip's protection against further lightning strikes. After that, I moved into the kitchen where sat a pan that was in need of a scouring pad. It had been there since the morning before and this seemed an opportune time to work on making it shine. Glancing over my shoulder, I saw Patsy still standing at the window and she was laughing.

"What's happening?" I inquired from the kitchen sink.

"Marsha Kotecki is forcing little Jake out into the rain to retrieve his baseball glove. I think she's trying to teach him a lesson, except it looks like he's enjoying getting soaked."

I looked out the window above the sink while I scrubbed. "It doesn't seem to be letting up, does it?"

"The lightning strikes are fewer," she said. A second later, a bolt illuminated the sky as if to prove her fallibility.

I carefully inspected the job I'd done on the pot, scraped off a stubborn splotch with a fingernail, and set it in the drainer. I dried my hands with a dishcloth and returned to the front room. I picked up my wallet from the bookshelf.

"How's the foot?"

"It'll do. Just no marathons for a while. Ready?"

"Ready as ever."

"Your car or mine?"

"Mine's at the curb," she said. "We'll take yours."

Valley Camp never hosted hurricane parties like those that are heard about in the Gulf states of Louisiana and Florida, but when the weather took a turn for the worse and it was certain the squalls, the winds, and the lightning with its thunder would persist throughout the day, townspeople weren't inclined to stay in their homes. No sir, not when Valley Camp had its prolific share of bars and clubs like so many small towns throughout the state.

"Welcomian?"

Patsy pointed a stiff finger to the road out front and I drove us there in a cautious hurry.

The parking lot for the popular bar was all to the backside of the building and it stretched to the property line of a house and its separation run of thick juniper bushes. When we arrived, cars and pickups had already filled the space. I managed to squeeze the Subaru into a corner and near the end of the bushes. It was raining hard and wasn't letting up.

"On three?" I said.

We pulled on our latches, jumped out, and Patsy made a dash for the entrance. I limped my own kind of dash. There wasn't even the smallest marquee above it and the rain was pelting us. I pulled on the door and instantly got pulled back.

"What the hell!"

I yanked on it again, it opened a couple inches and again slammed back against the jamb. Rainwater was clouding my eyes and Patsy was shielding her own with a hand. On my third attempt I quickly inserted my other hand on the inside when I was given the few inches and pulled and pushed it open. Two fellows on the inside with beers were having a laugh on us.

"Nice," I said to them as I entered behind Patsy. I exaggerated my hobble for their benefit.

One wobbled his head at us, which I interpreted as a kind of apology, and the other smiled.

"Apparently, he's unaware of your fast *riken*," Patsy muttered behind a mischievous grin.

"Shut up and look for a place where we can sit," I said.

Patsy threw a slow-motion *riken* of her own at my nose.

The joint was crowded and there weren't any places to sit. However, one of three chairless islands had only a can of beer on its top and the owner of that beer, while he kept a hand cupped around it, was talking with others at the bar. I pointed Patsy to the chest-high table, but she started in the opposite direction.

"We're getting waved over," she said.

"Who?" I said. "... Oh man, no."

"Wyatt!"

"By any chance are they—?"

"—I'm sure they're not."

"That only means that boneheads attract boneheads."

"Didn't you tell me you owed them?"

They were both waving now and when we made it to their booth, each rose and invited us to sit on the inside.

I waved off the invitation. "I like to stretch my legs." I said. "I'll sit out on the end."

"Get in there," ordered the bigger one, jovially. "We're leaving, so you'll just have to get up again to let us out."

"No, you can't leave just yet," pleaded Patsy. "Stay. At least have a beer with us."

"Can't do it," the shrunken head said. "We're already late for another engagement. But I'm so glad we ran into each other because I have a surprise specially for you."

"A surprise? What kind of surprise?"

"Turn around. Turn your head around. Go on."

"Why?"

"I don't want you peeking. You turn around, too," he said to me, "until I say it's okay."

I swung my head lazily around while inside it I was thinking that I wouldn't really know how to thank them, that you couldn't possibly find the words, Wyatt ol' boy.

"Can I turn around now?" Pats asked. "We're hungry and my throat is dry."

"Just a second.... All right, now you can both turn around and open your eyes."

"You didn't say I had to close my eyes," I said.

Patsy and I turned back in our seats and saw that the shrunken head was holding up a fountain pen.

"Here, this is for you, Patsy," he said. "Or Pats, I should say."

I looked at my woman and saw the "What's this about" expression forming with reluctance.

"There's an inscription on it," he said, jubilant. "Read it."

Patsy twirled the barrel of the blue and gold pen in her hand. "To Pats Lukehart, greatest writer of them all."

"That's very nice, except it isn't true," she said under a sheepish smile.

"It is in his book!" stressed the bigger bonehead. He turned to me to explain. "I don't know if you were dating Patsy when Earl started his bagel business, but she wrote an article about it for the local paper, and wow, did things take off after that."

"Your bagels are a delicious item that people around here crave," Patsy said. "That's why the business took off."

"Do you like the pen?"

"It's a very nice pen."

"I know you're not likely to use it. Who uses refillable fountain pens in this day and age, except for professional calligraphers! But I didn't think a ball-point or a felt pen had as much class."

"Thank you," said Patsy, trading the sheepish grin for one of genuine gratitude. "When I sign my first book, I'll use it with a flourish." She threw her right hand into the air above our booth and scrawled wildly. "Now won't you stay and have a drink with us? Maybe even a slice of pizza?"

"We really have to go."

"And we have to go NOW! Come on, Earl." The big guy tugged at the arm of the little one.

"Thank you again," said Patsy with a wink.

"You're more than welcome. It was really my pleasure to do something nice for you."

A minute following their departure Charlotte came by.

"Pizza!" I roared. "Half-pepperoni! Half-sausage!"

"Drafts?"

"Two," I said, but Patsy amended the order and told Charlotte to deliver us a pitcher.

"Be a few minutes," said Charlotte. She took two steps and turned back. "I almost forgot. Your friend was around here the other day, Wyatt."

"What friend is that?"

"I guess he isn't really a friend. The editor."

"He was in here?"

"To be truthful, I'm not sure. I was arriving for my shift and saw him in the parking lot. The lot was full. I think he probably lost sight of where he'd parked his car."

After Charlotte left us, I ventured an opinion. "You think Metheny might have been drunk?"

"It's not a stadium parking lot," Patsy remarked sourly.

"He wasn't drunk. And he wasn't searching for his car. He was hoping to find one of ours."

Although the days were becoming longer with spring ending and the summer solstice approaching, when we stepped out of the Welcomian an hour later, there was no proof of that. The rain had slowed and there were no further displays of lightning and thunder, yet the grayness of the skies was dark, thick, and dismal. Because of what Charlotte had said, I took Patsy's hand and picked our way through the parking lot to the car with utmost caution. As far as Metheny was concerned, he likely was unaware that we had identified him. And as far as we were concerned, it was of some comfort to know that Dempsey and Maines now had him in their minds and that they most probably had determined the kind of car he was driving, along with its plate number. What's more, they would have passed this same information on to the Valley Camp police.

"What's he call it?" I said as we pulled away from the parking lot. "Bonehead Bagels?"

"Are you telling me you've never been to Earl's West Side Bagels?"

"I've never eaten a bagel, period."

Patsy couldn't believe it. "This is my fault," she pretended to clamor. "I'll have to divorce you so that you can get out in the world more often. You can't claim to be a writer if you've never had a bagel."

"That's all it takes?"

She laughed and placed a restraining hand on my arm. "Let's think for a second, Wyatt. Is there anything we need before getting back to the house?"

Ah, I thought behind a smile, we're spending the night together.

Chapter 34

Once we were back at the Falkner abode, I told Patsy to lock the door and switch on the outside light while I went to the rear entrance and checked that its door remained locked. Having given over our information to the detectives, I felt confident the police would locate Metheny in a short time and detain him for a bout of hard questioning. All the same, on entering the neighborhood, I'd searched for his car with the darkened windows, and not only on the street, but also in the many nooks and crannies that come with the aging of a locale—like the array of bushes, now overgrown and widely spread, that when planted years ago went unnoticed by everyone's eye but the planter's; like the abandoned rusting vehicle amid a small jungle of high weeds, overlooked by the ordinance checkers; like the large recycling dumpster that hid a cop car on occasion. I stared through the window at the woodlot for a time, alert to any sign of unusual motion, particularly along its border. Finally I turned away and flicked on the yellow bug light.

Back in the front room Patsy had taken hold of her tote and removed her laptop. I powered on the flatscreen and switched to the CBS affiliate out of Philly. I wasn't looking to watch a program. Four murdered authors was an unusual story and in the beginning there had been mention of it on the morning, noon, and closing newscasts of the day. But when no sustainable leads developed, the story dropped from the headlines. An arrest, a quick one especially, would permit Patsy and I to let out our breath. As I moved about the house, I kept a studious eye to the bottom of the screen for a crawler that would say a suspect had been arrested.

The evening soon slipped into the late hours and around ten, because she was still immersed in the laptop, I asked Patsy if she had some new assignment underway. She always did, so it wasn't a question out of nowhere.

"I'm just browsing," she answered without diverting her eyes from the screen. "Seeing what manner of items are trending." She occasionally picked up a story idea by doing this.

No crawler ever appeared on the TV screen that evening that was relevant to the murders, and around midnight I decided to find my way to a pillow. Patsy, who continued to work the laptop, said she would join me in a few minutes. I told her to leave the lights on outside.

The next morning she was first on her feet and she moved quickly to turn on the TV.

"Anything?" I asked.

She shook her head, then addressed me with a thoughtful mien. "Wyatt, don't you think we're easy targets in this house? Wouldn't it be wise to get out of the area and away for a while? If there's any chance that Metheny could evade the police and find us, I want him to sweat a little for it."

"Where would you recommend that we go, Babes?"

"I thought maybe Clinton County," she said.

"Your friend Bethany... What was her name again?"

"Bethany Alsop."

A close friend of Patsy's I'd met only once, the woman had purchased an isolated hunting camp in some of the most wooded and remote area of the state. She'd wanted to paint and write and couldn't get it done at home. She hadn't explained why that was, and although Patsy, like me, was wondering of the reason, neither of us had pressed her for an answer.

"What makes you think she'll be there?" I inquired.

"She won't. She's at her mother's in Florida. She visits her every year around this time. But she told me where the key is and how to turn on the water. She's urged me several times to use it any time I want."

I smiled at her and to myself. If the place was anything like I remembered this Bethany Alsop describing it, I didn't think anyone would find us. Not even a coyote. And she'd said the crafty animals roamed the vicinity.

"Mind if I have my coffee before we pull up stakes?"

"Have all you want. Let's just get on the road sooner than later."

"Do you know how to reach this camp?"

"Ahhh," she intoned, like she had entered the tomb of some mummified pharaoh. She wagged her familiar finger at me and dug into the tote. She extracted a small green notebook from the bottom and thumbed through its pages. "Here we go," she said in a sing-song voice. She read the directions aloud. "Any of those words familiar?"

"Woolrich is," I answered.

"They make wonderful outdoor shirts and jackets."

"So you've heard of them. Yep, they're made in a tiny hamlet of the same name, which is included in those directions you're holding. I'm sure I can get us there. As for the rest, we'll have to pay close attention. We'll also have to make sure we get ourselves there before dark. Otherwise, it'll be impossible to navigate our way throughout those smaller roads."

I had my coffee, two cups, and was intentionally ready in little time because I didn't want to test Patsy's patience and start off the journey by being on edge with one another. Yet she made an adjustment to her "sooner than later" advisory. She wanted to wait until the traffic picked up, a couple of hours, she said. In the event Metheny was still in the vicinity, she guessed he would have a difficult time of following us, even in small Valley Camp, when more vehicles were filling the streets.

Whether he was in that traffic or not, I don't know, but her strategy worked. I wove the Ru through it and when we reached the city limits, I tore onto the highway where there were fewer cars and trucks; and although she and I continued to work our vision in a three-sixty, there were none that we saw revealing heavily tinted glass. And the dark tint of the windows remained all that we had to go on. Patsy, recall, had been unable to accurately describe the color of the car in Koldren's driveway, and the night that we watched Metheny scream the U-turn on Grant, the only thing we seemed sure of was that the color wasn't black.

About twenty miles out of Valley Camp where the land transitioned to farms and long stretches of forest, the highway became ours. Not exactly true, but it was rare when another car passed us, and throughout most of the trip the vehicle up ahead was out of sight and any behind were usually back at least a quarter-mile. We glanced at one another often, smiling because we were chilling.

Hours later, a few clouds were starting to open and a mile before Alsop's instructions said to leave the main highway for a gravel road, Patsy's cell sounded. She withdrew it from the tote and checked the screen.

"It's my editor," she said, raising her brow and bunching her lips. "Hello, Randall. What's on your mind?"

Editor Randall did the talking and it wasn't by asking questions of Pats, who spoke hardly at all. I glanced at her more than once while the phone was at her ear. Her eyes narrowed, her head shook, her brow transitioned to troubled. But I didn't see a frown or any other expression of disappointment, so that the call likely wasn't made to deliver bad news about her book. When she put away the phone, she pondered what she'd heard before looking over at me.

"What is it, Babes?"

"Schacter's dead."

"What? You're kidding!"

"He was murdered."

"How? A bullet through his forehead?"

"No. Not that at all. He was in New York and his body was discovered in his hotel room by one of the maids. His neck had been snapped."

"Was anyone with him?" My suspicion was immediate.

"Yes, his bodyguard. Do you think he's the same one you named the Muscle?"

"Good chance of it. Did your editor have any information on him?"

"Only to say he's disappeared and the police are searching for him."

A short time ago when Patsy and I had first heard that Schacter and the Muscle were missing because we presumed the law was closing in on them, my thought then was that the bodyguard had been killed to keep from testifying against his boss. Now I realized that Schacter must have ridiculed the Muscle one too many times.

I'd already swung the Ru onto the gravel road and within several hundred yards it narrowed. The tires were kicking up stones and a throaty hum was coming up through the floor as I pushed our speed at an accelerated clip. I slowed several times as Patsy returned her attention to the directions. It would have been too easy to get lost because one gravel road looked like any other and none were marked. Bethany Alsop had indicated items along the route for us to watch for, such as a massive boulder beneath the road level just outside a sharp bend and a rusting bus from decades ago that was once used as a hunting camp but now had a tree growing out its roof. There were other smaller points of interest, too, and we had to watch carefully so that we didn't miss even one of them.

"What impact might Schacter's death have on your book?" I asked after a while. "Did he say?"

"This will squelch it."

"He said that?"

"He didn't have to."

"Then how can you be so certain?"

"A month from today nobody will mention Tor Schacter. You won't even find his name on AuthorsRetreat without searching through old postings."

The Ru flew past an off-road with a chain and a snowmobile sign at its entrance and that brought us to the last bulleted direction in Patsy's notebook.

"Slow down."

"What are we looking for now?" I asked.

"Bethany said the drive leading to the camp is narrow and depending on the time of year, it could be overgrown and easy to miss."

In the past week, as the vegetation began to rapidly rise, the mowers in Valley Camp started to emerge from their hibernating slumber. There were no mowers in this part of wild Clinton County.

"Pull up," Patsy said as she placed a hand on my arm.

I brought the car to a stop.

"Could that be it?" She pointed to a section of the roadside where there were no trees, not even a sapling of the thinnest dimension.

"Is the camp visible from the road? Did she say?"

"She never said."

"'Cause I don't see anything up there, Babes. Tell you what. I'll get out and walk it a ways. I certainly don't want to roll up there if the ground is iffy."

"I don't want us to get stuck out here either. Go ahead. I'll wait."

I got out, straightened my back that had grown tight from the drive, and began to walk. I stretched my legs for about a hundred feet. The earth was solid underneath and crushed stone had been laid down once upon a time. Throughout the swath was an absence of trees. That indicated to me that the opening had once been cleared.

"We're in luck," I said after I walked back to the car. I slid behind the wheel and turned into the opening.

A quarter-mile uphill at the end of the drive, the camp revealed itself. It was a small one-story cottage painted forest green. It would not have been visible from the road below, except at night and when its lights were on. A walkway of flagstone extended further uphill from its left to a dilapidated outhouse.

"Don't tell me," I whined as my eyes took it in.

"And don't fret," Patsy said. "It's no longer in use. There's a bathroom inside the cottage complete with a shower and a toilet."

"What about hot water?"

She pointed to a propane tank on the opposite side.

"What if it's empty?" I said.

"I'm ignoring you," she said.

"Okay," I said, grinning. "So where's the key that'll get us inside?"

"In the outhouse. Just inside the door. It should be hanging on a nail."

The outhouse was an old piece of construction and its boards hadn't been stained for many a year, if they ever were. I walked up to it and worked open the door that was out of plumb and felt inside along a two-by-four for the key. When I didn't touch anything, I stepped inside to look. The nail was higher up, near the roof, and the key was there as promised. I removed it and rejoined Patsy waiting in a sketchy patch of yard outside the back door.

"Here you go," I said and handed her the key. "By the way, contrary to what you said, that single-seater is still in use."

She looked at me askance.

"Nooo," I said, shaking my head. "It wasn't me. But there is a roll of paper on a shelf and a gob of mud on the floor. It's rather fresh."

"Some hunter—"

"—Fisherman. This time of year it's trout season that's underway."

"I love fried trout," she said.

"I'll get right on it," I said, for which I received a poke in the stomach.

We moved out of the sparse grass onto the stoop that had been crafted from rocks relocated from the surrounding terrain, and Patsy unlocked the door. Once inside, the first thing to strike my senses was the rank odor of mildew. As a teen I had been to a couple of hunting camps belonging to the fathers of my friends, and that pent-up smell of mildew was always the first to greet us. Emptied for most of the year with their windows shut, each camp imprisoned the air within in solitary confinement, and the wet, moldy odor wasn't replaced until the next morning when a new scent, one of stale beer and teenage vomit, permeated the rooms.

"What made her buy this?" I asked. My eyes swept the interior space that had walls of a bilious yellow hue.

"I told you. She wanted—"

"—This particular camp is what I mean."

"It probably was priced as something she could afford."

"She hasn't done much to it," I said. It was a man's haven in the past and it hadn't changed much, although the room we stood in contained four paintings by her friend, only one completed. It showed a bridge with a man at one end and a woman at the other. The man had his back turned and was looking into darkness; the woman faced us and was surrounded by light. I wondered if it was an artistic interpretation of the woman's marriage.

The remaining decorations were cheaply framed photographs of the previous owner, his friends, and some of their whitetail kills across the years. Dead flies loomed behind the glass of each. A new owner who was a non-artist would have taken them off the walls within a day of closure. An artist, however, would have felt an undefined reason to leave them be, at least for a time.

"Let's see what Bethany's left in the kitchen cupboards," said Patsy. "Just in case we're forced to stay here for more than a day or two."

"Don't forget to turn on the water," I said. "I'll see what else is available."

There was no television, which wouldn't have pulled in a single station if there were. The tall, all-enveloping mountains throughout the region were a major hindrance. There was a radio on a corner table in the main room and I turned it on briefly but it wasn't far behind in weak reception. Two bedrooms formed the rear of the camp. In one were two sets of double bunks with brown military blankets spread across their mattresses. It was where visiting hunters from past years slept. The other room was where we would sleep. It provided a queen-size bed. It had a closet too, and on the dresser were a hairbrush and an atomizer of perfume.

The bathroom was an add-on. It extended outside the original walls of the cabin. The age of the fixtures indicated that it was probably only several years younger than the outhouse. The tile, too, was of old design and the linoleum on the floor had become soft, sticky, and yellow with age. Crooked on a wall was a framed photograph of a steam locomotive climbing a rail somewhere out west. There were dead flies in it, too.

I scanned the entire room and on a storage shelf beneath a small trellised window trouble was revealed in an empty plastic wrapper.

"Oh-oh!" I cried out.

"What is it?" Patsy responded from the outer room where I could hear her busily opening and closing cupboard doors.

"Gotta go back to the outhouse," I said.

"Please don't say the toilet's broken."

"Worse. There's only the slimmest roll of paper at the ready and none on the shelf. I'll bring down the one I saw up there."

Patsy doesn't often swear, but I heard her mutter an overused profanity, which made me laugh.

I went back outside and on my return to the outhouse, I paused halfway up the stone walk to look at the steep surroundings. The old camp certainly was nestled in a beautiful and quiet setting. The mountain behind it was carved from several huge outcroppings arranged as though it were a staircase made for a giant. Over portions of the lower stairs ran water from a generous spring and it was the same water that came into the cabin. Another steep rise, without the steps, loomed on my left and all of its trees, mostly oak, were but a day or two away from full foliage. When my eyes arrived at the top, I counted six deer cruising silently through brush and only one hesitated because it sensed there was something down below that could mean danger.

Far below and on the other side of the gravel road was a narrow stream. It was a winding feeder to a much larger flow south and wasn't visible at all from where I stood. Its water tumbled over rocks in a not-so-faraway section and that rippling sound was plain and wonderful to my ears. Out on the road and down quite a ways I listened also to a car making the same audio the Subaru had made. It passed in front seconds later and continued along the road, the crunch of gravel with it all the way. I could still hear its rhythm as it slipped over the crest of the mountain and into silence.

I stood in place, smiling to myself because of an odd thought. Patsy's friend, for whatever reason, might not have been able to write and paint in her home, and that must have been a major cause of anxiety. Up here amid the shouldering mountains she was probably thinking both activities would come easier, and perhaps it did for her. I wasn't sure it would for me were I to stay here for an extended period of time. The land was too stunning, too restful, quiet and exceptionally serene. I could sit here forever, I thought, and stare out at everything surrounding me and none of it would tire. I wouldn't care if I accomplished a thing. Neither would I feel guilty about my lack of production. Of course, while it was a soothing interpretation that I attached to the matter, others, my boss one of them, would have ordered me to get my head out of my ass.

I blew out the fantasy and continued the walk to the outhouse where I retrieved the roll of toilet tissue. I took to spinning it on my index finger and walked back. As I re-entered the cabin I added a John Denver tune. I smiled at Patsy and spun the roll off my finger and into the air in her direction. She caught it with one hand and realized immediately that circumstances were not registering with her beau.

"Look who's here, Wyatt," she said. "We have a visitor."

Despite her alert and despite the twisted nose and the gun in my field of vision, Metheny's presence still required an extra second before I ceased singing and realized our lives were in danger. And then I didn't move. I wasn't frozen, however. Rather, I was arrested by the atrocious appearance of Metheny and particularly by that sorry looking belt buckle that was again yanked under the brass button. Did he do that on purpose? I thought. And what would be the reason?

"Get over there next to your girlfriend," he ordered me.

"Ignore him. Stay where you are, Wyatt," countermanded Patsy in the calmest voice.

I wouldn't learn till later how he had tracked us, and what was parked out on the gravel road wasn't a car with tinted glass but a black Ford pickup that he had switched to in order to evade authorities. I also wouldn't learn till later that he had bugged my house; that he had not expected me to show up as I had that evening when he'd fired a shot; that his plan had been to use me to gather information on Patsy as to when she might leave her home and where she would go so that he could take her life. When I had read in his novel about the tribe in outer space who owned new technologies and yet had zero knowledge on how to use them, I had wrongly presumed that its author was equally ignorant of their use. Detective Dempsey would inform me that it was much the opposite. And that same tribe in Metheny's mind, I would learn from Detective Maines, deserved to be annihilated because of its ignorance.

"Move."

"Stay."

Patsy saw me staring at her. My look, questioning. I wasn't understanding something that she so obviously did.

"What's going on, Babes?" I said feebly.

"Mr. Metheny is intending to kill us with that revolver he's holding."

That much I knew.

"Mr. Metheny, Patsy couldn't identify your car. All she remembers are the tinted windows."

"It's too late. Don't waste your breath. When Mr. Metheny gets something in his head, it's got to be done. And that's the only quality he has in common with writers."

"Move!" said Metheny.

I took a step and Patsy raised a hand, as well as her voice. "Wyatt, stay where you are! Do exactly what I tell you! We're not going to allow this failure to end our lives."

"You're a foolish young woman," said Metheny.

"Wrong," said Patsy. "I know things about you, Mister. And the first is that you are a staggering failure. Your writing wasn't accepted anywhere, not even at Quotidian Release. Which you've stated time and again will publish anything.

"You got a mouth on you, that's for sure."

"So I'm right?"

"Turn around. I'll spare you watching the death of your boyfriend."

"Go to hell!" said Patsy. "I'm not turning around for you. Wyatt, you give him what he wants. You turn around."

Metheny advanced a step in my direction.

"But keep your back to him," said Patsy. "Don't let him get in front of you."

"How's the wrist, Oliver?"

"It's good enough."

"I was hoping I'd broken it."

"I'll bet you were."

"This time I will."

"Getting that close was a mistake. Now turn around and face me or take it in the back like a coward."

"Tell him what Op-Ed means, Babes."

"Pay no attention to him," Patsy said. "Remember the story about the hunter chasing the squirrel around the tree? That's what you have to do, Wyatt. Be that squirrel."

I didn't remember the story. At least not all of it. And I should have because it was about what we wanted words to mean. It was part of a philosophical discussion the first night I had met Patsy and the fellows who brought it up were the boneheads. That was already more than two years ago.

I shook my poor memory at Patsy and she responded. If she couldn't get through to me in one way, she would find another.

"The other night, Wyatt. Little Jake. Remember what was happening between the boy and his dog?"

I had to think. And yes, I did remember. Jake and his dog had been circling round and round in unison. The dog was the inside circle, little Jake the outside. And I realized at the same time that Patsy was intentionally not spelling out what I should do. She didn't want Metheny to realize that she knew his secret.

"You're getting on my nerves, young lady. Back yourself into that corner and turn around. I'm tired of looking at your face."

"I don't think so, Mr. John Growler."

Metheny noticeably twitched at her words and I saw it. The movement was faint, yet it rippled throughout his flesh, and the eyes shrank in their sockets. He and Patsy shared something of which I was ignorant.

"Schacter rejected you on the second book, too, didn't he?"

Metheny moved away from me and back in her direction. He jerked the revolver's barrel to one side, jerked it several times, to say that she was to turn around, he wasn't putting up with any more sass.

"You always thought Quotidian accepted anything and everything," Patsy continued. "What a slap in the face in must have been when they rejected yours, first by one name, then by another."

Suddenly, another movement. A flash of a movement. Only this movement came from the outside. Someone had passed by the small window in the bathroom. And it was definitely a flash, not a casual step. And my first thought was that Patsy and I had failed in our thinking. Metheny had never acted alone, there was someone else, and here was Metheny taking too long and number two was already tired of waiting and coming to hurry our end.

I swept my eyes throughout the room while he directed his attention at Patsy. Was there something I could take hold of and use to defend ourselves, to put Metheny and anyone who came through the door on his back? Surely there was something at hand in an old hunting cabin that I might grab with a little stroke of luck and use to brain this sonovabitch who was about to murder us. Alsop's easel pushed next to the window by the door could work, but it was spread apart and upright, displaying an unfinished painting. There was a poker, too, behind the woodstove. Only it was too far away.

Yet as I set my eyes upon that poker, another eye was stretching around the edge of the window near the rear door. Patsy saw it at the same time and she gave a furtive glance my way. It wasn't belonging to an accomplice; much the contrary, it was a possible rescue. Patsy sped up her talk at Metheny to keep him occupied, to make sure he would not turn toward the door and the window.

I watched the eye slide down to the bottom sill and the hump of the back, telling me this was a big, heavy man, then rushed across the length of the glass. Whoever it was was now at the door. I stared at the knob and watched it slowly turn.

And then a second later the door burst inward and a male body in a brown outfit, filling the frame and wielding a gun, leaped into the room. "PUT IT DOWN!" he screamed at Metheny.

Only Metheny was already in his turn and I watched the revolver swing with him. Two shots exploded from the doorway.

Just for a moment Metheny stood still and his eyes locked onto mine. Then he collapsed onto the floor.

The big man very carefully approached with his gun still trained on Metheny. He bent over and freed the revolver from Metheny's hand. Stepping back, he shifted his attention to Patsy and me.

"Are you two okay?"

We each took a deep breath before nodding. Yes, we were okay. We were both okay.

"Thank you," said Patsy.

"Thank you," I said.

Chapter 35

Metheny had two bullet holes in him and his blood was pooling on the cabin floor, but he would survive. Aided by the big constable we did our best to keep him alive until state and local police arrived along with a rescue vehicle. Patsy and I told the police everything. We also gave them the names Harley Dempsey and Verlaine Maines and said they were the Philadelphia detectives who had been heading up the investigation from its inception.

It was late and darkness had fallen when all was finished and the others and their vehicles had left. We had no reason to continue our stay at the camp, and anyway, after what had taken place, we did not wish to stay. Even so, we also didn't want to search for a motel and we didn't want to drive, and I was worried that we could even miss a turn and become hopelessly lost amid the mountains. In the end we decided to stay the night.

Patsy had to phone her friend and let her know what went down inside her cabin. It was a difficult call for my Pats to make and she waited until the morning. It was difficult because her friend had offered her hideaway as a chance for Pats to get away on occasion. A place where she could chill out if she ever felt the need. The offer might not have been made had Betsy Alsop known that a murderer was after us. I wondered awhile what her thoughts would be the next time she came up to paint and stood before her canvas in the room where her friend and her friend's boyfriend nearly lost their lives and where a killer had been shot and bled on her floor. Because she was an artist, I was inclined to believe she would be okay. That she would somehow internalize it in a positive way.

If he didn't plead guilty to the murders of four people, Patsy and I understood that in the months ahead we would be summoned to testify against Metheny in a court of law. Nevertheless, we shared the feeling that our ordeal was finished. This was manifested in how I drove the route back from Clinton County to Valley Camp. I set the Ru's cruise control at 60 once we entered upon a hard road. Hundreds of cars, bikers, buses, and big rigs overtook us throughout the return journey. Before either of us uttered a word, an hour would pass.

"You know we were lucky," I said.

"So what does a constable actually do?" Patsy mused. "Do they patrol like police? I've never really understood what their duties are. You talked with him and were getting the story. He grew silent when I appeared alongside. Which was the reason I went outside."

"He wasn't patrolling," I said.

"No? Then what was he doing out there?"

"He was fishing, Babes. He and his brother, they were fishing for trout. They each had favorite holes that were a distance apart, and his was just off the road on the other side, directly across from the cabin. The brother had dropped him."

"That doesn't explain his appearance at the window."

I laughed because the explanation is where the

constable had hesitated in Patsy's presence.

"What's so funny?"

"That toilet paper I stole from the outhouse? It was his. He'd left the roll behind for the next guy."

"But that visit was made before the two of us showed up. It doesn't explain his second visit."

I laughed again, then blurted out, "Babes, the poor man had the runs."

Patsy threw up her arms at once. "Whoops! You can stop right there. Sorry I asked."

"You wanted to know, so I'm explaining it."

"TMI."

I ignored her protest. We were still a little tight and this absurd ingredient to the finish of the entire matter, I figured, would loosen us up. "He said he didn't want to lower his trousers alongside the stream because it could get messy for himself"—Patsy was shaking her head from futility; she knew I wasn't going to stop with the story—"so he hiked up to the outhouse which he knew was there because he was friends with the previous owner of the camp. Well, it's the same explanation for his second visit, except when he approached the road, he spotted Metheny. Not that he knew who he was, of course. But what really made him suspicious that something was about to happen was that Metheny already had the gun in his hand, hanging at his side, and he was walking with it as though he meant business. So he stayed planted and watched. When he knew Metheny wouldn't be able to see him, he ran up to the camp. He saw our car and that's when he drew his own gun—first steeling his bowels, he assured me—and wound his way to the window to see what was going on inside. The rest you know."

We grew quiet again. After several seconds, I heard a

faint titter. "Thank God," she murmured

"What's that?"

"Thank God, the man had the runs!"

"Why do you say that?" I asked.

"They usually require a second trip."

That response made me smile and laugh. I reached over and took her hand in mine. We remained that way for the next mile and more.

"Babes, can I ask you something?"

"I left the gun in Valley Camp," she said.

"Oh... I did mean to ask you about that."

"What is it?"

"Well, you finally got through to my thick head why I needed to keep my back to him. He absolutely had to shoot me in the forehead like he did Underwood and Smmith. It was a screwball compulsion of his."

"But what's your question?"

"Well, he was ordering you to turn around and you refused. Weren't you taking a chance? He might have killed you just for disobeying."

"No," she said, firmly shaking her head. "No, he wouldn't have. The other night when I was surfing the web, it passed across my mind that we never learned how Lillian Purvis had been killed, other than she was shot. So I went searching. It took quite a while but I eventually found a piece in a blog by a police officer that said she had been shot in the back."

"Like Suter?"

"Yes. Just like what happened to Spectra Suter. And then I explored a hunch I was having about John Growler after we discovered that he and Metheny are the same person. I brought up Amazon and typed in the name. Five seconds later up came a novel by John Growler. And this one did not have to be purchased because the 'look inside' feature was provided."

"What did you find?"

"Another story and it was set in some galaxy other than ours. Only with this tale the protagonists and antagonists were women."

"And the one side, I'm guessing, was smashing the spines of the other side with an *iron malleta*."

"No *iron malleta* in this story. In this one a specialized laser gun was the chosen weapon and each time it was aimed at the base of the woman's back."

I thought about what she had said.

"Even so, Babes, he ran you off the road. He wasn't above making an exception to his compulsive rules. You were taking a chance. I could have lost you."

Her face all of a sudden adopted an expression that I'd not seen in the many months we'd been together. She said (and it was uttered almost plaintively), "I'm so glad this is over for you, Wyatt. I really am."

"For me?"

"Yes. I didn't realize until this moment how much you were affected by my mysterious absence. Wyatt sweet, you've already forgotten that he left the gun at the Koldren house with Koldren's prints all over it. It wasn't an exception he made. Oliver Metheny had no choice but to force me off the road."

I didn't say anything to what she had said. Maybe she was right about me. Patsy certainly knew me better than anyone else, I wouldn't deny that. Perhaps I had undergone a stress that I was reluctant to face.

"Anyway," she went on, "I read all that Amazon allowed of Growler's story and the thought that next came to mind was that Schacter must have turned down both his book and the one under his real name. Of course, I knew it was something I couldn't prove, yet I felt sure it had happened."

For the moment I resigned from thinking of Patsy, and of myself as well. I thought, instead, strictly of Metheny. "So on the one side," I responded, "he was fighting with Schacter and on the other side was the Nemesis Nine. And he most certainly must have been fighting with himself. Years spent believing you're a writer, only to learn that others think you suck? I'm not sure what I would do if that were ever the case."

"He'll plead not guilty and his lawyer will forward an insanity defense," Patsy postulated. "Furthermore, he'll win. The court will order him to an institution."

"Assuming you're correct in your prediction," I said, "do you agree he'll be confined until he dies? After murdering four people and attempting the murder of two more, I can't believe that any board of doctors would ever release him back into society."

"Want to know what else, Wyatt?"

"Oh, oh. I recognize that tone of voice. You're planning something, aren't you?"

"Your Babes intends to keep in touch with Mr. Metheny throughout the judicial process."

"Oh yeah? Are you sure you want to do that?"

"What is it that forced him to shoot men in the forehead and women in the back? Therein lies a compelling story."

"Let's hope you're right," I said. Then after a little reflection, added, "I guess I would like to know what makes him tick."

"You wouldn't be alone," she said.

We made the remainder of the return trip to Valley Camp in virtual silence.

Epilogue

In the days, the weeks, and the months to follow, several matters of importance would occur. The first involved Marley House. It said "No" to my second novel. I'll grant you that I was disappointed, but only for a short time. Afterwards, I telephoned Patsy and she gave me Atherton's phone number. The next day the manuscript was overnighted to his publisher.

The second matter of importance came after Metheny had been arraigned and a trial date set. Patsy contacted Editor Randall and explained her idea for a new book whose focus was Metheny and his eccentric compulsions. Randall loved the idea as she laid it out. So did I. The more I'd thought of it, the more I'd realized it was the exactly the kind of narrative that she does best.

With Randall's approval, she quickly took the next step and got hold of Metheny's lawyer. She apprised him of her intentions and he, too, got on board and why not, since his name as the accused's defense attorney would be prominently mentioned. Metheny, the last to be notified that he could be the subject of a book, readily agreed to the interviews and even lit up when Patsy informed him that Schacter's name would appear in the book as well and not in a very positive light. Before, during, and after the trial, writer Pats Lukehart met several times with the man who had tried to kill us. Her attention and the additional media coverage of Metheny and his unusual murderous compulsions spurred interest in both his novels, and despite dozens of one-star reviews, their sales numbers soon outstripped the purchases of Quotidian books, including my own.

Finally, six months to the day since our ordeal in Clinton County, the biggest matter of all to both of us took place. I asked Patsy to marry me.

She said "Yes."

About the Author

F. E. Mazur grew up in Western Pennsylvania near the Allegheny River and was educated at Slippery Rock University. After teaching in the public schools of his home state and New York, he worked for a regional advertising agency and often wrote the copy for his consumer and industrial clients. In the 90s he became employed as the staff writer for an avant-garde multimedia computing lab at Cornell University. His articles arising from the experimentation of bringing various media together in a computerized setting appeared in popular, trade, and academic journals. He has contributed to a wide range of publications. His fictional works include *The Buckseller, Spine, The Halftone Man, Unvisited Spaces and Twelve Other Stories*, and the story within these pages.

www.ingramcontent.com/pod-product-compliance
Lightning Source LLC
Chambersburg PA
CBHW020232260626
47156CB00002B/642